D0344282

HOW to SAVE a QUEENDOM

HOW to SAVE a QUEENDOM

JESSICA LAWSON

Simon & Schuster Books for Young Readers

NEW YORK LONDON TORONTO SYDNEY NEW DELHI

SIMON & SCHUSTER BOOKS FOR YOUNG READERS
An imprint of Simon & Schuster Children's Publishing Division
1230 Avenue of the Americas, New York, New York 10020
SIMON & SCHUSTER BOOKS FOR YOUNG READERS
and related marks are trademarks of Simon & Schuster, Inc.
For information about special discounts for bulk purchases, please contact
Simon & Schuster Special Sales at 1-866-506-1949 or business@simonandschuster.com.
The Simon & Schuster Speakers Bureau can bring authors to your live event.
For more information or to book an event, contact the Simon & Schuster Speakers Bureau at
1-866-248-3049 or visit our website at www.simonspeakers.com.
Interior design by Hilary Zarycky
Map on page 118 by Drew Willis
The text for this book was set in Horley Old Style.
Manufactured in the United States of America
0321 FFG
First Edition
2 4 6 8 10 9 7 5 3 1
Library of Congress Cataloging-in-Publication Data
Names: Lawson, Jessica, 1980– author.
Title: How to save a queendom / Jessica Lawson.
Description: First edition. | New York : Simon & Schuster Books for Young Readers, [2021]
| Audience: Ages 8-12. | Audience: Grades 4-6. | Summary: Life has been cruel yet quiet
for orphaned, twelve-year-old Stub, but now, charged with ferring a tiny wizard, Orlen, to
the country's capital, Maradon Cross, to protect the queendom, her life is suddenly filled with
adventure.
Identifiers: LCCN 2020030137 | ISBN 9781534414341 (hardcover) |
ISBN 9781534414365 (eBook)
Subjects: CYAC: Adventure and adventurers—Fiction. | Wizards—Fiction. |
Orphans—Fiction. | Fantasy.
Classification: LCC PZ7.L438267 How 2021 | DDC [Fic]—dc23
LC record available at https://lccn.loc.gov/2020030137

For those dreaming of journeys,
for those already on a quest,
for those feeling trapped and those breaking free,
this one's for you.

HOW to SAVE a QUEENDOM

1

How to Deal with Rats

S unrises were *not* my favorite part of the day. They
had a nasty habit of shedding light on my life's prob-
lems, both old and new. This morning's new problem
involved holes in a wall and rats. Oh yes, and a ransacked bag
of magically enhanced chicken feed. Also a whole bunch of
eggs. Really big eggs.

Even before Matron Tratte woke and surveyed the damage in the stone wall surrounding the Tinderbox Tavern, I
had a sneaking suspicion that I'd get the blame.

I was right.

Twelve hours later, with aching arms and a rusty spade,
I was still paying the price. I blended what I sincerely hoped
was my last bucketful of sand, dirt, clay, and water, hearing
echoes of the matron's furious words in my mind.

*If you had wiped the stone with wizard spray like I told
you, they would never have gotten in!* she'd bellowed. *You'll
patch the whole thing—every crack and cranny!*

I could have told her that the wizard-spray spell had worn out several days before, but I hadn't wanted to ask her for the coin to buy more. And I could have told her that filling the holes was completely unnecessary; depending on how much of the feed had been eaten, by tonight the intruders would be far too big to squeeze back through, at least for a week or so. But there were plenty of other vermin in Trapper's Cove, and, besides, the matron was not someone you "told things" to. Instead I kept my hand stirring as I peered through another gap in the wall, having the sudden wish that there was a bag of shrinking-feed handy so that I could make myself small enough to slip through and escape as well.

The Tinderbox was the very last tavern on a street that sloped upward from the harbor. A high place with a view of a low place. *Like a royal castle,* Matron Tratte liked to say, which was laughable in too many ways to count.

Below, I could see the market tents, the crowded docks, the moored trading vessels, and the bobbing fisherboats. Beyond it all, the glint of sunset flashed upon open water. It was getting late. I jammed a full spade into the hole, squelching the messy mixture into place and sealing off the view.

I stood and stretched. Behind the sharp-toothed peaks surrounding Trapper's Cove, streaks of gold and crimson spread across the sky with a sleepy, yawning glow. The lucky day was already tucking itself in. As for me, I was far from sleep. No doubt the matron would soon be screaming for me to help serve the evening crowd of traders and travelers.

As though hearing my thoughts, the back door of the Tinderbox slammed open. I flinched but didn't need to look up to see who it was. Matron Tratte's arms were thick and strong enough to throw troublemakers from the tavern when necessary. The flimsy door was no match for her frustration.

"Stub!" she yelled in her high-pitched, grating tone while glaring around the animal yard. "Stub-the-Nuisance!"

I stiffened. Whenever she used my full name, it meant she was feeling twitchy about something. A twitchy matron was a dangerous one.

"I'm over here," I said, careful to keep my words clear but soft. She didn't like the sound of my voice much. The feeling was mutual.

Eumelia Tratte was not as mean-looking as her voice suggested. Her eyes were a friendly blend of green and brown. Her skin was clear of blemishes. Her hair was long and dark and shiny from daily applications of horn-nut oil. And, unlike many in the trading village of Trapper's Cove, all of her teeth and facial features were present and accounted for.

Today she wore her very best outfit: a long-sleeved red tunic trimmed with frills over matching embroidered trousers. But while the owner of the Tinderbox looked very much like a delightful ripe piece of fruit, I knew very well that her insides held a rotten pit.

BOOM!

This time it was the matron who was startled. She stumbled down the steps, cursing at the blast of a fireburst rising over the harbor. The brilliant blue lights rained down over the cove, playing lively music and changing colors until they met the sea.

It was still a week until Maradon's annual Peace Day, but as it was the hundredth anniversary, the traders had been at it for a month, showing off wizard-made celebration goods. One fireburst had been set off every day at sunset in order to lure people to buy more. From what I'd seen at the market, it was working. Fizzy sparking sticks, blue smoke smackers, and the more expensive firebursts were all the rage. For some reason, celebrating a lack of war made everyone want to set things on fire.

I watched the last remnants of light fade while the matron regained her balance.

"Stub, I swear, if you're not done with that wall in the next five minutes, I'm going to swing you over it, right into the harbor!" She turned and stomped back into the tavern.

She was bluffing. Matron Tratte knew I couldn't swim. And I knew she didn't have anyone else who would work for free. Still, I quickened my pace. As I finished filling smaller holes along the wall, a familiar growl echoed against the stone. Though my arms ached from patching high holes and my legs ached from squatting to fill low cracks, it was my stomach that ached most of all.

"I'd rebuild this whole wall for a bowl of beans, wouldn't you, Peck?" I turned to grin at my feathery companion, who'd been quietly dust-bathing near the wall just minutes before.

The dirt was disturbed, but my best and only friend was nowhere to be seen. A quick survey of the yard revealed several chickens of varying sizes, six wizard-enhanced sheep the size of horses, and a good deal of extra-large animal droppings. I saw no scrawny, red-feathered, sharp-beaked best friend until a violent ruckus of *ba-GAWK*s echoed from inside the chicken coop.

A few copper feathers flew out the coop door, and then a scraggly, raggedy, squawking chicken flashed across the yard in a frenzy of panic. A rowdy horde of large birds ran after her.

I threw the spade aside, glancing once again at the tavern's back door. Everyone in Trapper's Cove knew that calling any sort of attention to oneself was usually a good way of starting trouble. But when my best and only friend was being threatened, I could never seem to remember that.

"Don't worry, Peck!" I called, dashing after her. "I'm coming!" Two of the chickens turned my way when I ran through the feathery throng, as though they sensed that I'd been the one responsible for the loss of their food. I tried to dodge their oversized beaks but winced at a sudden pain near my knee. I shoved the bully bird aside while Peck ducked under the door flap of my shelter in the corner of the yard. I followed her inside.

My home was the old chicken shed—a rickety structure that was most definitely built for nesting boxes, not people. When the matron had expanded the backyard flock and built a larger coop, she'd decided that it was time for me to be stripped of my sleeping spot near the kitchen hearth. I was six years old at the time, scared and cold and very much alone, until a runty baby chick wandered in one evening, trembling. She was even more scared and cold than I was. And that was when the alone part ended for us both.

Over the next six years, we'd grown so close that I almost didn't mind where we slept each night. Still, the space was growing tighter by the year. The flap door, made of heavy sailcloth, was low and just wide enough to for me to crawl through.

"It's only me, Peck," I said quietly. "You're safe here." I wiped away a thin line of blood near my knee. The damage had been done by Spiker, the biggest and meanest of the matron's flock. She was a real stinker when she was hungry, and that was especially true when she'd been temporarily enhanced to five times her natural size.

With the flap closed, it was pitch-black inside. A shuffling noise came from somewhere opposite me. By feel, I dug through a layer of dirt until I felt the smooth lid of a discarded cigar box from the marketplace. It housed my special collection, which included a way to light the darkness.

I hadn't noticed the stones' magic right away. I'd been sent to gather clams by the sea caves. It was a place where treasures from old shipwrecks sometimes showed up. Every now and then I found things I could trade at the market for food. When a weathered sack of rocks washed up, I almost left them behind. I don't know why I brought them back, other than the fact that I didn't think anyone would want them. I could relate to that. But as I spent more time with them, their magic was revealed.

One rock grew icy cold for several minutes if you squeezed it tight. Two stayed hot long after being placed near a fire. One was a sleek and shiny black stone, scattered with a few minerals that sparkled—if tapped in the right place, it whispered mysterious nothings that sounded like a soft morning wind gently sweeping up traces of moonlight. Another came back to me, no matter where or how hard I threw it. And two were glow rocks that lit up for an hour when shaken. I searched for one of those.

I grasped each rock in turn until I found one shaped roughly like a crab claw. I shook it hard until the shelter began to glow.

Peck crouched within reach.

With an unusually long neck, a sunken breast, and dusty-rose-colored wings too large for her scrawny body, Peck looked more like a starved dragon baby than a full-grown fowl. A patch of raw skin on her neck had joined a number of older patches where the other birds had attacked her, simply for looking different. Tiny slips of feathers were trying their best to grow back.

"Peck, stick!" I whispered. She bobbled over to my ruck-sack and rifled through until she found a stick with a sharpened end. She tossed it to me with her beak.

"Good girl."

I used the stick to dig a line into the wall of the shack. It joined many others. When I'd run out of space with my reaching arms, I'd stood on crates to make a ragged scratch for every ragged day I'd been there. The third wall was nearly full. I left a good amount of space between the marks each time, on the off chance I'd take up drawing and have something beautiful to fill the emptiness with. There was only one space with something nice carved. It was a six-year-old's drawing. A rough oval shape, with a triangle attached to the right side and two lines for legs on the bottom. I carved it the day I met Peck.

I dropped the stick and gathered her in my arms. I blew lightly on her fresh wound. "Oh, Peck," I whispered. "Those hens are awful to you." I kissed her feathers, took a crust of bread from my trouser pocket, and tore the food into pieces. "I swiped it off a plate during the noon rush. I've been saving it. Don't tell."

The chicken pecked at a piece, then looked up, waiting.

"No, you go on," I urged. "I'll have something tonight. Eat. And stay here. I'd best hurry back before I'm missed."

The back door creaked open. "Where are you, Nui-sance?" called a low, nasal voice.

"Too late," I whispered. I sucked in a breath and held it, not moving a muscle while the matron's son coughed loudly and spit a wad of phlegm that dinged into the alarm bell hanging near the back door.

Footfalls pounded down the stairs. Boots stomped close. Then, closer.

Frantically, I stuffed the still-glowing rock back with the others. Just as I'd smoothed dirt over the buried box, a long arm shot into the shelter and flailed around. The cloth door lifted. A hand closed around my ankle, squeezing hard.

Hut peered inside, then yanked me out by the leg. His brown hair fell in his eyes, all the way to his long nose with its slit nostril, the result of a broken bottle thrown across the tavern when he was small.

"Still keeping that naked-neck chicken as a roommate?" He wiped his hair from his face and grinned. His smile had grown steadily from mischief into menace during the years that I'd known him. "Mind that it doesn't wander over to the chopping block when you're not watching. Now get inside. Mother has a special guest coming tonight. A *captain*, Stub-Rot."

Mr. Tratte had passed away ten years ago, and after three years of mourning, the matron had decided to try to remarry. She'd been aiming for a sea captain, both because they had money and because they could get her away from Trapper's Cove. She hadn't landed a catch yet, but it wasn't for lack of trying.

"If you mess anything up, Mother says it's the closet." He grinned again. "Every night for a week this time."

The year before, Matron had locked me in the narrow broom closet for breaking a whole tray of plates. She hadn't seen Hut push me. I doubt it would have mattered if she had. Now I stood and dusted myself off so he wouldn't notice me shaking. One full night of being locked in the closet had been horrible. Seven in a row would be unbearable.

"And if everything works out, she says you're free of us and we're free of you."

I stared at him. "Free?"

Hut laughed at my open mouth. "She'll be gone and you won't be needed. Which would be quite convenient for you, wouldn't it?"

My heartbeat quickened. Yes, it would be convenient. Miraculous, even.

I'd been abandoned on the porch of the Tinderbox when I was only a few days old. The matron had taken me in. She had a letter from my abandoning mother, pleading for me to be raised and then given an apprenticeship. Her written words were as binding as a contract.

I was lucky. I'd been told that time after time by Matron Tratte. Proper apprenticeships were coveted arrangements. They were opportunities that allowed any child to follow their passions and talents and future aspirations. They were not often granted to orphans like me, who had no references or goals in life other than survival.

Under the apprenticeship laws of Maradon, the eight necessary years of service could begin as early as age ten, but could start anytime after. There were no age limits. Even a woman the age of seventy could begin an apprenticeship. The arrangement was meant to protect both sides. The apprentice got a guarantee of hearth, home, and knowledge. The mentor gave away secrets of their trade; in exchange they gained a faithful worker. At the end of the eight years, the apprentice was granted a traditional parting wage to launch their own business.

But that sort of dream was for other people. I knew very well that Matron Tratte was my owner, not my mentor. I locked eyes with the scar on Hut's nostril. "I don't believe you."

"Fine. Don't believe me." He shrugged, then smirked.

There was something about his smirk that bothered me.

Trapper's Cove was inhabited largely by well-armed women, shifty-eyed men, and crafty children—the sort of people who might trade their own mother away for a pair of used boots and a half-chewed leg of mutton. But still, there were apprentices here: fishers, gamblers, shippers, and market traders. There were even tavern apprenticeships, when there was no child to pass the business along to, or when the child involved chose a different path.

But as for me?

I would be given no closing wage. Or knowledge. I was twelve now and therefore committed to being the matron's property for six more years. There was no chance of ending the contract, unless both the matron and I agreed to end it. That would never happen, and escaping early was the equivalent of stealing—I was reminded of that daily.

Any apprentice who ran away with no notice would be publicly renounced and forced into a much longer work assignment, with no chance of a parting wage. That was the law. Matron had showed me the paper saying so, many times. I couldn't read it, but the royal seal at the top of the paper matched every other official document I'd seen posted in the marketplace and on the spell sheets that came with wizard-made goods.

So, yes, being freed would be *very* convenient for me. Too convenient. Still, if there was one skill that my time at the tavern had taught me, it was how to spot a liar. And that was the oddest thing. Because I could tell: Hut definitely wasn't lying.

"What about you?" I asked. "Wouldn't she take you along?"

His nose twitched. His eyes shifted over to the wall surrounding the Tinderbox. "No. I'll run the tavern. Mother plans to sign it over to me."

So the matron would leave him behind. It was true, he'd be eighteen soon—old enough to take over. But Hut hated the Tinderbox. I saw the way he looked at travelers, especially when they sang ballads of the sea. I'd heard him sing a song once, when he thought he was alone in the backyard. His voice was nice, but he'd stopped the moment the matron had opened the back door, yelling at him to hurry up with the eggs. He'd stared at that door as it swung shut, then walked in a hunched shuffle while completing his work, like his legs carried heavy invisible shackles that were as firmly clamped on as mine. But the extra weight had turned him into his mother's son, so I didn't feel bad for him. At least not any more than I felt bad for myself.

"What are you looking at?" Hut made a sheep noise and flicked my head. "Your wool is growing out," he said. "Might have to give you another haircut tonight, so you and your chicken match properly." He held out two fingers and made a snipping motion against my head.

I'd forgotten about my hair.

A week ago I'd been stupid enough to fall asleep while doing dishes. Normally, I'm quite good at sensing incoming threats, even when I sleep. I get buzzing, bristling sensations in different places when something's amiss. Sometimes my ear, sometimes my eyes, sometimes the back of my knee. I'd avoided a dozen or more thieves at market because of a sudden prickle. But I was so exhausted that I didn't even notice when Hut cut my hair off with kitchen shears.

He'd managed to snip it quite close to my skull in some places before I woke up. I was lucky he didn't shave me with a wizard knife, or I'd be completely bald.

"Make sure you wipe that dirt off your face before you come inside." Hut grunted, then snorted. "You look like a pig."

"You smell like a pig," I muttered.

"What?"

I shrugged. "Nothing."

He eyed me suspiciously. "That's right," he said. "You're nothing." He spit on the ground. "You've been nothing since the day Mother found you. She said she'd seen fish at the market wrapped with more care than you. She should have thrown you into the sea."

I nodded. If I could have breathed in water—if I'd been even *nearly* a fish—I would have jumped into the sea myself long ago. Given the choice of being lost and alone in a great big sea, or being here in Trapper's Cove? The two things seemed fairly equally hopeless, except that in the sea I'd have time for myself.

But then, there was my Peck. If I were a fish, I'd never have met her. And now, maybe there was a chance for us. There was a *captain* to please. True, there had been captains before—but never the promise of freedom attached. Perhaps I could even become a real apprentice and learn a trade.

Hut mounted the stairs to the tavern's back door. "Who knows?" he called over his shoulder. "Tonight's meal is squid, but this captain might want chicken." He turned and gave me a nasty wink, looking pointedly at my coop home. "And I might run out of plucked birds."

I waited until Hut was inside before ducking back into the shelter to drop a kiss on Peck's head. "He was joking, you know."

Peck nipped my finger doubtfully.

I sighed. Then I put my friend carefully into my market rucksack. "Right. Well, come along and keep quiet."

2

How to Take Orders

⤟

O f all the rooms in the Tinderbox, it was the kitchen that won the prize for having hosted the worst moments in my life. My body knew it too. Every muscle tensed in high alert as I pushed the door open.

Matron Tratte huddled over one of her larger money pouches, counting coin as I stepped into the kitchen. Hut fiddled with a massive knot of pale blue tentacles roasting at the hearth. I set the egg basket on the cutting table with a quiet thump.

The matron whirled around, clutching the pouch to her chest. "Stop creeping around like a wretched burglar. Make some noise for once!"

I shifted so that she wouldn't see the bulge in my rucksack. "Sorry, I just—"

"Quiet!" She jabbed a meaty finger toward trays of unbreakable glasses and full pitchers. "You're not going to market yet, so put that sack away and start serving. I want the worst of the riffraff fed and gone soon. This is a respectable tavern—or it will be by the time Captain Vella gets here. Wipe the dust off the Peace Queen paintings and light the lamps." She tossed me a small circular rug. "And cover the stain by the fireplace."

"Stain?" I asked, cowering a bit. She liked it when I cowered.

Matron wound and unwound the pouch string around her thumb. "Yes, *stain*. There was a fight last night while you were so very busy letting rats demolish the last of our big eggs and chicken feed."

Ah. A bloodstain. There was one of those right by the front door that wouldn't come out, no matter how much I scrubbed. It was shaped like a hand with a missing finger. Another permanent bloodstain was by a table. It looked like a large, spiky horn nut. She didn't mention those, though, and I wasn't about to bring them up.

Matron turned to her son. "Hut! You're burning the squid! I bought it especially for the captain. Squid chowder is supposed to be his favorite!"

I glanced at the hearth. She was right. The iridescent flesh was badly charred on one side.

"It's not my fault." Hut banged the edge of the metal spit holding the bulbous clump of seafood. "Stupid thing's supposed to turn itself." He thumped it once more to get it moving. "We need a new one. Wretched wizards with their faulty magic." He slid the squid off the spit and onto a cutting board, then began chopping it into rough, uneven pieces.

"Magic doesn't last forever," Matron snapped. "Any idiot knows that. You're supposed to keep track of when it will run out."

"It was supposed to last a year!"

"Said who? Did you watch a wizard do the spell?"

He sighed. "We haven't had a wizard in months, Mother. I got it at market."

"Did you see the maker's signed paper—the contract that it was valid?"

Hut paused to pick his nose, then rubbed the squid with a spice he used to cover the taste of his awful cooking. "Why don't you just marry a wizard instead of a captain, so you can get all the spells you want," he grumbled.

"Maybe I *would* if there were more around, and if any of them stayed in this toilet of a town longer than a day or two!"

While the Trattes bickered, I swiped one of the small bowls stationed to catch roof leaks when it rained. It was half full. I carefully tucked it into the broom closet along with my sack, making sure to lift the flap so that Peck could get out if she wanted to. "I'm sorry," I whispered. It had been a terribly tight squeeze for me, but there was enough space for a small chicken.

Hut reached for a bowl of pepper and accidentally breathed in the tiny grounds. He sneezed onto the mass of tentacles, making me very happy that the squid was too expensive to waste on me. "Like I just told you, I bought it from Greevy. He said the maker's paper was . . ." Hut's face fell. "He said it was lost."

"*Greevy?*" Matron groaned. "I told you not to buy from him. Those chickens were supposed to stay large for three months at the price I paid, and they're going back to normal after a week. He's a forger and a crook!" She filled a large pitcher from the water barrel and poured it carefully into the ale barrel, then repeated the process.

My stomach clenched. Watering down ale was like cheating at cards. It was done all over Trapper's Cove, but only those who got caught were punished for it. As the server, I'd be the one caught.

I slipped my apron on and grabbed one of three thick wizard matches that were tucked inside a covered spittoon on the floor. Wizard matches could be used over and over when scraped against any surface, at least until they wore out. I removed a single match and buried it deep in the apron's pocket.

Squeezing the small rug under one armpit, I turned to address the full tray of glasses. It was heavy, but experience and the matron's version of consequences had strengthened my arms and wrists. I lifted it with two hands, then carefully shifted it to one. Just the two pitchers were left. Fingers threaded through the handles, I gathered them both in my free hand and pushed backward through the swinging door.

The Tinderbox's wooden tables were packed full of sailors. A smell drenched the air—thick layers of body odor and foul breath and leaky bandages. One sailor was as tall and wide as the door frame, her arm muscles the size of babies. Most were average in height and sinewy of limb, not unlike me.

"Ale!" called a few of them.

"Stew!" called others, clattering spoons against the bars on the front windows.

Once the pitchers and glasses and bloodstain had been dealt with, I stood on a stool and used the bottom of my apron to polish the five small paintings hanging over the tavern's fireplace: Queen Alessa the Peace Bringer, Queen Barra the Peace Defender, Queen Rona the Peace Watcher, Queen Nadina the Peace Keeper, and our current leader, Queen Sonora, who had not yet been given her Peace title.

I rubbed the dust from Queen Alessa's young face first—she was only sixteen when she took the crown, after her mother and father died fighting in the war with Tartín, the bordering queendom. The war had lasted a very ugly ten years. Around Peace Day, Maradonian sailors sometimes

sang old songs into their mugs about Tartínian soldiers crossing the mountains that divided our two queendoms, trying to
steal our home for its convenient access to the sea.

By the age of seventeen, Alessa had managed to bring
an end to the war, ushering in the era of Peace. Tartín hadn't
bothered us since.

And where would I be at seventeen? Unless the matron
married the captain, I'd still be flinging the very large poop of
very large sheep and being jealous of hungry rats.

Through letters and negotiation, Alessa had convinced
armies to put down their weapons, retreat, and never return.
Meanwhile, I could barely write a word.

I spit onto the cloth and rubbed a dried splatter of stew
from Queen Barra's cheek. Queen Rona was her sister, and
the two looked nearly identical, down to matching moles.
They both wore simple necklace chains tucked into their
gowns. Both portraits had small tears at the bottom from a
tavern fight. I tried to press the curling pieces of canvas back
into place. Failing, I addressed the next painting.

Queen Nadina had remained unbetrothed and unwed
for all of her life. Her coronation portrait included her smiling eight-year-old daughter, Sonora. Nadina was a smooth-
cheeked, white-haired beauty. Her daughter had similar
features, but her hair was darker, so black that it nearly sparkled, like one of my wizard stones. The girl's earlobes were

marked by two sets of delicate blue earrings that matched the colors of Maradon's flag. Her head rested on the soft curve of her mother's elbow, filling the space as though it was exactly where it belonged. The pair fit together.

I let my eyes linger on the two of them.

"Stub!" Matron Tratte yelled, poking her head out of the kitchen. "Hurry up!"

Hastily, I moved on. The last coronation portrait had been created just a year after Queen Nadina's was painted. Sonora stood alone this time, looking very small for the size of the crown resting on her head. She wore a determined, almost defiant expression that seemed much too old for her years. It was as though the girl in the painting with her mother had aged fifty years, not one. She'd been nine years old when her mother died unexpectedly. By my calculations, she would be twelve now. My age.

"Bet you'd like to switch places with our young queen, eh, Stubby?" A canvas bag smacked against my bare calves.

I jumped down from the stool before the bag could whack me again.

The old sea woman was a regular. She cradled a half-full mug in a well-callused hand and snorted into her glass. "The only queendom you'll inherit is that dirty pen behind this dirty castle—but, no worries, I'll drink to your long life. To Queenie Stub the Muck Cleaner, who's always there to mop up other people's messes." Ale trickled down her chin, splashing her own small mess onto the floor as she turned to babble to the woman beside her.

I left them, traveling the room to light the wizard lamps, striking the match against the wall each time to spark an extra-bright flame. Gentle puffs of odorless, colored smoke rose from the lamps, filling the tavern with a pleasant haze that helped mask the general dinginess of the place. I was versed enough in serving at the Tinderbox to know that you only had to bend down a bit to see through the light fog. I was good at noticing things from that angle.

I noticed a large man at the corner table, arm-wrestling a small, muscled woman and losing badly. I noticed a thick-necked woman trying to pry the magical music box off the wall. She didn't know it was fastened with enchanted nails and wouldn't budge. I noticed Hut picking up a tooth from the floor and glancing around before trying to fit it into the space in his mouth.

But I failed to notice Matron Tratte until a tingle of warning swept over my ears and a thick pinch caught me at the tender back of my arm.

A sheen of sweat shone on the matron's peachy cheeks. She looked anxious as she marched me back to the kitchen, but she sounded scarily calm when she spoke next.

"Listen to me carefully, Stub. Captain Vella is coming

this way after he settles his trades. I've paid the dock manager to send him here and here only. He'll be spending two nights in our rooms. He is handsome and, more important, rich and without a wife." She licked a bead of moisture above her lips. "Do you understand?"

I nodded.

"I'm told he drinks wine. You'll buy two bottles. I can't afford to lose this chance just because we get all the cheap, low-class travelers who only drink horn-nut ale."

Matron Tratte herself only drank horn-nut ale. She kept her own private barrel. In fact she had a tall mug clutched in her hand at the moment, but I thought it best not to point this out. Instead I grabbed my rucksack from the broom closet, closing the flap over Peck before I hefted it to my shoulders.

The matron breathed deeply through her nose and fluffed her hair. She opened the back door and fanned herself, gazing in the direction of the harbor.

"This is it, Nuisance. The fresh start I've been waiting for. I've wanted to leave this place since I was a little girl. I'll have a new husband and a proper home by Peace Day, mark my words. And who knows?" Her voice grew higher. "Maybe we'll be able to hire an expensive house wizard." She drummed her fingers across her lips. "Perhaps I'll have a title. Lady Tratte and Captain Vella," she murmured. "Or Captain Tratte, if he wants to take my name. Or Lady Vella, if I take his. They all sound wonderful, don't you think? And a manor—I *must* have a manor for my own little queendom."

She smiled at me strangely, and it took me a moment to realize that the strangeness was because she looked genuinely happy. I'd never seen that.

"I might even keep you with me. Imagine that, Stub— you could be cleaning a fine house. We might even get you shoes."

Then her gaze shifted from the docks to the yard, where the sheep crowded together. Her nose wrinkled at the sight of my shelter, and her tone shifted as well. She straightened her shoulders. "Or perhaps you belong here. In that case, if all goes well, I'll tear up the contract letter in my safe and you can do as you please."

I felt my heart quicken. The letter from my mother was in her safe. My own mother's words were less than a dozen feet from where I stood.

"Shear all the sheep when you get back from market, so you can sell their wool tomorrow. Use the money to buy me the most expensive dress you can find." She smoothed her red tunic. "This will do for tonight, but I want to wear some- thing new tomorrow night."

I gaped at her. There were six wizard-enhanced sheep. Each was taller than me. "I can't finish all the shearing tonight," I blurted. "It takes hours just to do one."

"Does it?" Matron Tratte smiled a dangerous smile and leaned down. "Then you'd best hurry. You will shear every last one of them. *Tonight.*" She emptied a coin purse into her palm and counted the *clink, clink, clink* of the money. "When you buy the wine, you may buy a wizard blade to make the work go faster. If you can't find a wizard blade, you'll use a kitchen one."

My heart sank. Wizard blades were rare at the market. If I couldn't find one, there would be no chance for sleep before the next morning's chores began.

"And *Stub* . . ." Matron Tratte pointed to my rucksack. "Any hen that's not laying should go in the pot. If you don't come back with the wine in time, I'll be serving the captain your pet chicken this very night, instead of squid. And even if you deliver the wine, if the sheep aren't shorn by the time I wake up, it'll be roasted chicken for breakfast. That's a promise."

I shook my head ever so slightly, and backed toward the door.

The matron advanced, arching an eyebrow. She crooked a finger under my chin. "That hen is my property. Just like you. Get the wine. Shear the sheep." She winked. "Or I'll make you do the plucking."

I swallowed a sour taste in my mouth. I knew the matron well. The threat was not an empty one.

"Now go," Matron ordered. "Do as—"

"I'm told," I finished for her. "Yes, Matron."

As the matron swept back into the dining area, I took the bundle of coin and turned just as Hut was coming inside from the yard with a basket of small eggs. He sank his elbow into my side as I passed, and I fell, scraping my belly down the steps into the backyard. I held in a moan and stood, grateful that Peck was on my back, not my front.

"That's for me having to do your serving job while you're at market." He glared down at me. "Face it, Stub-Rot. The captain probably isn't even coming. You're never getting out of here. None of us are." Piling plates on a tray, he stalked bitterly into the tavern.

Peck and I hurried out the back gate and trotted down the main street toward the harbor, weaving between travelers who were on their way to food and rest.

I passed the village flagpole, where a green cloth flew whenever a wizard was in port. It had been empty for months. Though I'd learned from travelers that there were wizards scattered throughout all of Maradon, most lived in Maradon Cross, the royal city. Any wizard who came into port was mobbed with requests. Matron was right—they never seemed to stay more than a day or two.

My mind drifted to the matron's excitement about this year's Peace Day, and the fresh start it could bring, should her wish to be married to a sea captain come true by then.

Though my life was anything but peaceful, I always looked forward to the holiday. The Trattes and their patrons got caught up in the celebration, so much that they didn't notice if I took a few precious minutes away from cleaning the last of the night's dishes. While the entire village flocked to the cove for an hour-long fireburst display, Peck and I stayed behind. I sat on top of the Tinderbox's crumbling wall and Peck sat in my arms. Together, the two of us celebrated the queendom's Peace.

The wideness of the night sky and the brightness of the lights should have made me feel even smaller—even less than I already was. But instead, somehow, for one golden hour each year I felt like I belonged in the world.

As I approached the motley rows of market tents, my rucksack wiggled. I turned the bag around so it rested against my chest. I squeezed Peck twice, then twice more. *I'm here. You're here.* Three gentle pokes on my belly responded. *We're here together.*

The exchange was normally a reassuring one. At least we had each other. But somehow, this time felt different. Peck was already six years old. I wasn't sure how long chickens could live, but she deserved better than to spend her final years in the animal pen. Would the matron really free me if she remarried? Would life on the streets of Trapper's Cove be easier? Or was Hut right, and nothing would ever change?

I whispered the only certainty I could to my friend. "One week, Peck. Just seven more days until we'll see the Peace Night firebursts again. We'll watch them together. I promise you that."

I placed a secure hold on the coin purse around my neck. The open-air marketplace was full of thieves. "But first we've got to make it through tonight. My eyes steady, your beak ready."

3

How to Be a Dagger Thief

ᏨᏆᏫ

Matron Tratte was right—the greasy-haired, beady-eyed man at the stall in front of me was a dirty cheat. But the knife in his hand was the only wizard blade I'd seen in the entire line of market tents.

"Do you want it or not?" Greevy asked impatiently, his eyes shifting to the other market-goers. "There were only ten in the shipment, and they all sold lightning fast." He raised a piece of paper in his hand. "Like I said, it's indestructible, good for two years. The wizard signed it."

I ignored the forged paper. "If it's so indestructible, throw it in there," I told him, nodding to an empty steel bucket beside him.

Greevy frowned. "What for?"

I frowned back until he shrugged and tossed the blade. It hit the bottom of the bucket with a clatter.

I leaned over, looking closely at the knife. The wooden handle carried a small carving of Maradon's emblem: guard-

ian gates to symbolize protection, a Book of Peace to symbolize the letters Alessa wrote, and a shining jewel to represent
the value of peace. That meant it had been created in Maradon Cross, the royal city. The knifemaker's initials were
carved into the metal.

I took a polishing cloth off Greevy's table and covered the
bucket, then peered underneath, like I'd seen a tradesman do
with a load of wizard knives the previous year. Sure enough,
the maker's mark glowed slightly with traces of strong magic.
The knife was genuine.

Matron Tratte was probably tapping her foot on the front
porch of the tavern, waiting for wine. I should've bought the
drink first, I knew that, but the wine vendors had all had long
lines when I'd first made my way through the market. And
the thought of shearing all those sheep with a kitchen knife
made my hands throb.

I cleared my throat. "I'll give you seven for it."

Greevy looked greedily at the coin purse hanging
around my neck. He kneaded his hands together, mentally
counting the contents, and then grinned, flashing yellow
teeth tinged with black flecks of tumbleleaf. "You've got
more than seven," he said, snatching the bucket. "Ten.
No less."

I had twenty coin with me. I'd never bought wine
before, but I guessed I'd need to save at least six coin to buy

two bottles. The wizard knife was worth fifteen, easily. But Greevy didn't seem to know that.

"Your paper's a fake," I said, keeping my voice stern. "The knife's sharpness won't last a month, let alone two years." I opened the purse. "Eight."

Greevy leaned forward, crossing his arms. "Ten."

I crossed my own arms. "Nine."

Greevy rubbed his stubbled chin and glanced behind me, hoping to catch the eye of another customer. He rang a small bell. Its sound was harsh and aggressive, more like clinking swords than beckoning music. "Knives and pots here!" he called to the people streaming along the rows of tents. "Enhanced and otherwise, best you'll find in Maradon!" When no one approached, he grunted. His eyes narrowed in defeat. "Fine, nine it is," he said. "Dagger thief."

Relief and impatience washed over me. The knife had taken far too long. I still needed to find the bottles, and it was getting late. At least half my time had passed. Peck shifted inside the rucksack and poked her beak out, telling me to get a move on.

But as Greevy started to wrap the blade, a breathless woman in uniform ran up to the tent. "Wait! Is that the last one? I need that knife!"

The Roamer was tall and thick-limbed. Her eyes were the green-blue of the sea before it turned deep and dark. Her chestnut hair was wrapped into several small knots, as was common with those in the messenger trade, and her skin was the color of dry sand, paler than most Maradonians'. She wore a medallion stamped with a messenger bird on the top half and Maradon's emblem on the bottom. A strongbox perched on her back, boasting three imposing locks.

Roamers were paid handsomely for the messages and packages they delivered. The woman was sure to have plenty of coin. And Greevy knew it.

He stopped wrapping the blade and swished it in the air for the Roamer to admire. "Indeed, this is the very last," he told her. "Came all the way from Maradon Cross. They're very rare—only two came in the shipment! Top quality, never go dull, sharp as my wit, but enchanted to never slice so much as a fingernail from the bearer's hand."

"Perfect. I'll pay double the price this child's offered for it."

That knife was mine! I clenched my rucksack, and it offered an encouraging poke back, courtesy of Peck. Taking a deep breath, I turned to face the woman, who held out a coin purse twice as stuffed as mine.

But none of my words came out right. In fact, barely any words came out at all. "I need that for . . ." I stopped talking and felt a rush of heat creep up my neck.

"I'm sorry," the Roamer said. Her voice was not unkind

as she bent to look directly into my eyes. "But I need it more. I have plans for this knife."

With bony, scarred knuckles, Greevy pounded agreement onto his table. "Excellent! Now, perhaps you'd also be interested in these fine Maradonian pots." The stall owner hastily shoved me. "Go away—we're done here." He scowled. "Do as you're told."

"Come on, Peck," I whispered into my satchel, trying to keep my voice hopeful. "We'll look for the wine now." The wizard knife would have made the work go five times as fast, but I could shear with a kitchen knife. It would be all right. It had to be.

But the wine tents I'd passed earlier were all closed up for the night. The few that were open were all sold out.

"Sorry," said a toothless vendor. "Fancy captain's in port, didn't you hear? Every tavern owner in town wants his business or his hand in marriage or both. Word is, he's not staying long." She reached up to close her tent flap.

I felt my chances at freedom closing along with it. And Peck's chances as well.

Frantically, I searched for anyone still selling wine. Instead I only found more vendors promoting the upcoming holiday.

"Peace flags! Get your Peace flags, especially made for the anniversary!"

"Peace mugs! Celebrate one hundred years of unbreak-able Peace with unbreakable mugs to toast with!"

"Royal Peace portraits and firebursts here! Just ten coin for any item, in honor of one hundred years of Peace!"

I rushed past the paintings, feeling the steady gaze of a dozen Queen Sonoras following me.

I threaded past tents still selling barrels of fish and bread, cloth and weapons. Past candles made of enchanted wax that wouldn't melt, rings that never lost their shine, teas that encouraged wonderful singing voices. I didn't need any of that.

A two-tone horn sounded in the harbor. It was the wharf manager, announcing the closing of the evening market.

"Where can we buy two bottles of wine, Peck?" I mut-tered. *Think, think, think!*

Most of Trapper's Cove was set on the west side of the harbor. In general, the whole village was the type of place where it was wise to sleep with all your belongings. But there was a small section of village to the east of the harbor. That side had slightly more respectable establishments and a few shops. I could see them now, on the other side of the market tents.

The nearest tavern was cream-colored with clean brown trim and a fine torch on either side of the front door. A mer-chant was reaching for the door. She wore loose blue trousers embroidered with gold thread. Her blouse and hat were equally fine, and her thick brown ledger bag had tassels. The woman's posture was confident.

A person like that, I thought, *might be someone who expects to be served wine.*

Matron Tratte had not given permission for me to go anywhere other than the market. I had never in my life taken a step beyond it. But the soft heartbeat in my satchel gave me courage. Slowly, I tried sounding out the tavern's name, feeling a surge of hope. "Fork and Cork."

I licked my fingers and tried to smooth my rough-chopped hair. I swung the rucksack to my back and looked down at my too-short trousers and too-long tunic and simple apron. My clothes were splattered with a lifetime of stains, both from the animal pen and from my tavern duties.

"Right, Peck," I said over my shoulder. "We'll try the back door."

I passed the last of the market and felt something tighten inside me. A fierce sea gust whipped around into the cove as though it knew I was heading to a place I didn't belong.

I leaned hard into the blowing wind and moved steadily forward.

The back gate of the Fork & Cork had a flimsy lock that I could have picked with a wizard match. There was no need for that, as it was already propped open by a bucket of coals. The back door was cracked open a hand's width. The glorious smell of baking bread and something savory wafted through the space.

I peered through the crack. A young cook, no older than me, thrust a thin wooden slab into a clay oven beside the hearth. He swiftly transferred six fresh loaves and a pan of rolls to a butcher block. Wisps of steam rose gently from the bread as he sliced it. He placed the pieces into small baskets, then turned and stirred tomatoes and olives in a sizzling pan.

His sleeves were rolled up, revealing dark lines on his thick arms that I recognized as oven scars. Half his hair was pulled up into a high bun. The rest hung loose, long and wavy and brown, with a single white streak running through one side. He wore an unusual belt around his waist, with a dozen or more small glass jars attached at intervals. His kitchen sandals were half-covered with leather, to protect his toes from spills and any falling pots or pans. They were like Hut's, only nicer.

Beside him was a middle-aged man with no hair to speak of. He sang a soft, cheerful tune and patted the boy gently on the shoulder, then took a tray of the still-steaming bread out to what I presumed was the dining area.

Placing the skillet aside, the boy turned to address a bag of enormous potatoes. He was shorter than me and didn't look particularly strong—he had the healthy softness of a well-fed child. Still, he lifted and poured the tubers into a stone sink with ease. As he scrubbed them, he hummed the same tune the man had sung. His foot tapped along with the melody. He thought he was alone.

He was not. I ducked down as a familiar figure appeared in the room.

There in that same doorway was the woman who'd so rudely stolen away the wizard knife. She held it now. She watched the boy, unwrapping the blade from its cloth as she silently crossed the kitchen.

I have plans for this knife, the woman had said.

My heartbeat quickened and I felt myself freeze. Just as the Roamer reached the boy, he turned and gasped, his eyes widening at the sight of the woman behind him.

"Green gravy," he breathed. He dropped the potato he'd been holding. It rolled across the floor and out the back door just as I came to my senses.

I picked up the potato, ready to hurl it at the attacker, just as the boy launched himself into the woman's arms.

"Mother!" he shouted. "You're here!"

I stopped myself just in time.

The Roamer laughed and released him from a long embrace. "Come, Beaman. I've brought you something." She stepped over to the stovetop and dipped a finger inside the saucepan. She brought it to her lips and closed her eyes. "Mmm, my dear. You have such a gift, you could make grass dance on my tongue. What's that spice?"

I shrank back into the shadows, feeling my cheeks flush. I'd been so sure the woman was about to attack.

The boy called Beaman reddened with the compliment. "Tamarindle seeds. I sautéed them first, in the tinadub oil you always bring me. You're right—it draws the best flavors out of everything it touches. And it's wonderful when we're running low on wood—just a sprinkle keeps the hearth flames burning nice and long."

His mother nodded thoughtfully. "Excellent for wound care as well. Heals like a dream. But here—look." She passed the blade to him. "It's wizard-made, Beaman. Sharp as a royal sword, with no chance of cuts for the bearer." She cupped his cheek. "It's so good to see you."

The boy unsheathed the knife and admired the blade, turning it this way and that to catch the firelight. "How long are you here for this time?" he asked. He stepped over to a small table, where two wheels of cheese rested. He cut into one. "Try some. I made a batch two months ago. My own recipe. It's just finished aging."

My mouth watered. The cheese was a rich, buttery yellow. The stuff we served at the Tinderbox looked nothing like it.

The Roamer popped a slice in her mouth and closed her eyes. "Tastes like a sunrise spent with you. I'm staying a few days. I've got some deliveries here and I'll see who's in need of my services." She kissed his head. "Then I'm off to the Queendom of Katara." Her eyes sparkled at his expression. "Yes, all the way across the sea. It'll be an adventure, that's certain. I've already started a fresh Roaming journal. And a warm hat. I've never traveled in snow."

Beaman sheathed the knife. "Can I come with you?"

She smiled sadly. "You know that's not possible. Oh! But wait." She rummaged through her pack and came up with a massive skein of squishy blue yarn. Attached to it were two knitting needles and a long, foot-wide scarf. "It's getting ridiculously long. I've been making it for ages. I'll finish it while I'm here and give it to you."

I should have been relieved that nobody was being murdered, but as I watched them, I suddenly felt like someone was stepping on my chest. Every time I took a breath, my insides felt a hard pinch, like Matron Tratte's rough fingers had somehow found a way inside me.

The boy took the scarf. "Thank you. But I'd rather . . ." He reddened once more.

"Rather what, darling?"

His voice grew small. "I want to travel with you."

"Oh, my Beaman. You were so young when we stopped

in to say hello to Pap all those years ago. Even then you couldn't stop asking him happy gibberish questions about the bits of spiced gourd he fed you. You were so excited when he offered you an apprenticeship. This what you wanted." She picked a piece of herb from his hair. "Besides, the life of a Roamer is not for you. You trust anything with a heartbeat."

Considering the unlocked gate, I suspected the Roamer was right.

"Listen to me." She put her hands on his shoulders and smiled at him warmly. "You are a fierce adventurer in the kitchen, but you don't like the cold. Have you ever spent a night outdoors?"

Beaman shifted out of her grasp. "No, but—"

"No is enough." She laughed fondly. "The only fires you've built are inside a hearth. You, Beaman Cork, were meant for this life, in here. Not that life, out there. It's too dangerous. Continue with your cooking. It is your gift to the world, my love. The knife should be of use to you, don't you think?"

Beaman looked at the knife. "Yes. Thank you. But if you would only talk to Pap, maybe—"

"Stop asking." The Roamer ruffled his hair and stood. "I need to know that you're safe." She pointed at the stove. "Save me a bowl of that for after my deliveries. I can't wait for a good night's rest after filling my belly with your wonders.

I might be home very late. Can I sleep in the guest room? I don't want to wake you or Pap."

I watched the boy's face fall. "Of course," he said. "It's empty tonight."

"Good." She nuzzled her nose against his, then yawned. "We'll talk more over breakfast."

He blinked several times and nodded.

The Roamer strode to the back door. She inhaled deeply and smiled. "You have such talent." She blew her son a kiss. "Remember, Papredon Cork is one of my closest friends. He chose you. He needs you."

I pressed myself against the outer wall of the tavern as the Roamer passed.

"But I need *you*," Beaman said to the empty kitchen.

The tall woman stepped through the back gate, muttering to herself about carelessness as she locked it. She took off toward the main street. I waited a moment, then knocked on the back door.

There was no answer. I leaned an ear against the wood. I could hear a muffled sniffling noise buried beneath the heavy sound of aggressive chopping.

I knocked again. "Hello?" I called. "Can I come in? I need help."

"Go away!" The boy's voice shook. "I'm not supposed to give to beggars."

I knocked a third time. "I've got money. I'm from the Tinderbox, on the west side of the cove. We need wine."

The chopping slowed. "Then go to the marketplace."

"It's closed."

The chopping halted altogether. A moment later, the door swung open.

The young cook motioned me in. His face was streaked with tears. He sniffed and wiped a strand of hair from his face. He had light brown Maradonian skin, but his mother's turquoise eyes. His ears were pierced with small silver discs. "Make it fast, please." He sniffed again. "Your eyes might water from the onions."

He returned to the large table, where a scattering of onions, some sliced and some whole, took up space where none had been before.

Stepping into the kitchen, I noticed three paintings hanging above the fire. One was of seafood stew, and one was a trio of vegetables on a cutting board. The center painting was the same coronation portrait of Queen Sonora that hung on the Tinderbox wall.

Beaman wiped his hands. If he thought anything rude about my appearance, he said not a word with his mouth or eyes. "How many bottles?"

"Two. I've got a few coin. I can get more later if—" I stopped myself. There was the knife—*my* knife—sitting on top of the rubbish bin, resting on a pile of potato peelings. He'd thrown it out!

The boy walked over to a large trunk beside a tapped ale barrel. He opened the lid. "Berry wine . . . I've got one bottle left." He opened the trunk wider to reveal a dozen or more empty bottles. "And that's all. A new shipment is coming tomorrow."

I felt Peck shift in my rucksack, as though she, too, felt the invisible blow. One bottle would not be enough. I looked at the knife again.

He glanced over his shoulder. "What are you looking at?"

I pointed to the rubbish bin. "I tried to buy that blade. The price was agreed on, but then your mother paid more."

He picked up the knife, still in its thick brown sheath. He brushed off a stubborn peeling, held it for a moment, then thrust it toward me. "You can have it. I'm done with her gifts. She means well, but she doesn't listen."

I stepped back. "Oh no, I couldn't." I tried to ignore a series of indignant Peck pokes on my back.

Beaman flipped it, caught the sheath with two fingers, and held the handle toward me.

"Are you sure?" I nearly refused again, but Peck helped me come to my senses with one final, firm use of her beak. I snatched the knife before he could change his mind.

"I'm sure," he said. "I've got plenty of sharp blades." He reached into a butcher block, pulling out a chopping knife. With lightning speed, he turned the last uncut onion into hundreds of tiny, perfectly even pieces, then threw the blade fiercely at the wall. It spun several times, then buried itself into a hanging cutting board. He grinned. "My mother taught me that trick. I'm up to five in a row before I miss. You see—it's not the knife, it's the hand that holds it, right?"

Inwardly, I gulped, noting his facial features so I wouldn't accidentally try to out-bargain him if we ever met at the market. "Nice throw." I looked down at the wizard blade in my hand and shook my head, wishing I'd better absorbed the Tratte trait of taking advantage of people. Despite Peck's urging, I held the knife out toward him. "I can't take it. It's too valuable."

"Then you'll owe me a favor."

A *favor*. It was a dangerous business, owing people favors. As a newborn baby, I'd made the unfortunate mistake of being abandoned and dropped on the porch of the Tinderbox. Matron Tratte reminded me nearly every day that she had done me the favor of plucking me from the loose draping of sailcloth I came wrapped in. Now I owed her my life.

"No," I told him. "Besides, I have nothing to offer."

"Then I'll owe *you* a favor, for taking it off my hands." The boy smiled again, waiting for me to make some sort of reply—as though he wanted me to be there. To say some-thing. To simply talk to him. It was unnerving. While he was busy grinning at me, a complete stranger, I could have snatched up a frying pan and bopped him on the head, then stolen all his food.

His mother was definitely right about him.

I put six coin on the table. "I'll take the wine." My eyes fell on the empty bottles in the trunk. I bit my lip. "Can I have an empty bottle as well?"

Beaman's eyebrows rose, and then he winked, grabbing a bowl of round, fleshy fruit from beside the sink. "Surely someone will notice if they taste it. But they'll *look* exactly the same. And if you add the right amount of vinegar, it stands a chance of fooling someone who's had too much. Pap sometimes does that when he feels someone's a danger to themselves. Are the bottles for the same person?"

Baffled, I nodded, and watched as the boy—the strange boy who'd never met me before this day—filled the empty bottle with water and squeezed berries into it until the liq-uid turned a deep crimson. He smiled wider as he poured a small amount of clear liquid inside and shook the contents together. "I'll put a notch on the cork with the fake wine. Start with the real wine, and maybe they won't get to the other. You can come tomorrow and replace the false one."

I put the knife and bottles in my bag.

"Today is a bread day. I made extra." Beaman held out a handful of small brown rolls, speckled in seed. "For you." He grinned. "And for that chicken poking out of your bag."

The room had grown uncomfortably warm. I didn't want to come tomorrow. I didn't even want to be here now. I did, however, want the bread. I could imagine the feel of it, gloriously crammed into my mouth. But why was the boy behaving so oddly? It made no sense at all.

The knife had already been in the rubbish bin when he gave it to me. That was acceptable. But I ignored the bread. I added two more coin on the table and stepped back, not looking at him. "For the berry juice. I'm going now." I turned and ran, glad to be out of that place.

I sprinted past the closed market, looking once more at the center of the harbor. This year the queen herself had sent every port town in Maradon an enormous magical sand clock that connected to the tides and stars, keeping track of hours and days. This one was made of light blue glass and navy sand. It had thin, glowing tick marks on one side, counting down the time until the momentous Peace Day anniversary.

Seven more days.

The waxing moon sent flashes across the sea waves, and the clock glinted too, sending pulses of dark blue into the night.

· · ·

The matron was waiting by the back door with a sour, angry plum of a face, wringing her hands. She dragged me in by the collar.

"You're late! Thank goodness the captain is late too!" She looked past the wall, toward the harbor. "Did you see him?"

I swallowed hard. For all I knew, the dock manager had taken multiple bribes and the captain was already three drinks in at the Bitter Crab Tavern or the Salty Shark Inn. "He's probably busy. There's still lots of trading going on down there," I lied.

With a sigh of relief, she let me go and smoothed her dress. "Oh. Good. Well, what are you waiting for! Go shear the sheep! That wool brings in a fortune, and I need a dress that's worth a fortune! Now, where's the wine?"

I pulled the bottles from my sack.

She tore them away, hissing like a starving cat. She placed one on a tray scattered with flowers and a single unbreakable glass.

Oh no. The bottle on the tray had a notched cork. The captain might still show up, and if he didn't, I had no doubt the matron would be drowning her sorrows in the bottle.

I slipped the coin purse from my neck and tossed it on the table behind her. The purse still bulged.

The matron studied it with narrowed eyes. "Didn't you get the wizard blade?"

I hesitated. The boy had given the blade to me. I'd never been given anything.

"Well?" Matron demanded.

"I was about to buy the last one. Then a thief took it."

"How much is left?"

I shrugged. "I can't count that high."

She grumbled and turned to count the purse's contents. As she did, I quickly switched the bottles, then reached into a high cabinet for the fine glasses that Hut had pilfered from the room of a trader the week before.

"What are you doing?" the matron barked, turning around sharply.

I raised the glasses. "Would the captain like these? Maybe two, in case he's sharing with you?"

Matron looked over at the glasses. Her cheeks grew rosy. "Indeed," she murmured. She stuffed the coin purse down the front of her dress and swiped the glasses from my out-stretched hands.

"Never mind the stolen knife," she said, with a milder tone. "This entire cove is a prison of thieves. You'll use one of our knives." She fixed me with one final, meaningful glare. "Just be done shearing those sheep by morning or it's chicken for breakfast. Understand?"

"Yes, Matron."

"Good." She looked me over. "And stay away from the

serving area tonight. In fact, stay out of the tavern altogether. I don't need Captain Vella thinking you're family."

I waited for the matron to leave, then stashed the false wine out of view before heading to the backyard for my next task.

Peck wandered the moonlit yard while I led the first sheep to the shearing stocks.

The sheep was taller than me and twice as round as the biggest ale barrels at market. The wizard couple who'd enhanced the animals had been traveling with a trading ship. They'd consulted with each other, then pointed their hands at the sheep, doing some sort of finger dance while whispering words beneath their breath. And, just like that, the animals had grown. Quadruple the wool. Quadruple the quality. Their young daughter had watched and clapped her hands. It was such a wondrous sight that I'd clapped as well, and for once, Matron Tratte didn't scream at me for making noise. I was completely enchanted until I realized that it meant quadruple the sheep mess to clean up.

Whispering an apology, I clamped iron rings around the animal's legs and neck, tightening the attached chains so it would stay put.

"Don't worry," I said gently. "You'll be free again soon." But the sheep still twitched, and the words sounded empty, even to me.

The wizard blade made for fast work. In an hour's time, I finished the first. Five hours later, all six had been shorn, the wool stuffed into large canvas sacks. I shook out my arms and tunic, sending soft remnants of the wool flying. I was filthy. Well, filthier than usual. The new day would begin in a matter of hours. I yawned. "Let's get cleaned up."

Peck and I jumped the wall and walked to a nearby stream that trickled down from somewhere in the mountains. Stepping into the cold water, I bent, scrubbing off wool and dirt with a flat stone that I always left on a nearby boulder. I kept my trousers on as I cleaned them. Wild dogs had shown up once, and I'd had to choose between pants and Peck. The choice was simple, but it had not been fun to climb rough tree bark with naked legs while holding a terrified chicken.

As I lowered myself farther, ready to apply the same treatment to my top layers, a prickle ran through me. It wasn't my elbow that tingled. Or my ears or my neck or my toes. It was everywhere—a warning unlike one I'd ever felt before.

Something was coming.

I scanned the streambed and the moonlit water. I saw nothing unusual.

Not until I looked down.

A *poof* of green smoke drifted up from my waist, lingering in front of me. It came from my apron pocket.

I blinked, and the smoke was gone. Had I imagined it? Hunger sometimes made the world waver a bit. I dismissed the emerald cloud as an illusion. But then my apron pocket grew heavy on the right, as though I'd dropped one of my magical rocks inside.

The weight jerked to the left.

It made a grumbling sound.

And then it spoke.

4

How to Greet a Pocket Lump

The scrubbing stone fell from my hand. Saying that my pocket "spoke" was an understatement. My pocket was shouting.

"I'm trapped!" it cried. "I'm being drowned!"

I stared at the lump hidden beneath the damp cloth. There had to be a logical explanation for it.

Surely, I'd heard a noise, not a *voice*. After all, I was tired. I was hungry. And Hut sometimes slipped screeching, large-pincered insects or harmless, frightened mice inside my apron for giggles. Yes, of course—that had to be the case. Whatever it was thrashed mightily against the cloth.

"Where am I?" the voice demanded.

I stumbled out of the water, still gawking at my apron. Were the words all in my head? If they were, then why did my head words sound like an angry, scraggly voiced man?

"Peck," I whispered. "Whatever you do, do not panic."

Peck looked at me briefly, then continued scratching at the

water's edge. "That's right." I swallowed, not wanting to look down again. "Well done."

I shook out the tremble in my fingers and pressed a hand lightly against the cloth. The bulge roiled beneath my palm. I relaxed. It *did* feel like a mouse—a small, squishy, feisty, squeaking mouse. I let out a long breath. "I told you not to worry, Peck."

Peck ignored me. After wading quickly back to shore, I emptied the pocket onto a streamside boulder. And then I nearly fainted.

The moonlight did not shine down on a mouse. Or an insect.

I rubbed my eyes, sure that I was seeing things.

On the boulder stood a tiny man, no more than a thumb's length in height. He wore a red nightdress that grazed the tops of his delicate but filthy slippers. A limp, long, wet nightcap of the same color draped over one of his shoulders. His sleeves were rolled up, and around one of his wrists was a delicate bracelet, marked with a single green jewel.

"What dream is this?" I muttered, careful to keep my voice soft so I didn't startle the tiny thing.

He was so busy coughing and whirling about that he didn't appear to see me. He held the wizard match I'd forgotten to return to the spittoon, hefting it straight and using it as a tall walking stick. He marched to the edge of the boul-

HOW TO SAVE A QUEENDOM · 55

der opposite me and leaned down for a look, almost tumbling over the side. He stumbled backward and angrily threw the match down beside him.

"What nightmare is this!" the man cried. Then he griped and fussed and hurled surly, insulting sounds into the world. His face grew redder and redder, like an angry, wrinkled, newborn piglet. I watched him, fascinated. It was like seeing a miniature Matron Tratte having a fit.

Shivering, the man began furiously twisting water from the fabric clinging to his substantial stomach. He tore off his sodden nightcap and threw it next to the match. The bald spot on top of his head took up a large residence, with long, thin, ivory hair covering the rest of his skull. Wild chops of thick facial hair sprang from his temples and extended down the sides of his jaw. The hair clump narrowed only as it made its way around a rather prominent and deeply dimpled chin. He was completely wet, and if he had not looked so very fiery as he paced across the boulder, I might have offered him a bit of sheep's wool to dry himself off with.

"Blasted curse!" he grumbled.

"Um . . . hello?" I said quietly.

The man froze, then turned. Slowly, his gaze traveled up the length of my body, stopped at my eyes, then journeyed back down a few inches to rest on my open mouth. A small yelp burst quietly from his lips. He waggled his fingers and firmly said something that sounded like *Sleep deep!*

"What?" I asked.

He repeated the gesture and sound with more force, and I suddenly felt a sensation in my nose, as though I were Hut, sniffing pepper. I sneezed.

The man scowled at his hands, then pointed behind me and gasped. "Oh! Oh my! What could that be?"

I looked behind me. Nothing unusual was there. When I turned back, the tiny man was attempting to scramble down the side of the boulder. Peck came over to investigate the small ruckus. She bobbed forward and lowered her beak, prodding the fellow in the rear.

He shouted and managed to bop her on the beak until she retreated.

I quickly reached over to pull him off the boulder and set him on the ground. "Please, don't, sir. You'll hurt yourself. And don't hit my chicken. She's just curious."

Holding his nightdress, he darted across the bank of the stream, aiming for a shock of tall grass ten feet away. Just before he reached it, he jerked backward and was flung onto his rump, into the mud.

"Are you all right?" I stepped forward and placed him afoot.

The tiny man wrestled free of my fingers and ran between

my legs in the opposite direction. Again, when he was about ten feet away, he was pulled to the ground. He sprang up, trying one last direction. Once more, he fell. This time he did not get up. Instead he pulled himself to a seated position and hastily yanked up the bottom of his nightdress, just enough to reveal his bare ankles. Each was encircled by a faint, green glow. He looked up at me with an irritated sigh.

"Binding spell," he muttered. "Most inconvenient. Well, giant, it appears that we are attached by a magical leash. Are you going to bash me or gobble me up or both?"

I laughed nervously. The small wind I created made the man's nightdress flutter. "I'm not a giant. I'm not going to hurt you. Don't be afraid." I bent at the knee and faced the man. "I'm only a child."

"A child?" The wary expression disappeared as the tiny man stood and crossed his arms. His lips twisted back and forth, as though this new information were a puzzle he was attempting to put together inside his mouth. "If you're not a giant, then I'm . . ." He trailed off, then stared at his hands. Then he stared at my hands.

I cleared my throat. "What exactly are you? I'm sorry if that's a rude question."

"Of course it's a rude question!" The tiny man's puzzled expression was replaced with annoyance. He crossed his arms and looked at me as though I were the small one. "*I* am a wizard. To be more specific, I am Orlen, the royal castle wizard to Queen Rona, Queen Nadina, and now Queen Sonora. Scholar, advisor, keeper of the royal library, and provider of necessary acts of magic."

"A wizard!" Despite the fellow's sour expression, I was charmed. Taking care not to crush the man, I sat down beside him. "I didn't know that wizards could be so small, Master Orlen."

"Hmph. I'm normally twice your size." He crawled onto my knee and warily looked at Peck, who had wandered close again. "Hand me my walking stick."

Walking stick? I searched the ground for the wizard match and passed it over.

He wielded the match like a spear, taking two shaky hops forward to poke Peck on the beak. "Keep that beastly thing away from me."

I lifted Peck and tossed her gently toward the shelter. She fluttered and landed softly. I crossed my legs neatly and put my hands in my lap so he wouldn't think I was going to snatch him up. "Sorry, Master Orlen."

"Just Orlen. Titles are for formal occasions, not disasters." He studied me in the moonlight and coated his frustration with politeness. "Forgive me for not asking sooner—what is your name?"

My cheeks grew warm at the question. Matron Tratte had

told me of my naming many times. After I'd been left on her porch, she'd stumbled into me while dumping the contents of a full spittoon. Though she managed to avoid squashing me, she stubbed her toes most painfully in the process, and drenched her dress in filth. As a result, she thought it fitting to give me a name that would help me remember something important: I was nothing but a burden and a bother from the very start.

I cleared my throat. "Stub-the-Nuisance."

Orlen wrinkled his already wrinkled nose. "That's unfortunate. Can you do without the Nuisance part?"

I nodded.

"Good." He paced uneasily up and down the length of my calf, looking at the stars as if orienting himself. "Now. Am I . . . still in Maradon?"

Funny. Having a tiny person pop into my pocket had me wondering the exact same thing. Feeling the tickle of Orlen's steps, I glanced at the Tinderbox, hoping, as I had many times, that it would be gone. That *I* would be gone, and would wake up somewhere better. That the past twelve years had only been a bad dream. But none of that was true.

"Yes, you're still in Maradon," I told him. At the confirmation, I thought I saw a flicker of disappointment in the wizard. Was he hoping to be somewhere else? I could certainly relate to that. "What were you doing in my pocket?"

He scowled at me. "Another rude question. Where are we, *exactly*? How long until Peace Day?"

"There's one week until Peace Day. And you're in Trapper's Cove. It's a trading post on the queendom's southwest edge."

Orlen let out a glum breath. "About as far from the castle as possible while remaining within the queendom's borders. Still, it could be worse." He climbed to my knee and slipped, tumbling into my hands. He rubbed his hips as he rose. "There's plenty of time to get back to Maradon Cross, if we hurry." He tugged one of my fingers. "Lay your hand flat."

When I obeyed, he marched purposefully onto the center of my palm. "Now raise your thumb so I can hold it. Yes, that's right. Now, up. More . . . more! All the way to that very large face of yours." He waited until we were nose to nose. "Now look me in the eyes, so I know you're listening."

I felt a bit cross-eyed trying to look him in his tiny eyes—his face in general was easier. A wine-colored birthmark splashed over one side of his forehead, trickling down the edge of his cheek. Each part of his face was a mass of wrinkles, as though he'd been soaking in the sea for years.

"I'm listening," I said.

"Take me to the nearest, most talented wizard in Trapper's Cove. I am in need of enhancement."

I shook my head. "There are no wizards here."

He glowered. "Then take me to the wizard district."

"The wizard district?" I'd never heard of such a thing.

"Yes, the *wizard* district! Where most of Maradon Cross's *wizards* live and work in the royal city," he added impatiently. "They all have different talents and enhancement specialties. People go there to buy from our shops or request services. We must get there well before Peace Day. Your *Peace* is in peril." He waited for my reaction.

I didn't know what to say. The Peace didn't mean much to me. And I suspected that it didn't mean much to anyone in Trapper's Cove, other than a celebration once a year. But the wizard was clearly an important person. That I understood. And Matron Tratte had told me time and time again that people, especially important people, didn't like children who talked. So I said nothing.

"Are you listening, child!? I believe that Queen Sonora is in terrible danger!"

My mouth flapped uselessly. A shrunken wizard had *appeared* in my pocket. I was now holding that wizard close to my face while being told about a threat to my queen—and to the entire queendom. There were a million questions I could start with. I went for the first ones that sprang to my mind. "Why are you so small? Did a wizard make you that way?"

He rolled his eyes. "Well, it wasn't a chicken, was it? Of

course a wizard shrank me!" He tapped my nose with a finger. "Now take me to Maradon Cross. Immediately."

I let out a baffled laugh as I shifted him. He made his demand as though I were a seasoned traveler who'd been to the royal city often. I'd barely been to the other side of the marketplace.

Orlen crawled onto my shoulder and thrust his chin up. "I assure you, there's nothing funny about this situation," he said sternly.

I looked sideways at the tiny, cross-looking man dressed in the fancy nightgown. The puffball at the end of his nightcap dangled beside his nose. "No, sir, of course nothing's funny," I said quickly. "But I have bindings that keep me here."

"Ha!" Orlen scratched at his ankles. "Do not talk to *me* of bindings. My sister Gwenda's repair shop is only a quarter hour from the castle. She's talented enough and can be trusted. Let's hope she can break the curse." He drummed his fingers over his lips. "I haven't talked to her for fifty years—she got a bit snotty when I left the wizard district to live in the castle. But family's family, right?"

I didn't respond. I had no family.

"Take me to your quarters. I could use a quick warm bath before we set out. Do you have hot pudding? I'll take a large portion with a side of buttercrust berry pie." He raised a finger. "*Cow* butter in the crust, not goat."

I slipped over the wall and into the corral with the wizard perched by my neck. Peck trailed behind. A window candle at the far end of the tavern illuminated a crouching, Hut-shaped shadow moving slowly in one of the top rooms. The room's patron would likely be waking up with less than they had before.

I bypassed a pile of snoozing goats and pigs and paused in front of my shelter. Despite the cool night air, my cheeks felt suddenly hot. I'd never had a guest. And this was the royal wizard to the queen of Maradon. I cleared my throat. "These are my quarters. I'm . . . all out of pudding and pie. And there's no place to take a bath."

"This just gets better and better. Sit down. We'll discuss things here."

I settled against the ancient shed.

Orlen fussed with his nightdress and cap, mumbled a few words, and patted his sides. Nothing happened. He frowned, then repeated the spell. Still nothing. Then, with extreme effort and grunting, he wiggled his fingers as hard as he could.

The sleeping gown changed into a long tunic and leggings that looked only slightly less like a nightdress. The nightcap became a scarf piled on his head. He swiped at the scarf until it fell around his neck. He frowned at his tunic. "Brown? I was trying for maroon. It looks like a goat-feed sack." He slapped his forehead. "Stupid, stupid, stupid!"

"What's wrong?" I asked.

The wizard snorted. "So much is wrong that I hardly know where to begin." He counted on his fingers. "The queen is in danger, I'm cursed and wearing a goat-feed sack, and there's no pudding or pie or bath. And it seems my talents have faded, along with my height."

Peck bobbed over to my side. Seeing the wizard's wary expression, I picked her up. "She's harmless. She knows you're a person."

"Harmless, you say?" Orlen eyed Peck with skepticism. "Just keep a tight hold of that beast. Now, Stub. We must fetch provisions and begin our journey. We're at the south end of Maradon. Perhaps a ship will be fastest, then."

I shook my head. "No ship will have me aboard. They all know my owner and that I'm contracted to be an apprentice. There are laws against running away." I looked at the Tinderbox. "The matron took me in as a baby. I would have died otherwise. I owe her six more years."

He slapped his side. "Don't be ridiculous! Look at where you sleep—she didn't take you in, she only *took* you. The queen will clearly pardon you. You'll tell them the circumstances when all this is over."

"They won't believe me. They won't believe you, either."

"Of course they will! You believe me, don't you? Well?"

I stared at the tiny man. He was a wizard, that much was

clear. And he was desperate. But how was I to trust that he really worked in the castle? My instincts told me that he was telling the truth, but what if my instincts didn't work on wizards? What if he didn't even know the queen? I would still be breaking the law, and I would be caught eventually. "It won't work," I told him firmly.

Orlen grimaced. "The mountains, then."

"There are trails in the mountains, but I have no knowledge of where they lead. And there are dangers—I've heard travelers speaking of them. One woman said that a starving caravan had their hired wizard enhance a mountain rat, but the spell went wrong, and it grew to the size of a house—the caravan had planned to eat it, but it ate them instead. Now it roams the peaks, feeding on people."

Orlen's eyebrows rose. "After how many glasses of ale was that particular tale told?"

He had a point. "We can wait for a wizard to come break your curse," I offered. "Usually we get a visiting one every few months or so."

With a great deal of effort, Orlen jumped over to my sleeve and climbed it until he was resting against my neck. He caught his breath, then patted my shoulder. "I understand that you're afraid. I am also afraid—afraid of what will happen if I don't get back to the castle before Peace Day. And you are the only person who can help me."

I looked up at the stars, half expecting them to start falling from the sky. I was *bound* to a wizard. He needed *me* to take him on a journey to save the queendom.

My stomach tossed like sea waves. Leaving would be too bold, like the moment the very first sailor had lost sight of the harbor behind her with no land in sight ahead. What a foolish, brave thing that had been. I had never been foolish enough to be so brave, nor brave enough to be so foolish.

Of course, I knew that things were not good for me in Trapper's Cove. In truth, there were days when I felt like the last egg Peck had laid, which was so light in my hand that I hadn't been surprised—only saddened—to crack it open and see that it was empty, save for the dried remains of what could have been a life. And I knew that I was not ever *truly* safe, not with the daily threats to Peck and with Hut taking shears to my hair while I slept.

Six more years of the same, plus a week of nights locked in the closet if Matron Tratte's plan was unsuccessful, especially if it was due to a fake bottle of wine. But if the matron married Captain Vella, I could be free right here, within a week. Without risking my life in the mountains.

"What happens after we get to Maradon Cross?" I asked. "Will you send me and Peck back here?"

"If you wish," Orlen said. "Once you take me to my sister, we should be free of each other and you can do as you please. If you'd like to stay in Maradon Cross, I promise to find a place for you, as payment for your service."

A place for you. He said it so easily, as though people found their place all the time.

Hope was a delicate thing that did not survive well in my experience, and I was unsure what to do with the small bit that was tapping away at my insides. I took a deep breath and decided. "I know where we can get maps."

The wizard clapped. "Excellent. Fetch supplies and the pair of us will be off."

"We'll be a trio. My chicken must be brought."

Orlen gripped my earlobe. "Your chicken is eyeing me as though I were a juicy worm. I don't like the idea of keeping pets. They have no purpose."

Clutching the bird close, I mustered a smile. "Peck cannot be left behind. She has a purpose."

His expression relaxed. "Ah, she is the best egg layer, then? Excellent. I do love a good egg. Six minutes boiled and not a second more. Now, then. What I don't like is a damp traveling carriage." He wiggled his fingers with determination and muttered a spell. His face grew red, then purple before he exhaled in exhaustion.

A soft wind whirled around me. My apron fluttered. From the waist down I'd been soaked with the stream's water. Now everything was dry. "Thank you."

Orlen was bent over, breathing heavily. "Yes, well, one doesn't like to be traveling in wet aprons when one can help it. I don't have much magic left. The curse seems to have drained most of it from me. But Maradon is not a large queendom. Between my brain and your legs, we should get to the castle soon enough. Place me back in your apron, please. I'm feeling a bit woozy. Then gather your belongings. Don't bring too much."

That was easy enough. After gently depositing the wizard into my apron pocket, I put one glow rock in my trouser pocket and piled the rest of my rocks at the bottom of my rucksack. A thin sheet of paper clung to the wall. I reached for it.

Two years earlier, the paper had torn away from the dock's notice board during a gust of high wind. It had whapped me in the face as I passed by with a basket full of fresh fish. I'd bartered a salvaged bead necklace to have someone read me the words. Then I'd taken it to my shelter to help me practice reading and writing.

> *Much Needed: Ship Crew*
> *Leaving port soon—sign a contract before*
> *it's too late!*

Of all the words, the first two and last two stood out the most to me. *Much needed. Too late.* Such cradling words at

the beginning and such haunting ones at the end. After reading it one last time, I left it on my wall. Maybe it would make
the Trattes think I'd tried to join a crew.

Along with my new wizard blade, that was the lot of my
belongings. Peck hunkered on top, as though guarding a nest,
looking as excited as a chicken possibly could. I couldn't help
but smile. She'd be safe from the stew pot. Then I looked
down at the wizard in my pocket and my smile drooped.

What dangers would we be facing instead?

Shoving the thought aside, I crept into the tavern kitchen
and lifted six loaves of flat brick bread from a stack near the
oven. Keeping quiet, I emptied two flasks of ale and filled
them with water from the barrels. Little by little, I stacked the
stolen goods around Peck: one tin of fat, three lard candles, a
small cooking pot. Three dried fish, four starchy tubers, and
two hunks of hard cheese. It was more food than I'd eaten in
the last week, and the wizard wouldn't eat much.

Hoping that Matron Tratte hadn't bothered to change
her hiding spot, I opened a cabinet beside the ale barrels and
reached past bottles of clear liquor, searching for a small
box. *Rat poison*, it said—one of the very few letter combi-
nations I knew by heart from seeing the words so frequently
at the marketplace. Highly unimaginative, but effective, as
I was banned from the cabinet upon penalty of death and
Hut would never touch the box. He'd had a nasty incident

with magical rat poison as a boy. The rash and scabbing had lasted weeks.

Inside were two small packets of powder, one blue and one red. They were most definitely not rat poison. They were the locking-and-unlocking powder she'd sent me to market for years ago. The vendor had stressed that the matron would need to read the instructions, which allowed the buyer to personalize the powder to a specific location. That way, nobody could simply use their own unlocking powder to steal from you. I happened to be outside, cleaning the kitchen window, on the day she placed the packets in the box, then in the cabinet.

There it was! Quickly, I pulled the box out and poured a little of each powder into the palm of one hand.

"What are you doing?" Orlen huffed in the apron pocket. "Hurry up!"

"I'm hurrying," I whispered back.

After putting the powder back in what I hoped was the same spot, I pressed open the door leading to the tables and snuck over to the fireplace. I hadn't thought twice about the safe until today, when she'd mentioned my contract. Feeling slightly sick, I stood on a chair in front of the mantel and sprinkled the blue powder on top of the frame holding Queen Alessa's portrait, the way I'd seen the matron do once.

Click. The frame opened like a book.

"Um, I just . . . I have to . . ." The next words wouldn't come. I had to what? I struggled to justify breaking into his home. I took a step to the side until I was beneath the painting of Queen Sonora. I pointed up. "I have to save the queendom."

His gaze rose to the painting. His eyes softened for a moment and the pan lowered again. Then he shook himself free of some thought. "You have to do what?"

The Roamer stirred. Beaman looked uncertainly between his mother and me and the painting. "Give me the journal," he ordered quietly. "Then get downstairs. *Now.*"

I obeyed. I felt sure that if it came to a fight with the boy, I would come out on top, but still, all the way down the stairs I could sense the heavy pan right over my head as I held the glowing pebble to light my way. He didn't seem the type to hit me with it. But he might get scared and drop it by accident. It would be the same outcome for me, either way.

Once in the kitchen, Beaman squinted in the low glow of the rock. His face was a blend of surprise and hurt. He gestured to the back door, still holding the pan and the journal. "Go. Don't come back."

I put the rock on the table near the bread baskets so that the room was dimly lit. "I can't. I need your mother's maps. I need to find a way over the mountains to Maradon Cross."

Looking puzzled, he slowly set the pan on the table. "Why? Are you running away?"

"No—well—yes," I stammered. "I told you: The queendom is in danger. So much danger that I'm breaking my apprenticeship. I can't go by water—someone will send me back to the Tinderbox."

"What kind of danger? And how do you know?"

"Oh, *enough!*" Orlen popped his head out of the apron pocket. "Give us the maps!" He sniffed the air and saw the bread basket. "And those rolls as well. They look much better than the ones we have."

Beaman jumped back, his eyes wide. "What in the world? What *is* that?"

Orlen cleared his throat. "Stub, introduce me."

The boy looked shocked and afraid. I wondered if I'd looked the very same way an hour before when Orlen had appeared in my pocket. But, somehow, Beaman's open face made it easier to speak to him. I placed the wizard on my open palm.

"This is Orlen, the royal wizard to Queen Sonora. He's been shrunk and banished to Trapper's Cove by a curse that binds the two of us together." I put Orlen gently on the table next to the glow rock and stepped backward until the wizard began to slide toward me against his will. "You see? He needs to return to the castle immediately."

Beaman shook his head, still baffled by the sight of the

tiny man. He ran a hand over his bun and stepped closer to the glow rock's light. "*Pickled carrots.* Is this really happening? Are you real?" He reached out a finger.

Orlen slapped it away. "I'm not a toy; I'm a wizard. An important one!"

While I casually moved the iron pan out of Beaman's reach, he bent closer still.

"You *are* real! Amazing! And you're from the castle? What's the food like there? I'll bet they have all kinds of meats and cheeses and vegetables to work with! Oh, and the sauces! What are the sauces like?" He took three steps to a nearby shelf and lifted the lid of a jar, ruefully scooping a handful of white powder. "I've only got horn-nut flour to thicken mine. What kinds of flour does the castle have? Mother said that my Peace Day pastries are the best she's ever tasted, but if I had better-quality ingredients, I could—"

"ENOUGH!" Orlen stamped his foot. "I've been cursed, child! Can't you see a crisis when it's in front of your face! The queen—and the entire queendom—may be in the gravest of dangers, and you're standing there babbling about Peace Day pastries. There may not be any more Peace Days if we don't get to the castle!"

"What do you mean, no more Peace Days?" Beaman frowned. He glanced at the painting of Queen Sonora. "Are you saying we'll be at war again?"

I suddenly had the same questions myself. My life was not pleasant by any measure, but at least I wasn't being forced to fight battles to keep my homeland.

Orlen let out a sigh. "Enough questions and interruptions. You're both too young to be involved. I only need transport, not talkers. The maps—hand them over. Stub, pick me up."

Beaman looked carefully at Orlen. Then his eyes darted to me as I placed the wizard on my right shoulder. "If it's so important, why can't we wake my mother and have her guide you? Or have her deliver a message?"

Orlen's eyes darkened. "Your mother is a messenger. She likely has many contacts. Too many. She'll feel obligated to tell someone. I cannot trust her. I can't risk the wrong person being alerted."

"Why should I trust you?" Beaman straightened and gripped the table edge. "And how do you know that *I* don't have contacts too?" He attempted to raise an intimidating eyebrow but ended up looking as tentative and apologetic as unleavened bread.

Orlen sighed. "I said that's enough questions."

Beaman glanced toward the staircase. "Mother says it's smart to ask lots of questions."

I stared at the ridiculous cook. Asking lots questions was nothing but a recipe for a beating, in my experience. And while I knew Beaman Cork had a misguided sense of trust, as he'd gifted a trespassing stranger a knife, I was astonished that he didn't seem to grasp a basic truth I'd learned long ago.

"You can't fully trust anyone in this world," I informed him. "The only person I completely trust is my chicken." My head yanked to the side as Orlen pinched my earlobe.

"Ow! Um, that said, Orlen is a royal wizard to our Peace Queen and he's the size of my thumb and I'm magically bound to him and he's telling the truth. That will have to be enough for now." I rubbed my ear, then held out a hand. "The maps."

"Not so fast." He held the journal to his chest. "What's this plot against the queen?"

"I told you, I'm in the process of uncovering things," Orlen snapped.

"Then at least tell me what you know."

Orlen glared at the boy's unmoving arms. "Fine," he grumbled. "Each year, the queen invites representatives from all over Maradon to a grand feast in honor of Peace Day. As this year is the hundredth anniversary, it's much more of a to-do. As you must know, Queen Sonora rules along with her regent. Before her death, Queen Nadina chose her steward to be that regent—a man called Renart. He is to guide the queen in her ruling until she is sixteen."

"I've heard of him!" Beaman said. "Mother delivered a letter to him once."

Orlen grunted. "He's in charge of royal correspondence. He's also an idiotic control-monger who's out to get me fired. He keeps silly lists for everything, including Peace Day festivities." Orlen rolled his eyes. "He actually ordered me to change all the draperies in the castle to blue in honor of Peace Day. Ordered *me*! Like I was a common servant! So, to annoy him, I slipped into his quarters and changed everything to blue."

"Everything?" Beaman asked.

He smirked. "From washcloths to underclothes. In any case, while I was there, I happened to see a locked trunk with an old royal seal—one from before Maradon's reign of Peace. It was from a display in the Remembrance Room, a large chamber in the castle where the Tartinian War is chronicled. The lock had scratches around it." His eyebrows rose, and he looked at both of us, clearly waiting for a reaction.

"So?" Beaman supplied.

"He was trying to break into it, of course! It could hold hats and diaries for all I care, but clearly it wasn't meant for him."

I kept quiet. The queen's steward looking through old trunks didn't sound too ominous to me.

"There was also part of a letter on his desk. And," Orlen added rather dramatically, "there was a Wintrellian swallow."

Beaman and I exchanged bewildered glances.

"It's a small bird native to an island far north of here.

Light brown with golden wings. Bit of a furry head. They're extremely rare, astonishingly intelligent, and nearly impossible to catch. I've been longing to see one for years."

Beaman scratched his head. "So he's got a pet bird? And you want one too?"

Orlen sighed. "It brought the letter to Renart! It was from the queen of my homeland—Wintrel. Her name is Lacera, and she is a kincain."

"A kin-what?" Beaman asked.

"Kin*cain*. A wizard with unusually powerful magic—a prodigy with fewer limits than the rest of us. I've done extensive research on them. They're typically born with an unusual birthmark on their arm or face." He straightened. "My mother thought I was one for a few years, but then I came into my magic early. Kincains always come into magic later than others, but are extraordinarily talented from the start, and their life span is twice as long as normal. There's only one born every two or three generations."

Orlen's jaw tightened. "She is the most power-hungry, controlling leader my people have ever seen. There's not an ounce of empathy in her. I don't use the word 'wicked' lightly, but it suits her. I only saw one page of the letter—it said that she would arrive in one week. Just as I was reading it, a blasted servant came in. But rest assured, Lacera can only mean to harm Queen Sonora. And Renart is in on the plot. There's no honorable reason he would be communicating with her."

I listened to the two of them, astonished, not only by the revelation that a wicked wizard queen would be coming to Maradon, but also by the fact that Beaman had somehow gotten Orlen to tell him all that. It was like he had his own strange, talking-to-people kind of magic. Why wouldn't Orlen have already told me those things? Why hadn't I demanded more answers?

Beaman looked at the paintings. His hand rose to his heart. "Will Lacera harm the queen?"

Orlen nodded curtly. "And the entire queendom, I should think. I doubt Sonora is aware that she's coming. And I suppose it's possible that Renart is innocent and doesn't know that Lacera has ulterior motives—maybe she sent a letter under the guise of coming here for a friendly visit. He's so eager to make this hundredth-anniversary celebration huge, he'll latch on to any exciting guests. A wizard queen would likely seem glamorous to him." He frowned. "But no. His behavior over the last few weeks has been far too suspicious for him not to be directly involved in a plot."

Something bothered me as I looked at the paintings of the young royal. "Wouldn't it be better if Queen Lacera didn't come at all, then? Can't you just send a message, asking Queen Sonora to instruct Renart to refuse her?"

hens are awful to you." I kissed her feathers, took a crust of bread from my trouser pocket, and tore the food into pieces. "I swiped it off a plate during the noon rush. I've been saving it. Don't tell."

The chicken pecked at a piece, then looked up, waiting.

"No, you go on," I urged. "I'll have something tonight. Eat. And stay here. I'd best hurry back before I'm missed."

The back door creaked open. "Where are you, Nuisance?" called a low, nasal voice.

"Too late," I whispered. I sucked in a breath and held it, not moving a muscle while the matron's son coughed loudly and spit a wad of phlegm that dinged into the alarm bell hanging near the back door.

Footfalls pounded down the stairs. Boots stomped close. Then, closer.

Frantically, I stuffed the still-glowing rock back with the others. Just as I'd smoothed dirt over the buried box, a long arm shot into the shelter and flailed around. The cloth door lifted. A hand closed around my ankle, squeezing hard.

Hut peered inside, then yanked me out by the leg. His brown hair fell in his eyes, all the way to his long nose with its slit nostril, the result of a broken bottle thrown across the tavern when he was small.

"Still keeping that naked-neck chicken as a roommate?" He wiped his hair from his face and grinned. His smile had grown steadily from mischief into menace during the years that I'd known him. "Mind that it doesn't wander over to the chopping block when you're not watching. Now get inside. Mother has a special guest coming tonight. A *captain*, Stub-Rot."

Mr. Tratte had passed away ten years ago, and after three years of mourning, the matron had decided to try to remarry. She'd been aiming for a sea captain, both because they had money and because they could get her away from Trapper's Cove. She hadn't landed a catch yet, but it wasn't for lack of trying.

"If you mess anything up, Mother says it's the closet." He grinned again. "Every night for a week this time."

The year before, Matron had locked me in the narrow broom closet for breaking a whole tray of plates. She hadn't seen Hut push me. I doubt it would have mattered if she had. Now I stood and dusted myself off so he wouldn't notice me shaking. One full night of being locked in the closet had been horrible. Seven in a row would be unbearable.

"And if everything works out, she says you're free of us and we're free of you."

I stared at him. "Free?"

Hut laughed at my open mouth. "She'll be gone and you won't be needed. Which would be quite convenient for you, wouldn't it?"

"What are you doing?" Orlen hissed.

"Getting something. I need it."

Matron Tratte was an organized woman, and the safe mostly held coin, not paper. But at the very back of the safe, I found an envelope with frayed edges marked with a single word that I was able to sound out: *Stub*. I took out the single sheet of paper inside, rolled it up, and stuffed it into my sack.

Hastily, I rubbed the red powder on top of the blue and waited until I heard a soft click. Then I wiped the powder off the frame and returned the chair to its place.

"And now," Orlen whispered in a harsh voice, "I'd like to go save Maradon's Peace if you're quite finished with your personal thievery."

"Just one more theft," I said quietly. "And this one's for your benefit."

My stomach lurched with guilt at the thought of my next task. The young cook at the Fork & Cork had saved my hide with the wine bottles. And the ridiculous boy had given me a fine knife, then said he owed me a favor for taking it.

Letting me steal his mother's Roaming maps was probably not the favor he'd had in mind.

5

How to Coax a Cook

Two twists and a lift of a wizard match was all it took to open the gate of the Fork & Cork. When I went to market, Hut made a regular game out of locking the back gate of the Tinderbox, and I usually had to fiddle ten times as long before getting to my shelter.

All was silent. No shadows lurked in the candlelit windows at this tavern.

"Leave the chicken," hissed the wizard in my apron pocket.

"Please be quiet," I said, approaching the back door. I could have argued about Peck. She only ever squawked in self-defense. But I placed the rucksack on the ground. "Be right back," I told her, shaking the smaller of my two glow rocks. It was no larger than a pebble, and its light was dim but steady.

The back door was even simpler than the gate. My bare feet made no sound as I crossed the kitchen floor. Step by step, testing for creaks before applying my full weight, I crept past a table with half-empty bread baskets and up the staircase.

There were two doors on the second floor. The first opened to a room with three beds. In the far bed, Beaman's mentor faced me, sleeping peacefully. The middle was empty. The bed nearest the door appeared to hold Beaman, as the shape under the blanket was smaller than an adult. Perched on a table beside him was a miniature version of Queen Sonora's coronation portrait. I closed the door quietly.

The other door was locked. I tried the match. No combination of twisting, pushing, or lifting worked. "Orlen," I said, keeping my voice low. "If you have any magic left, now would be the time to use it."

There was silence; then came a muffled sound, like someone straining to twist off an extra-tight lid. The lock gave way with a dull *chk-shwk* and I felt the wizard collapse. When I placed my hand against the apron to check for breathing, he grumbled and elbowed my palm.

I pressed the door open. The walls were bare, other than small paintings of the Peace Queens hanging opposite the single bed. The Roamer's head lolled to one side. A tiny line of drool dampened her pillow.

Timing my movements to the woman's guttural snore, I held the glow rock outward to light the room and stepped inside. A chair beside the bed was piled with clothes. At the chair's feet was the heavy box with its locks.

A small table to the right of the door held a water pitcher and basin, and a half-full bowl of stew. I nearly swooned at the sight and smell of it. *One lick!* a naughty inner voice begged. *Just one.* I might have listened if Orlen hadn't poked me squarely in the belly button. I looked down at him, then followed his pointing finger. A small leather journal lay face-down on the floor, near the bed. I picked it up.

As I started to flip through, I felt a prickle in my wrist. Then I heard the softest of movements and sensed a change in the air.

Danger.

I turned quickly, then ducked at the sight of a dark object poised to strike me on the head. My legs were too stunned to spring away, so I crouched, raising both arms, and closed my eyes, bracing for the vicious blow from what was undoubtedly a fierce thief, after the contents of the Roamer's lockbox.

The blow didn't come. In its place was a voice.

"*You?*"

I opened my eyes. Beaman was dressed in a long night-shirt. His bun was mussed and he looked frightened, not fierce. The young cook lowered the cast-iron pan, then frowned and raised it again. "What are you doing?"

I risked a glance at the Roamer. She was still sound asleep.

He snorted. "Oh, certainly, I could. And then Renart would convince her otherwise and continue with his plotting. Sonora's mother trusted him, so she has little choice but to take his advice."

"If Queen Nadina trusted him, maybe you should too." Beaman hesitantly reached for his pan. "Maybe it's you who's plotting an uprising."

Orlen looked as though he wanted to throw a roll into the cook's mouth to shut him up. "I'll have you know that I've been living in Maradon since I was twenty-six years old." He held out his brown gown. "I'm two inches tall. Do I look like I'm planning an uprising? And Lacera is the last person on earth I'd form an alliance with. Maps!" he snapped. "Now."

"What about the evil wizard who cursed you?" Beaman asked. "That person must be here in Maradon. Are they going to hurt the queen?"

Orlen's face reddened. "No."

"How do you know?" Beaman pressed.

Orlen mumbled a word.

"What was that?" Beaman leaned closer.

"*Accident,*" Orlen said scornfully. "I was trying to shrink Renart and bind him to my pocket so I could interrogate him. I don't know what happened, but I ended up here."

Hmph. Orlen had told me that a wizard had cursed him, banishing him far away. He'd been telling the truth, but not the whole truth. I wondered what else he was holding back.

Beaman looked at Orlen, then me. "I believe you," he said with a sigh. "But I can't let you have the journal."

Oh my. I really didn't want to steal from Beaman. His heart, I suspected, was made of sugar and butter and edible flower petals. There was no rotten pit inside him. There had to be something he would trade. Everyone had a price. I looked around the kitchen and spotted the three knives he'd juggled. "I'll give you the wizard knife back. The one your mother gave you."

He shook his stubborn head. "I told you, I don't want the knife."

"That's right—you want your mother," I said, keeping my voice smooth as a market vendor. "We can give her to you. Would you like to have her closer for much, much longer?"

The question should have made his eyes narrow in suspicion. But they widened instead.

His face was so easy to read. I felt sorry for him, for not knowing that it was always safer to hide feelings. Beaman lacked common sense when it came to leaving doors unlocked and passing out knives and showing an undue amount of kindness to complete strangers. Still . . . he was good with Orlen and better with people in general than I'd ever be. He might prove to be an asset. The decision was made.

I cleared my throat. "If you don't want to give us the journal, Beaman, then keep it—and bring it yourself. Come with us."

He shook his head and swallowed. "I can't. I'm Pap's apprentice. He's already given me his last name."

I'd forgotten that apprentices took on the last names of their mentors. Not that Matron Tratte had ever mentioned it. "So? Break your contract. You can give him his name back later." I said the words with a shrug, as though it had been a simple decision for me. As though I'd been given a last name and had flung it away with ease. "Show your mother how tough you can be, and then you can travel with her for months instead of only seeing her for a day or two. She said she was going overseas next—she won't need maps of Maradon."

Beaman's cheeks flushed pink. "How do you know what she said?" He took a step back. "And how do you know my name? I never told you."

I thought fast. "She was talking about you to the market vendor. Before she stole my knife."

"What did she say?" he asked warily.

Taking a cue from Orlen, I waved away the question. "The important thing is that you can prove you are more than ready to travel with her. She said that you weren't meant for the hard life of being a Roamer. But if you make it all the way to the castle, you'll prove you are. She can make you *her* apprentice. All she has to do is talk to your mentor once you've proven yourself."

Beaman bit his lip and looked around the kitchen. His eyes softened. "But I promised Pap."

A wave of envy rolled onto my shore. Beaman had two professions that he could learn. As for me, I had only the vague promise from a shrunken wizard that the queen could release me from my servant duty at the Tinderbox. "Pap will forgive you," I said rather sharply. After seeing the man for only a moment, I knew that was likely true. "In any case," I added, "after a journey across the queendom, your mother will surely give you a chance to travel with her. Don't you want that?"

His eyes grew shiny as they shifted to the door the Roamer had left through, as though he were chopping onions again. He blinked away the moisture. "Yes," he said quietly. "Yes, I want that."

He turned the journal sideways and flipped through it. He stopped at a page near the front and showed me a large shape with ragged boundaries. "This is where we are in Maradon." He pointed to a dot along the sea.

With a slow finger, he traced a line straight over a strip of mountains all the way to the other side of the queendom. "And this is Maradon Cross, where the castle is. It's miles and miles from here. It might as well be the end of but first pass me some of that cheese I saw you take from your larder. Yes, that's it. A bit more."

While Beaman dealt with Orlen's cheese craving, I dug beneath Peck's rump for the other glow rock, then handed it to Beaman, pointing at a spot on the jagged surface. "Follow me. If the light goes out, shake it hard."

I led the way down the thin trail. We pressed our way through large coastal ferns that sprawled into the path as though trying to warn us against leaving. I half-wanted to take their advice. Above were tall leafy trees, towering like sentries. Ahead was the moonlit silhouette of the Serpa Range. As we walked, the sky's clinging stars faded away. The terrain grew hard against the soles of my feet as soil turned to rock.

Hours later, my first day away from Trapper's Cove dawned. Ahead, the rising sun bathed the mountaintops in a blend of warm amber and pale pink light. I turned occasionally, looking back at the green lowlands.

In the distance, the curve of the cove looked calm. Almost peaceful. Would I ever return? Were the queen and the Peace really in danger? And how was the queen's regent involved? There was so much I didn't know. I suddenly felt smaller than the shrunken wizard in my pocket.

It was nearly midday when the last views of the sea disappeared, right as I felt a prickle of warning.

The wind blew, making a swishing sound somewhere overhead as it collided with mountain crags and slid over outcroppings. There was a buzzing sensation just behind my left eye. I turned to call for Beaman. Though much of the trail had twisted and turned for the last hour, the path behind me was relatively straight for a hundred yards.

And my cook companion was nowhere to be seen.

the world." His lip twisted. "There are peak wolves in the mountains. Big ones, Mother said, that attack at night. One of them climbed a tree to attack her once. It *climbed a tree*. And there are other creatures and I'll get cold and . . . we might run out of food," he whispered in a worried voice. The last part seemed to bother him the most.

"All the better," I said brusquely. "Just think how impressed your mother will be."

I touched the harbor that was my home, then regarded all the things beyond it. There were rivers and valleys and towns. There were question marks and sketches and short notes dotting the landscape. A strange stirring rippled through me. This was my queendom. And I was actually going to see it. If only I could get the boy out the door.

Orlen glanced up at me, then at Beaman. He cleared his throat. "There are wolves everywhere, child. And nights with cold weather as well." He wisely didn't touch upon the possibility of a food shortage as he stepped over to the basket of rolls.

"But what about Pap?" Beaman said. "He needs me."

"Oh, he'll be fine," Orlen said. The words were garbled, spoken through a fistful of bread. He swallowed and eyed the basket. "We'll bring this with us." He let out a tiny belch. "And anything else you've got."

Beaman ran a hand over his hair's top knot. "This is crazy. It makes no sense at all. No, I can't go."

A strong, restless wind blew outside. The house creaked. It would be wise to grab the journal and leave before the Roamer woke. But somehow I felt as though I owed this young cook more than that. Silently, I cursed him for his decency. Making decisions was so much less complicated when people were awful.

I looked at the belt of spices hanging on the wall from a nail—that was it! The boy was obsessed with food. "The castle, Beaman," I said. "You can visit its kitchens if you join us. Right, Orlen?"

Orlen rolled his eyes. "Fine. I'll introduce you to the queen and you can talk about sauces and baking the entire time." He clasped his hands together in fake joviality. "And we'll go to the cooking shop in the wizard district—enhanced pots! Extra-sweet humming honey! Magical flavoring salt! Rubbish like that. I daresay you'd love it." He slapped his thigh. "Now, for the last time, let's go."

"Humming honey?" Beaman's stared at the painting of Queen Sonora, lingering on the girl's face. He said nothing as he put the journal on the table. He remained silent as he lifted the belt free, buckled it around his waist, and filled a near-empty container with red powder. Then he faced me and Orlen.

"I'll come," he said, passing me a roll. "But I'm doing the cooking."

I stifled a snort. Did he think I'd be cooking? I'd been

planning on living on cheese and dried meat. I conjured my best beaten look from the marketplace. "You drive a hard bargain, but okay."

He straightened the belt with a grin and held a hand out to me. "I'm Beaman Cork. Though you already seem to know that. What's your name?"

I took a bite of the soft roll, avoiding his outstretched hand. What a very strange day. For the second time in my life, someone had looked me directly in the eyes and asked for my name. As though I was a person worth knowing.

I picked up the journal. "Orlen is right: We need to leave the village. Gather your things quietly, and we'll meet you out back," I said, forcing myself to sound much more confident than I felt. Then I placed my free hand in Beaman's and shook. "My name is Stub. My chicken is named Peck. Don't even think about cooking her or I'll shove you off the mountainside."

Huddled in the cover of night, our small crew sat at a trailhead leading into the thick underbrush at the base of the mountains that encircled the cove.

"Can we have more light?" Beaman asked.

I shook the crab-claw rock until its brightness joined the fading moon and starlight. In the journal drawing, the tallest peaks curved like a cupped hand toward the coast, but in several places, smaller branches broke away like forked tongues. Beaman traced the trails.

"According to the map and notes, it should only take a few days to make it through the mountain passes, as long as we keep a swift pace," Beaman said, pointing to a few lines of writing. "See, Stub? What do you think?"

A warm flush came over me. "I've never read a map."

"It's like reading a recipe. Look at the directions."

I glanced at the letters, trying to sound out the words in my mind and feeling both the boy's and the wizard's stare. Peck scratched at the dirt nearby. I stood and placed her in my rucksack. "You're the one with Roaming in your blood. I think you should decide."

Orlen gave an impatient grunt from his perch on my shoulder. "Well, I think we'll never get anywhere at this rate."

"I'm trying to find the best way," Beaman said. "That's what my mother would do." He winced as a horn nut fell from the tree above and bopped him on the shoulder. The fist-sized nut was covered in tiny barbs.

"You see? Even the nuts are moving faster than you! There are some things you can't plan for—like being shrunk and flung to the far reaches of a queendom, for example. The best way to get where you're going is by walking away from where you've been. It's not magic. Now put on your packs—

-Vicious, but only attacks things smaller than it

-Unique hunting techniques

-Excellent source of protein

"A snake and a mouse? I thought—" I dropped my knife and bent over to catch my breath. "I thought something had attacked you," I said shortly.

"The mountains have been attacking me." He stood and stretched. "I needed a break. You walk too fast." He smiled shyly and handed me the journal. "I added to it—just like a Roamer would. That's important, right?"

Beside the Roamer's neat handwriting were new notes. I silently sounded out a few of the words, then passed the book back to him.

"It's a recipe," he said. "I couldn't decide whether it should be tenderized before poaching, or which spices would work best, or if a lemon-herb butter would work, or . . ." He trailed off. "Do you think she'll like that I added to it?"

I doubted that any Roamer traveling through these mountains would care about a snake recipe. And I didn't truly believe that Beaman even *wanted* to be a Roamer's apprentice. But he seemed so eager to please his mother. He had both a passion and a family to grapple with. What had I ever grappled with? The short list included giant sheep, Hut Tratte, and full trays of ale. I felt a strange ache in my chest.

Probably from running. I busied myself with a cough so that I wouldn't have to answer.

"She wouldn't like you taking breaks so often, that's for certain," Orlen snapped. "That's the third time you've rested since we set off." He started to climb up my apron, then poked me. "Put me on your shoulder, Stub, so I can keep an eye on him while we walk. We'll never get through the mountains at this pace."

Beaman's face fell. "Right," he said.

As midday melted into afternoon, the trail twisted and turned. Twice, the way was blocked from rockfall and we had to find a different path. Without the maps and the landmarks, it would have been impossible to tell which direction we were walking. Even with them, I wasn't confident. I'd never read maps before. Neither had Beaman. Orlen would likely know, but he was keeping unusually quiet, other than the occasional insult, which I supposed were meant to encourage us to move faster.

We moved at a brisk but careful pace. If the prickle hadn't been about Beaman, then what had my instincts been trying to warn me about? As we climbed higher and deeper into the Serpa Range, the air, like me, had started to feel restless.

There was a strange crispness to it that hadn't been there an hour before. The landscape, too, seemed increasingly stark. The sky had grown as gray as the rock. Was a storm approaching? The only sounds were the wind and the shuffling of my trousers as I walked. Other than mouse droppings, I'd seen no evidence of life for hours. There was nothing much to do except count my steps. I counted over and over in sets of six: the number of days left until Peace Day.

And then, as we shifted to a new trail for the third time in as many hours, the prickle returned.

I felt as though I were walking through an empty version of the Tinderbox, just waiting for something awful to happen. Or like certain nights in the pen, when the animals should have been sleeping but were skittish instead. The change in their behavior nearly always meant that a shift in the weather was coming. Or that a predator was lurking.

I lifted my rucksack's flap to look at Peck. She stared back. "Do you feel it too?" I whispered.

She nipped my finger and crouched deeper in the sack.

I listened for the one noise I'd heard off and on since we'd entered the high peaks. It sounded like a distant waterfall, though the map showed no such landmark. The first time I'd heard it, a small part of me had feared it was the matron's footsteps. I knew it was silly, but the fear was like a horn nut, spiked with hooked barbs that were hard to shake loose once they sank into your clothes or skin.

There it was again. The noise, from somewhere above us, high on the peaks.

"Beaman," I said, turning sharply. "Orlen. Did either of you hear that?"

Orlen clung to my earlobe and turned side to side, scanning the path ahead. "Hear what?"

Beaman cocked his head to the side. "Is it like a shuffling?"

I nodded, fingering the knife at my belt.

Beaman shifted nervously as he saw my hand gripping the sheathed blade. "Pap says that ears are great cooking tools. I'm always listening for the smallest sizzle and bubbling in the kitchen." He swallowed. "You know, I've had the strangest sensation that we're being followed. Probably me missing the hissing of my pots and pans. I only brought my no-burn sauté pan and a regular pot. The rest know I've left them, and they're wondering why."

"Mm-hmm," I muttered. Then I stopped, and Beaman ran into me.

"I'm sorry," he said, bending over with his hands on his knees. "I need a break."

"Again?" Orlen asked, exasperated.

"I'm not traveling in someone's pocket or on a shoulder," he countered.

I looked ahead to where the trail split. Our path, the left

one, was blocked again by rockfall. I consulted the map. The valley was far below us. Still, based on how long it had taken us to pass certain landmarks, if we increased our pace, there was a chance we could make it down there by nightfall. Then we could start up the next peak at morning's first light.

Beaman took a long drink of water. "Speaking of pots and pans and, um, food . . . maybe we could have a small sandwich?" He took a jar from his belt and shook it. "I could add some paribo powder to a cheese. The spiciness is good for the lungs." He plucked another jar, his eyes brightening. "And just a hint of rosa root to add a touch of . . ."

I stopped listening to him and looked again at the sky. The clouds were lower. They clung to the peak just above us. Somewhere within the clump of fog, I glimpsed a long, dark shape moving along the highest part of the mountainside.

I tightened my grip on my rucksack straps. "Let's keep going while the weather holds."

Beaman sighed. "All right." He paused, tilting his head again. "Wait. There's that shuffling again. Where is it coming from?" He twirled in a circle, swaying toward the edge of the trail from the weight of his pack. I pulled him back toward the mountain. There was a treacherous drop-off on one side, and the trail had grown narrow.

Peck began to fidget against my chest.

I looked up again. The fog parted.

The shape was heading down the mountainside. Toward us. I held in a scream.

"Orlen," I said, trying to keep my voice steady. "Do you remember the story about the rat the size of the house? The one that was enhanced so that the starving travelers could eat it?"

Orlen snorted. "Yes. Highly unlikely. Enhancements can only make the creature as large as natural elements allow. Unless the spell went terribly wrong."

The storyteller at the Tinderbox had been right. He'd just gotten the details wrong. "Could a terribly wrong spell create a Serpa snake the length of a ship?"

He followed my gaze, then let out a strange squeak, like a cornered mouse.

A *mouse*—like the one stalked by the snake Beaman had observed. That snake had made tiny pebble walls. The reason behind the prickle I'd felt was now crystal clear. The avalanches that had plagued our travel weren't just natural rockfall. They were part of a conspiring trap. All those other rockfalls we'd seen—had travelers been buried, then uncovered for feasting?

Beaman looked up. His voice rose an octave. "But they only eat things that are smaller than them. Right? That's what my mother wrote."

The snake was massive. I wasn't exaggerating when I'd said it was the length of a ship.

"I hate to point this out," I said grimly, "but we're a bit smaller than that thing."

He gripped my tunic. "What do we do?"

The serpent slithered back and forth across the mountainside, creating a strange dust cloud. A deep rumbling sounded overhead, like thunder.

"Oh great, a thunderstorm?" Beaman asked, his voice panicked. His breath came in short, fast bursts. "I'm outside with a giant snake *and* a thunderstorm?" He shook my shoulders. "I could have been home with my mother!" He released me and mumbled to himself hysterically, bending his head over his belt. "And the rest of my spices!"

I let him panic. I was too busy panicking myself to calm him. I knew perfectly well that there was no thunderstorm. As I watched the cloud, the rumbling sound grew to a roar. The cloud grew larger. It swept down the mountain with terrifying speed.

Beaman stopped fiddling with the ingredients in his belt and looked up. His face turned gray as the stone around them. "Not a storm," he gulped.

"No," I said, unable to look away.

"Avalanche," he whispered.

"Avalanche," I agreed.

"AVALANCHE!" screamed Orlen. He jumped down from my shoulder, into the rucksack with Peck, closing the flap behind him. "STOP STANDING THERE! MOVE!"

"Beaman!" I screamed above the earsplitting sound of rock fall. "Move!"

"I just said that!" Orlen screamed, his shrill voice muffled by the canvas. "Go, go, go!"

I shoved Beaman back the way we'd come, hoping to make it to the turn in the trail. "RUN!"

First came the pebbles, whizzing through the air, spraying us with hot flashes of pain. Then larger stones bounced all around. The worst of it was coming.

Beaman's foot slipped on the scree pouring down the mountainside. He flailed, letting out a desperate cry, as the flow dragged him to the lip of the drop-off.

I lunged and caught his hand just as he began to tip over the edge.

"Don't let go!" he screamed. "Please don't let me go!"

"Hold on!" I yelled back. A rock the size of my head flew by as I tried to pull him up from the mountain's deathly slope. The larger rocks were all coming. Soon we'd be pummeled with boulders. Teetering on the edge, nearly losing my balance, I yanked him up with all of my might. His entire body shook as his belly landed back on solid ground.

I was still holding his hand when my foot slipped and we both went over the edge.

The dropping sensation was cushioned by the wild sea

of smaller scree rocks. I was buried alive, then forced to the surface as we smacked into a landing and continued rushing down the mountainside.

"Swim through it!" Beaman yelled, coughing and letting go of my hand.

"I can't swim!" I yelled back. Plus, my arms were busy trying to protect Peck from being crushed. Desperately, I flailed one arm to keep my head above the rocky sea. Beaman was in front of me. I followed him. The flow began to subside, and I felt the ground beneath me. The torrent beneath us slowed, then ceased.

I waded out until only my battered feet were covered. Beaman stood at the edge of the rockfall, bent over.

"Peck!" I lifted the flap anxiously. Though trembling, my chicken friend seemed relatively unscathed, though her scabs had broken open in places. "Oh, thank goodness!" I lifted her out and nuzzled her close.

"I'm fine as well." Orlen emerged from beneath Peck's back feathers. "Not that you seem to care." He climbed onto Peck's neck, pressing his hands gently against her battered wounds. "There now," he whispered. "I told you we'd be all right, didn't I?"

I managed a glimpse up and saw that we'd been swept to the far side of the avalanche. A chunk of outcropping the size of the Tinderbox bounced down the mountain twenty feet from us, crushing everything in its path. I'd been there just moments before.

Despite feeling like a pounded piece of meat, I was grateful the rock flow had carried us to the valley. According to the Roamer's journal, the serpent couldn't breathe at lower altitudes. In minutes we'd traveled what would have taken us the rest of the day. The giant snake was visible far above, no doubt upset that its prey had fallen too low to retrieve.

Staggering over to Beaman, I joined him in coughing out rock dust. Then we both collapsed on the grass, heaving with breath, and looking over in astonishment at the buried path we'd stood on moments before.

"I lost my sandals," he finally said.

I looked at our matching, scratched-up feet. "You did."

He looked dizzily at my legs, then my feet. "You were never wearing any. Why not?"

"I like the feel of the ground," I lied. "Your ear is bleeding."

He raised a weary hand to his ear, then looked at his red fingers. "It is." His eyes were slightly unfocused as he looked at my earlobes. "Why aren't your ears pierced?"

It was Maradonian tradition for parents or guardians to pierce their children's ears soon after they were born. It was a bonding gesture, so the baby would always feel connected to the parents, even if they weren't right there. The jewelry was never taken out. Every person I'd ever seen in Trapper's

Cove wore earrings. Some people wore two pairs, one from a parent who'd died, and one from their new family.

I didn't answer Beaman's question. I wasn't connected to anyone. As Hut had said, I was a nothing, raised to be a nobody. "Break time?" I asked instead.

He nodded weakly. "Break time."

7

How to Dodge a Question

᠙

I never knew a person could have so many things to say about cooking food.

I listened to Beaman's chatter as I slumped beneath the shelter of a thick-trunked tree, my body feeling like a dusty, beaten rug. Peck stretched her wings beside me and poked at a line of ants marching up the trunk. My sore feet stuck out beyond shadows cast by the branches above.

The afternoon sun's warmth blanketed my toes, making me sleepy. Beaman seemed the opposite. The promise of a good meal revived him completely. He dropped his bag beside mine and immediately went to wash his hands in the stream that ran through the valley.

"A good cook starts with clean hands!" he called over his shoulder.

I pictured Hut Tratte, wiping his nose just before he rubbed salt onto a roast of meat. "If you say so," I muttered.

"That child talks entirely too much," Orlen griped beside me.

I looked up through the leaves, then out toward the horizon.

"And you talk too little," he added sharply, crawling from
the apron to my shoulder. "What are you thinking about?"

"Nothing," I answered. And I was being truthful. I was
thinking about how nothing lasted. Not a calm moment with
Peck and not a hike without incident. The mountain weather
was unpredictable. Gray clouds had given way to blue sky. It
was nice—beautiful, even. But I didn't trust it.

". . . back at home, there's so much baking to do," Beaman
was saying as he walked back and began sifting through his
pack. "Rolls and loaves and sweet buns and flatbread and seed
cakes—I would die for a sweet bun right now, or even a . . ."

I glanced around for Peck, then stretched my own wings
and let the sound of Beaman's voice burble over me like the
nearby water.

Beaman touched my shoulder. "I said tell me something
about you." He grinned. "I don't know anything, other than
the fact that you work at the Tinderbox."

"Oh, um . . ." I didn't feel like sharing stories about me
and Peck and our life. In any case, what tales would I share?

Stub and the Awfully Rude Tavern-Goers

Stub and Peck and the Day with No Food

Stub and Peck Almost Freeze to Death

None of those were pleasant. But Beaman was staring
at me eagerly, waiting for me to say something. Despite my

exhaustion, his interested expression made me wish we were hiking. Like the weather, I didn't trust it. I glanced around for firewood and spotted a tree with a dead limb. I picked Orlen up and placed him on my shoulder. "I'll make a fire."

With the wizard blade, I easily sawed finger-width branches from the dead limb. I started a neat blaze with the wizard match, then placed two large rocks in the center so that Beaman could balance the pot and frying pan he'd brought. As I knelt and returned the match to my rucksack, my fingertips brushed the roll of paper on the bottom.

Burn it, I thought. *It would only take a second to disappear.* My inner voice was right. The letter was the only proof that I belonged to Matron Tratte—the only way she could lay claim to me. My hand hovered over the paper. I pulled it out of the sack, fully intending to scrunch it, then scorch it in the flames. But my hand didn't seem to be behaving.

The letter also happened to be the only connection I had to my mother. And maybe the only explanation about why she'd left me to this life.

"Stub?" Beaman called. "I said we'll need more wood. Can you throw a few branches on?"

"Right." I dropped the paper back in the rucksack and stood. "Okay." I left my rucksack and walked to the small stack I'd gathered. I pushed a few of the thicker pieces into the blaze. The mountain air was growing chilly. We'd need more wood if we were going to keep a fire through the night.

Beaman scrutinized his belt, then picked a jar filled with yellow powder. He threw a pinch of it on the flames, then saw my curious look. "It's a balancing powder for cooking— Mother brought it back for me last year. It keeps the temperature of the fire nice and even." He frowned. "It's a bit old. I hope it still works." He added another a pinch, then hummed to himself as he filled the pot with water and a cup of milled grain from a sack.

While he chopped an onion, I went to look for more wood. "Peck, stick!" I called.

Peck ran to the nearest thick twig, tossed it my way, then looked eagerly back at me.

Orlen snorted. "Is Peck a chicken or a fetching dog?"

I ignored the wizard and pointed again. "Peck, stick!"

The game continued until we reached the end of the narrow copse of trees. Then I looked to my left and froze in place.

A caravan of traders with heavy packs was traveling along a trail I hadn't seen. A Maradonian flag flew from the top of the leader's pack, marked with the same royal emblem that was on my wizard knife. They were from Maradon Cross.

"Orlen, please get in my pocket."

"Why?"

I plucked him from my shoulder. "Shh!"

As they drew closer, the line of ten or so women and men

stepped along the opposite bank of the stream with a weary, resigned march. I recognized the hollow, haunted look about them—I'd seen it in sailors who'd been out to sea longer than they'd expected. The line's leader saw me and startled.

I tried to see myself from her perspective: a lone child with a tattered tunic and nearly chopped-off hair. A runaway apprentice who'd been punished and shamed. Even without the proof of the letter in my rucksack, the royal trader would make assumptions.

I hurried back to Beaman. "Traders are about to pass. Don't talk to—"

"Hello, hello!" Beaman waved to the group who looked as exhausted as I felt. They stood directly across from us now, at the same lazy part of the stream that was convenient for wading. Several of them dropped packs and soaked their feet.

A burly woman at the front of the line returned Beaman's wave, but her eyes were serious. "Are you children lost?" she called.

I shook my head. "No."

"Big group you've got there!" Beaman called, resuming his stirring. "Where are you heading? We're off to the royal city. If you go to Trapper's Cove, be sure to visit the Fork & Cork for a meal!"

"Beaman, stop talking to them," I said in a low voice.

The leader jerked her head toward the back of the trading line. "We have food if you need it. And Peace Day goods, made especially for the hundredth anniversary." She shrugged at the second offered item, as though she knew we didn't have coin for buying such things.

Beaman eagerly tugged my arm. "Should I ask what food they have to trade? I forgot to bring parsley."

I shook my head again.

"We have a hired wizard with us," called a skinny man in the middle of the line. He smiled and licked his lips, looking at our rucksacks. "Do you want to buy any services? We'll give you a discount." He pointed to a young woman of Hut's age toward the back of the line.

The wizard carried no pack, but walked slightly hunched, as though she carried a great weight. Her emerald earrings were shaped like teardrops.

Beaman looked pointedly at my apron pocket and raised his eyebrows. He shuffled close to me. "Maybe she can fix Orlen."

I looked down and saw Orlen frowning from my pocket, studying the young woman carefully. He looked up and shook his head. "No," he whispered.

Oh, thank goodness. I had no doubt that if the curse was broken, I would be sent back to Trapper's Cove. There was a reward for returning stolen goods.

"I'll come negotiate." The man's eyes were friendly, but a prickle told me the intent behind them.

I was no fool. The man was only asking if we wanted to buy services to find out if we had coin with us. If he thought we weren't runaways, he could overcharge us. And if he thought we were . . . well, then, he would either take all of our coin for silence or force us to join the royal party until our story could be proven.

"We have no money to buy goods or magic," I called across the stream. "But we can both perform for you, for five coin. We're simple performers, sent to Maradon Cross to find apprenticeships." I lowered my voice. "Beaman, listen to me. Throw your knives into that tree," I said quietly and evenly. "Like you did with the cutting board."

"What? Why?"

"Just do it."

Something in my voice shut him up. He stepped quickly to his pack and took out a large cleaver, three razor-sharp chopping knives, and a dicing blade.

I nodded toward Beaman. "Here's a taste."

One by one, Beaman sent his five knives careening into the tree. They landed inches from each other in a straight line.

Beaman turned to me, arms raised in triumph. I ignored him. Instead, I watched the middle man and was pleased at his grimace.

I clucked my tongue. "My brother's usually a bit faster.

I'm much better than him. My aim is flawless. You should see me with flaming arrows."

To my satisfaction, the leader of the group shook her head. "We have no time for follies. We're here to fill water flasks and move on."

I looked up at the mountainside. "There's a snake up there," I told her. "A big one."

"We've heard about it." She jerked her head toward the wizard. "That's why we brought her." Without another word, the group gathered water and returned to their trudging line formation.

Once they were out of earshot and eyesight, I took Orlen from my apron and placed him near the fire.

Beaman sat on the ground beside him. "I don't understand—that was your chance. Why didn't you want her to fix you?"

"If they think a wizard that age can handle that snake, they're gravely mistaken," Orlen said. "She couldn't be much older than you both. She probably only came into her magic ten years ago, at the most. That's not nearly enough to face that beast. Or to restore me to the way I was. And that was a royal trading party."

"So?" I asked.

"So I can't chance them contacting Renart."

"When do wizards come into their magic?" Beaman asked.

"Usually at five or six. I was four," he said smugly.

Peck wandered over to Orlen and followed him with interest.

"What are you looking at?" the wizard snapped. He made a move to shoo the chicken away, but Peck bent and flattened her body to the ground.

I smiled. "She likes you. That's what she does when she wants to be picked up or cuddled."

"Hmph! Do I look like I could cuddle a giant chicken? Now, if you'll excuse me, I have to answer nature's call. Don't move far, Stub, or I'll get yanked around and make a mess." He stomped off toward a bush.

I dropped a kiss on Peck's back. "I think that wizard is warming up to you."

Orlen looked back toward the caravan as he entered the bush. There was something other than worry in his gaze.

Beaman returned from retrieving his knives. He stared after the retreating caravan, puzzled. "They didn't like it?" He sounded disappointed. "I hope I didn't frighten them."

"I hope you did." I set Peck down to roam. "That was the point."

"But . . ." He frowned. "They were friendly. It was a royal trading party—they wouldn't have hurt us."

I looked at him sharply. "People will nearly always hurt you, especially if you don't expect them to."

He slipped his knives into their leather safety sheaths. "You should always look for the best in people. That's what I've learned from Pap. There's good in everyone. What do you think of that?"

I think that's a pile of enhanced sheep plop, I thought. "Maybe there's good in everyone." I arranged the firewood in a neat stack. "But there's bad in everyone as well."

He shifted uncomfortably. "I guess we have different views on people."

"I guess we do." He looked really uncomfortable now— like he was holding his breath and didn't know how much longer he could last. "In any case," I added quickly, "you're really good with the knives. That was even better than what you showed me when we first met."

"Really?" He released a breath. "Because I—"

"Can I help with dinner?" I asked.

When I cut him off, he paused for only a second before smiling. I liked the smile, and I hated it too. He'd been taught to ask questions, but no one had taught him to lie low. Or to know when people were dangerous. Or to cower. His mild manner and faith in people would get him in trouble one day. I hoped I wouldn't be there to see it.

"Sure," he said. "Any chance Peck has laid an egg in your sack?" Beaman reached a hand out and patted her. "How often does she lay? Eggs can be cooked so many ways." He slurped from a wooden spoon, then frowned and rummaged through his spice belt. After unscrewing the lid of a jar, he pinched light brown powder between his fingers and tossed it in the kettle.

"She doesn't lay." I reached down to stroke Peck's feathers. "She can. She has. She just . . . stopped one day. Every now and then she goes in the coop with the others to try, but nothing ever happens, other than her being chased out."

"Aha, I knew it!" came a harsh voice from the bushes. "I knew that chicken was worthless. I knew she—AHH!" Orlen shrieked again and sprinted out, holding his long cloak up over his knees. He scurried to Peck and climbed up her feathers, panting. "Ants the size of pigs and spiders the size of boats," he muttered. He shook his trembling hands. "And I can't shrink them a bit. Stupid curse!"

"Pap says the right food can heal anything, especially if you take the time to taste it." Beaman wiped the knives and handed me the dicing blade, a small hunk of cheese, and a roll from his pack. "Can you cut this up for Orlen?"

I cut slivers from the cheese and bread, while sneaking glances at Beaman. His lips quivered and his shoulders were hunched. He wanted to be back in a proper kitchen. His apprenticeship was well suited, and I'd stolen it from him. What sort of person did that make me?

I plucked a leaf from the tree above and arranged the food

on it. The ground below the tree was scattered with round seed pods. I hollowed one out and filled it with water. "Here you go," I said, passing the plate and cup to the wizard. His wrinkled face looked weary. "Orlen, can I ask how old you are?"

"You just did." He bit into the cheese and took his time chewing. "Nearly one hundred and twenty-seven," he finally said. "Why? Were you thinking of getting me a birthday present?" He chortled and took another bite.

"Ha!" Beaman cried. "No wonder you look so old!"

Orlen managed to cough and glare severely at the same time. "Wizards live twice as long as you Maradonians. We mature at the same rate, but simply keep living."

While he kept nibbling with a miffed expression and Beaman sautéed onions, I picked up the journal and flipped through it until I came to the map of Maradon we'd looked at in Beaman's kitchen.

"Orlen . . ." Against my will, my arms curled inward, bracing for a potential blow, the way they always did whenever I was about to ask a question. "Where is your queendom?"

Orlen touched a spot high on the page, where nothing was marked. "Wintrel is far north of here, in the middle of the sea. It's small—about half the size of Maradon." He handed me his leaf plate and grimaced as he slid down Peck's feathers to the ground.

Beaman leaned over me, looking. "Mother's never been there. She once told me she'd like to travel to wherever it is the wizards come from."

"Your Roamers cannot venture there." For a moment the wizard said nothing more. He traced circular lines on the page, far north of Maradon and other lands. "The winds are different in that part of the sea. The waters there breed magic—or maybe they feed off the magic that's already there. Whatever the reason, the waters tend to naturally steer ships away from the isles that far north. Only those with magic or creatures like the Wintrellian swallow can pass through the sea winds. Which might be for the best. The dragons don't particularly like your kind. There was a kerfuffle around two thousand years ago, and you've yet to be forgiven."

"Dragons?" I stared at him, to see if he was joking. He wasn't.

Beaman looked up from his pan with interest. "They really do exist? I thought they were only in stories."

"Certainly, they exist. They have their own lands. We used to be friendly with them—we traded our island's gem-stones for favors. My father used to say that a single spelled dragon scale dropped in the sea could woo an entire tide of fish. But Lacera stopped the trade when she came to power— she said the dragons would turn against us one day. I haven't seen one since I was a little boy."

Dragons and wizards and magical winds. It all had my head spinning.

"She didn't like the thought of us mingling with you humans, either. She said that the world beyond our island would only fear us for our differences. Perhaps kill us. She lied, obviously. But when you're fed lies on a daily basis, that's all you have to grow on." His hand fell on a blank spot on the map and lingered there. "No one out, no one in. We would be nice and safe that way, she said."

Before Orlen had arrived, I'd barely crossed the market tents in Trapper's Cove. Maybe I never would have tried to go farther.

"Well, I'm certainly glad that some of you decided to come here!" Beaman tapped the side of his wizard pan with a stick. "I've never overcooked a thing with this beauty." He poured the onion mixture over the grits and scooped out a steaming bowlful for me. "Humming honey," he sighed happily. "I can't wait to try it."

I lifted Orlen back onto Peck and passed him a hollowed horn nut full of the meal along with a toothpick to use as a spoon. Then I took the bowl Beaman handed me. It was filled to the brim. A thin line of the porridge dripped down one side and plopped onto the ground. I stared at the food.

In my hands was the largest meal I'd ever received. It was

a beautiful, thick pond of creamy yellow, topped with onions seeping with sweet glaze. I took a bite and nearly closed my eyes—and not from sleepiness. This food wasn't just food. It was something beyond that. It filled something in me that I couldn't describe. It was like Peace Night.

Beaman must have seen my expression. His brow furrowed. "Don't you like it?" he asked.

I looked down as I ate. Slices of sausage were buried halfway through the bowl. By the looks of things, he'd used nearly all of his portion of the food supply. I wanted to point that out, but instead I took another bite and held it in my mouth. Then I swallowed. "It's the best thing I've ever eaten in my life."

His cheeks glowed with pride. "Oh, you don't mean that. I just threw it together." He wiped his hands on his trousers looking pleased. He refilled Orlen's tiny bowl and passed it to him. He stuck a hand in his pocket, holding whatever it was he was keeping there. "So . . . Lacera sounds awful. Do you really think she and the regent would hurt Queen Sonora?"

Orlen opened his mouth, then closed it. "I believe I'm done answering questions. Beaman, put some of that tinadub oil on my hands, please."

"What for?"

At the wizard's scowl, Beaman searched his belt and dipped a finger into a jar.

He held out his fingertip and let the wizard rub his hands in the oil. Orlen rubbed Peck's skin, where new feathers were trying to poke through. The hen's eyes closed in pleasure.

"I'm—I'm sorry for prying," Beaman sputtered. "All I meant to say is that I feel bad you had to leave your homeland, but we're lucky to have wizards in Maradon. My mother says she's never met a wizard in other queendoms she's worked in."

"We don't all advertise, you know," Orlen snapped.

Beaman looked at the royal emblem on the handle of his pan and brightened. "It must be the Peace. After you've lived with a tyrant, Maradon must feel extra free and safe, so you wizards come here. And I'll bet it's much easier to make a living selling magic here than back home in a place where everyone does magic. I'm surprised more wizards don't leave Wintrel."

Orlen slid down Peck's side and marched as far from me as the curse permitted. "There are quite enough wizards in Maradon."

I watched as Orlen sat against a rock and raised one hand to his forehead. Even with his small stature, irritation sailed off him in waves that I couldn't make sense of. Was it the queen being in danger? Or the fact that we hadn't traveled farther?

I fought the urge to look at Beaman and his easy smile. I didn't understand him, either. Maradon wasn't a free or safe place for everyone. The fact that he didn't seem to know that simple fact made it clear just how far apart the two of us were. But his words did bring up a point I'd wondered about.

It would be a bold question, and possibly a rude one. But as my life had become quite odd in the last hours, there seemed to be little harm in asking.

"Orlen," I said, "if Lacera is as talented with magic as you say, do the wizards of Maradon have enough magic to stop her? Or could she cast a spell that would overpower all the wizards here if you tried?"

For a moment Orlen looked as though he wanted very badly to say something, but couldn't. Instead he held out the empty hollow nut. "More food, please, then let me rest."

I did as I was told and filled the bowl. He took the food and slowly began to eat. His face was tired. And maybe a little sad, like when he'd talked about his queendom. But why would he be sad to leave such an oppressive place? It would be like me mourning Trapper's Cove.

His other responses seemed very carefully worded. I'd dodged a question or two in my day, and I was certain that he was holding something back. I felt a faint prickle as I watched him set aside his tiny bowl and close his eyes.

Looking around, I saw nothing unusual—other than a tiny wizard, who was keeping secrets.

8

How to Fight with Fire

᠗

Click . . . Click . . . Click.

Matron Tratte's steps were slow and deliberate. She stepped toward me in the kitchen.

"Another broken glass?" she said softly. "Oh dear." The corners of her eyes crinkled. "Well, that's one too many. Isn't it, Nuisance?"

I backed away from her, falling against the broom closet. I quickly opened it and squeezed inside. Peck was there at my feet. Her feathers ruffled against my shaking legs.

The matron approached. There was a gap where the closet's hinges had grown loose. As she neared me, her shadow darkened the line of light. "Stay in or come out," she murmured. "Either way, you're trapped, aren't you, Stub?"

I startled awake.

Beaman jolted beside me. "What! What is it?"

I raised a hand to my heart. I'd fallen asleep with the empty bowl in my hands. A dream. It was only a dream.

There was no matron and no closet. Around me was nothing more than a flowing valley stream, a fire circle, and a very harmless cook. Peck napped near us against the large tree's trunk. Orlen lay on his back on her feathers, his eyes closed. It was twilight, the unsettled hour between sunset and darkness. We'd all drifted to sleep without a lookout, which was extremely careless.

"It's nothing." My forehead and palms were drenched in sweat. I wiped them both and calmed my breath. "But get up." I added wood to the fire.

He groaned and stretched, then leaned back on the tree trunk. He pulled something from his pocket and rolled to his side, looking at it.

I poked at the fire with a long stick. "What's that?"

"What?" He startled and dropped the small frame.

I picked up the picture. It was the miniature painting of Queen Sonora—the one that had been on his bedside table.

Beaman blushed furiously. "I thought it would be good to motivate us. That's all."

Orlen yawned and stepped toward the fire, warming himself. "You like the look of her—just say it. She's got quite a brain, as well, you know." He shook his head ruefully. "She was always in the library before her mother died. Since Nadina's passing, she's taken to rather unroyal behavior—acting up and sneaking out. She's been faking being ill lately, just to get out of her royal duties. Not that Renart minds. He's quite happy, playing at being king."

"So you know her?" Beaman asked eagerly. "I mean, of course you know her. She and I are the same age, you know? Twelve, but she'll be thirteen soon—on the day before Peace Day. Mother delivered a birthday package to her once, and said she asked all about Roaming. Orlen, do you think you could maybe . . ." The blush returned to his cheeks and he shoved the small frame into the bottom of his pack. "Oh, never mind."

Orlen rolled his eyes.

"Where does she go when she sneaks out?" I asked.

"I wouldn't know." He stood by the fire, alternately warming his back and front. "When she was ten, I found her in the midst of the Peace Day celebration in the city's market square, dressed as a peasant, frolicking in the dance circles, and helping to set off firebursts." He sighed. "It wasn't the last time she did it, either. She doesn't like being queen. Says the castle is stuffy and cold in spirit." His expression softened. "I suppose it is, with her mother gone."

A mother gone. I looked over at my sack, thinking of the letter inside. If I knew how to read better, would I want to see what my own mother had written? Why would I? It didn't matter. She'd abandoned me. I was nothing to her, and nothing was what I'd grown up to be.

Orlen nudged my foot. "Speaking of cold, keep this fire up, Stub. It's starting to get chilly."

He was right. Once again, the weather had changed. The clouds that gathered overhead would cover the moon and stars. Soon the world would be completely dark. As I stoked the flames, I suddenly felt a sharp ache in my elbow. I scanned the area around us and saw nothing. Still, something was amiss.

I swiftly walked to Peck and put her in my rucksack. Swinging the sack onto my back, I stepped around to see what was on the other side of the trees.

"Stop dragging me!" Orlen shouted.

"Sorry." I hurried back as he picked himself up. He shimmied up my leg and into the apron pocket. He started to argue more, then saw my face.

"What's wrong?"

"I don't know," I said.

Beaman laughed. "That's quite a belly growl you've got." He smiled and stepped over to the scorched pan of remaining grits. He scooped some into my used bowl. "Have more. You must still be hungry."

My belly hadn't made a sound. I scanned the small campsite again and froze.

A gray wolf snout poked through the tall grass across the stream.

"Beaman . . ."

"Oh, fine. One more," he said pleasantly, scooping another spoonful into my bowl. Then his face fell at the sound of another growl. He held the full ladle over the bowl and looked down at my belly. "That wasn't you."

"Beaman," I said, my voice quiet but firm. "Get on this side of the fire. Now." When he only looked puzzled, I reached out and grabbed him.

Another wolf appeared. Then another.

Three growling wolves loomed. The first one crossed the stream slowly, never taking its eyes off me. The others followed. They were no more than twenty feet away.

"Boiled beets." Beaman's voice trembled.

"Get your knives, Beaman."

He gulped and pointed. "They're by the water. I was washing them, all except the cleaver." He tilted his head. "And it's in my pack. By the tree."

The wolves were closer than the tree. So much for that. "Orlen," I said, trying to control my voice. "Please tell me you have some magic left."

The wizard let out a bark of frightened laughter. "I'd love to tell you that, but no, I don't. Not an ounce." His voice was tinged in annoyance. "And anyway, why do Maradonians think wizards can do everything? We have specialties, and none of us specialize in repelling wolves!"

"Beaman," I said quietly but firmly. "Get behind me."

He jerked his head toward me. "But you—"

"Do it."

I'd faced wild dogs before, but the wolves looked harsher. They were leaner. Hungrier. And much bigger. Without Beaman's knife skills, I wasn't sure what to do. It was too bad I didn't actually have fire arrows. But were peak wolves even afraid of fire?

Only one way to find out.

Thrusting a hand at the fire, I grabbed the untouched edge of a fiery stick and hurled it. As soon as the stick hit its back, the wolf howled and retreated.

But only for a moment.

I eyed the remaining firewood pile. "Beaman, help me make a circle with the wood. Now."

But Beaman stood frozen, paralyzed by the sight of the three enormous wolves creeping closer. *"Piecrust,"* he said. His hands rolled an imaginary pin across an imaginary table. His breathing came in short, frantic bursts. *"Bread dough."* He began kneading the air. The cook's eyes watered as he made chopping motions. *"Onions . . . oh, I miss my onions!"*

As fast as I could, I used the rest of the wood to form a loose circle around us. I struck the wizard match again and again, lighting it.

The largest wolf crept forward with short, testing steps.

Its jaws hung open as though already unhinged for feeding. Saliva dangled, then splattered on the ground.

I saw the pounce before it happened. I dug beneath Peck and gripped my largest wizard stone. I cranked my arm back.

The wolf lowered its haunches. Then it lunged.

I threw the wizard rock, and the beast howled in pain and retreated to the others as the rock sailed back into my hand. They prowled around the fire circle but held their distance.

I added the rest of the wood, and the flames rose. The wolves stayed just beyond the fire, so close that we could see their sharp jaws, opening and closing in anticipation. They didn't seem frantic. They were waiting.

"Build up the fire!" Orlen yelled.

"We're out of wood," I said hoarsely.

Even if we hit them with my rocks, it wouldn't keep them away for long. There was only one rock that would come back to me. And there were three wolves.

There was nothing left to do. I switched my rucksack to the front and lifted the flap. I kissed Peck's shaking feathers. Or maybe it was me doing the shaking.

I gripped Beaman's shoulder. "Listen to me. The biggest one—there." I pointed. "We'll tackle it first. The others will stop when they see us attack it."

He stared at the wolves. "They will?"

"They might."

"They *might?*" he cried. "Wait! The tinadub oil!" Flustered and frightened, Beaman pawed through his belt beside me. "Here!" he said, shoving a bottle in my hand. "It burns long—maybe it'll help! I've got two of them!"

I tore out the cork of the first bottle, hoping upon hope for a reaction. I poured the entire contents over the ring of fire. The flames shot into the air.

"It worked!" Beaman shouted.

He was right! The wolves were backing away, unsure of what to do next! But wait . . . oh . . . oh *no*.

The flames were getting lower.

Then they flickered.

Then they died altogether.

I shot Beaman a quick glare. "I thought you said it burned long."

He gulped. "Must have been an old batch."

While the wolves regained their bearings, I jerked Beaman's hand. "Tree. NOW!"

We both sprinted to the nearest branch and swung up. Beaman screamed at the nip of a wolf beneath him. I shoved him higher and higher, my heartbeat slowing enough to realize that we needed a better plan than climbing a tree.

"Stub, stop!" Beaman suddenly shrieked. "STOP!"

I stopped. I looked up. Okay, we needed a *much* better plan.

There was a fourth wolf before us, larger than the rest.

And it had been hiding in the tree. I couldn't believe the higher branches weren't breaking beneath its weight.

"Go down, go down!" Beaman yelled.

I glanced beneath us. "Um . . . I don't think that's a good idea."

Below us, two wolves were steadily digging their claws into the trunk, keeping their eager, flashing eyes on us as they advanced. The last wolf stayed on the ground in case we jumped. We were trapped.

"*Spiced gourds!*" Beaman wailed, his eyes closing against the nightmare.

The wolf above us paused. Just as I was preparing to jump and take our chances with the single wolf on the ground, I noticed that the animals below us had stopped climbing. Their heads shifted side to side. They sniffed the air.

"Spiced gourds and warm milk with Mother and Pap," Beaman babbled. "Spiced gourds and warm milk and butter rolls and cheese and—"

"Beaman!" I hissed, tugging on his trousers. "Look!"

He squeezed his eyes shut tighter and shook his head. "No, thank you."

"Look!"

Beaman opened a single eye and gasped. "They're backing away!"

It was true. The wolves below us had lowered themselves

to the ground. There was a tremendous cracking noise as the wolf above us sprang from the branch it was on, leaping to the ground to join the others.

Their hair bristled, and their ears stood straight and alert. They raised their snouts to the sky and whined, then backed away even more.

"It's a miracle!" Beaman shouted, climbing down to my tree limb. He opened one of his arms and leaned toward me. I leaned away. He hugged the tree trunk instead.

Then a black cloud darkened the sky above us.

I followed the wolves' gaze and felt my stomach plummet to the ground.

It was as though one of the bats that sometimes nested in the eaves of the Tinderbox had been grossly enlarged, then given the beak and flight patterns of a hunting bird. A bird that happened to have teeth that looked like swords and two pairs of enormous glaring, glowing eyes. Its fur-covered body was over twenty feet long and as wide as a tavern table, with black, leathery wings extending thirty feet on each side.

The wolves bolted and split, each desperately running toward wherever it had come from. The flying creature went swooping after them.

"What *is* that?" Beaman shouted. "Another wizard spell gone bad? You know what, I don't even care! It's chasing the wolves!"

I knew the creature had nothing to do with magic. Traders at the tavern had sung war songs about them before—giant, four-eyed creatures called batterals that lived in the swamplands of Maradon. They'd been trained during the war with Tartín because of their excellent night vision. But they had all been killed off. That's what everyone said.

Apparently everyone was wrong.

Before I had time to think about what else I'd heard, Beaman let out a whoop of relief and pulled me and Peck into an excited embrace.

I felt Beaman's heart beat against my own and was suddenly aware of how close the two of us were.

I yanked back, breathing hard. The only time I'd been that close to people was when I was being shaken or thrown to the ground.

"Oh," Beaman said, putting his arms awkwardly behind his back. "I'm sorry, I just—um—"

"It's fine," I said shortly. I dropped from the tree and adjusted my pack so that Peck was closer to my heart than Beaman had been. There, that was better. "Grab your pack, then come back to the tree. We can hide among the leaves."

Beaman dropped beside me and trotted over to the stream. He whistled a tune while adjusting the pack's straps so it rested snugly against his back.

A low grumble came from my apron pocket. "What kind

of idiot whistles during a crisis?" Orlen raised a hand and made a rude gesture in Beaman's direction. "Hurry up!"

Obediently, the cook ran back. "What for? It's gone."

I sighed at his innocent, if dirty, face. "If that thing doesn't catch one of those wolves, it'll be coming back for us."

"Whatever you say." Beaman nodded, then looked past me. His jaw dropped. "Like that?" he whispered.

I turned and felt my stomach twist. The colossal bat-hawk creature shot toward us like cannon fire—fierce, deadly, and completely unstoppable. "Like that," I agreed.

There was no question of running away. The batteral was flying at an impossible speed. Before I could even scream, it gathered both of us in its talons and rose.

I felt little emotion as we left the ground. There was no time for that. There was only the grip of talons around my middle and a cold, cold air whipping into my face. The beast's toes were rough and thicker than my legs, forming a tight circle around me. I beat against them, then quickly stopped as the ground grew farther and farther away. An escape at this height would be a death sentence.

The air grew thin as the batteral flew high above the clouds. My vision became muddled. My thoughts came slowly. What . . . what was I doing? Where was I? Was I in danger? Or not? If I were in danger, my heart would be racing. Instead it felt deliberate and slow . . . so . . . slow. And my eyelids . . . they were like spades filled with wet sand. I struggled to lift them.

Maybe this was all a dream, and I'd soon wake to a kick of a Tratte boot. Ah, yes, there—tiny kicks were battering my stomach. I relaxed. The dream kicks didn't hurt nearly as much as Hut's. They were more like tickles from Peck.

Peck. Where was Peck?

I forced my eyes open and immediately wished that I hadn't.

I was, indeed, flying over the Queendom of Maradon. And there was Beaman, flying across from me, with limp limbs and windswept hair. I fought the fatigue addling my brain.

"Peck," I muttered. "Where are you?"

My best friend's toes scratched against my rucksack, scraping my belly. It was an oddly soothing sensation. Like she was scratching an itchy spot for me.

"There you are," I whispered.

The scratching felt a bit intense, though. "Not so hard, please," I said.

"STUB! WAKE UP!" The voice sounded more frightened than angry.

Now I'm hearing a voice, I thought. *Is that Peck? Has she learned to speak?*

"STUB!" Orlen bellowed from somewhere near my waist.

That's right, I thought, relaxing. *I have a tiny wizard with me. Orlen. He needs me. He's going to find me a place. I have a place waiting for me.* Then, feeling very light-headed, I used my trapped arms to give two squeezes to the rucksack smashed against my chest.

I'm here.

You're here.

There was a hard but comforting poke on my belly.

We're here together.

Then the dizziness overwhelmed me, and the world went black.

9

How to Feed a Nestling

I had never slept in a bed. Not once in twelve years.

I'd imagined it often, while cleaning the five guest rooms at the Tinderbox, but now I had the actual sensation of being tucked under tight covers. It felt good and safe and right for a moment. My eyes wanted to stay closed, so I let them. I relaxed, then moved a hand to scratch an itch on my neck. Or at least I tried to. But my arms wouldn't move.

Then the itch became a repeated poke. The jabbing grew more insistent.

"Peck?" I asked groggily. "Where am I?" My muscles slowly and painfully awoke. "And why do I feel like a wet rag that's been wrung out?"

I blinked my eyes open. The first sight that greeted me was a mass of brown lines. My eyes focused. Not lines— branches. Many pine branches and slinking vines, forming an enormous nest. The sun was midway through the western sky. It was well into the morning. How far had we flown?

And how long had I been sleeping? And where in the name of the Peace Queens was I?

I tried to move again, but my limbs were stuck to the branches with a layer of stiff, odorous mud. I looked down and saw three branches across my ankles, legs, and chest, barring me from moving. I was fastened to the inner side of the nest.

I looked right, then left, and saw Beaman, equally tucked among branches. There was only a body's width of space between us. His eyes were closed, but his chest and lips were moving.

A strange, high-pitched purring noise came from somewhere in front of me. I looked for the source and two creatures came into fearful focus.

"Babies," I muttered, though the word seemed highly inappropriate, as the two batteral nestlings were larger than me. Miniature versions of their mother, they were sleeping, curled up against each other.

"Beaman!" I whispered with urgency. "Wake up!"

He moaned, then tried to stretch. His eyes flew open. "Stub, I can't move!"

"Neither can I." I looked down. Peck was cramped against my chest inside the rucksack. Orlen was astride her neck.

"In case you're wondering, I can move," Orlen said,

straightening his robe. "Thank you again for your stunning concern, by the way," he said dryly, climbing onto my shoulder. He clung to my ear, surveying the scene. "At least the big one isn't here. Do you think that the two of you are Mommy's new children or food for the ones she's already got?"

"Food," I said grimly.

Beaman groaned miserably. "I love food. But I don't want to *be* food."

A strange, growling chirp rang through the air, across the nest. Another menacing chirp joined it.

Our chatter had caught the attention of the nestlings. They woke and teetered awkwardly, opening their mouths to reveal four-inch-long, razor-sharp baby teeth. One of them hopped and fluttered its wings, hovering in the air for a second. The other did the same, then sank back into the nest.

I remembered what the traveler at the Tinderbox had said about young batterals being trained like hunting dogs. Perhaps the nestlings could be distracted by a game of fetch. It might buy us time while we thought of an escape plan. "Orlen, can you get me a rock from the bottom of my pack? It's one of the big ones—the one that's cold."

He slid down Peck's back and disappeared into my pack. A series of grunts sounded. "It's no use," he said, crawling back up. "It's too heavy."

When I looked up, one of the baby batterals had hopped

over to Beaman, probably curious about the frozen-in-place prey. Beaman whimpered, closing his eyes as though it would make the batteral baby go away.

As for me, I thrashed against the branches, trying to break free. Peck tried desperately to flap her wings, but she, too, was trapped. The other baby heard the ruckus and waddled over to me. I slammed myself back into my branch prison.

The baby cocked its head. Then, letting out a loud chirp, it stabbed at the part of my foot that still stuck out of the bottom branch restraint. It missed, then raised its head for a second try.

Wrenching with all my strength, I twisted to avoid its beak. The nestling's beak still sliced down along my foot. It was better than if it had gone through it, but the pain was searing. A line of blood dripped into the nest. "Go away!" I screamed.

"Get away!" shouted Beaman and Orlen.

Our combined voices startled both creatures, and they hopped back. It was a reminder that although the beasts were bigger than us, we'd been in the world much longer than they had. But soon enough, the larger nestling found its courage and lunged at Beaman's face with an open, toothy beak.

He screamed. "It's trying to eat me! Get a knitting needle!"

A knitting needle? I really needed to have a word with him about methods of defending himself—if we survived the nest.

Orlen clearly felt the same. "Knitting needle?" he shouted. "Are you serious?"

"I only have the cleaver left—it's too heavy for you to lift!" Beaman shouted. "Stop talking and hurry, before the mother comes back!"

Where *was* the mother? Hunting for more food? If that was the case, she could be back any minute.

Orlen leaped over to the pack squished against Beaman's back. He slipped inside, then emerged, awkwardly hefting what looked like a jousting tool on his tiny frame. He lunged forward just as the bolder beastling charged toward Beaman again.

"Aha!" Orlen shouted. "Right in your mouth—serves you right! Wha—ahh!" The creature clamped down on the needle and flung it aside, Orlen still gripping the other end. The wizard smacked against a restraint branch. He fell, managing to grab hold of Beaman's tunic.

"What do we do?" Beaman cried. Orlen climbed to his shoulder.

"Scream at it!" I shouted.

While Orlen cursed and Beaman shrieked and bellowed threats about baking the nestlings into a pie, my mind raced.

The wizard blade had been light in my hand—if Orlen could manage to lift it, maybe its magic would be sharp enough to slice through the branch bindings.

"Orlen, shut up, please! Are you all right? Can you manage to get the wizard blade? It's lighter than the cleaver and the rocks."

"I can try." Orlen crawled from Beaman's arm to the nearest branch. Kneeling on the stick and scooting inch by inch, he grunted his way over to me. He dropped into my rucksack and I felt him digging around near Peck, who was pressing herself against my belly. He cried out in pain. "Who put a horn nut in here?"

"Just hurry!"

"Ooooof!" With a great thrust, Orlen pushed the dagger out.

"That's it," I said. "Now take the sheath off and put it in my hand." I glanced anxiously at the babies. Orlen was taking too long. The batteral nestlings were gathering close again. "Beaman! Distract them!"

A loud grunt sounded as Orlen removed the sheath. "Take it!"

I felt the smooth hilt of the knife and gripped hard. With difficulty, I twisted my wrists to saw up through my middle restraint branch. It broke with a satisfying *snap*!

One done, two to go.

"SOUP!" Beaman shouted, his voice shaky but loud. The larger beast was eyeing a good-sized opening near his waist. "I swear I'll turn you into soup! With spicy vegetables sautéed in—wait a minute!" His arms still restrained, Beaman twisted his wrists and used his hands to search the jars around his waist. "Pepper powder, pepper powder, where is it, where is it?" he muttered. "Yes!" He untwisted a jar that looked full of red sand as the batteral bent close and opened its jaws. The other one approached and bent as well.

"Take that!"

A well-aimed flick of the fine red powder flew into both babies' mouths. One clamped down. The other followed suit. Both beaks flew open and they began squeaking, their mouths opening and closing as though trying to expel the powder. They tried to fly but bumbled into each other and collapsed.

"Well done!" I sawed through the bottom branch. One more to go.

Beaman let out a strange, terrified laugh. "A little goes a long way." The pine branches above him swayed in a sudden wind. Beaman scanned the sky above and his smile faltered. "Oh *no*."

The adult batteral plunged through branches with a crash, landing heavily on the nest's edge. The branches quaked and swayed. A crack sounded beside me. The top branch barring Beaman had snapped from the impact.

"Try to get out, Beaman!"

"I'm trying!"

The mother nudged her nestlings together, then pushed them toward us. The top branch was firmly at my neck. I sliced through the last branch as both babies sprang toward Beaman's face.

He screamed, straining against his bindings. I thrust my arm out, swiping the knife against one of their wings. It barely made contact, but the nestling jumped back and made a whining sound.

The adult looked pointedly at the babies, as though disappointed. She lowered her head and shoved the nestlings back toward us.

"You're a horrible mother!" Beaman shouted, his voice shrill. "They need flying lessons, not eating lessons! Everyone knows how to eat! Why don't you shove them right over the edge of the nest and then follow them!"

The threat backfired. The adult lowered her head and screeched in Beaman's direction with such force that his cheeks rippled.

I slashed through his bindings. Beaman's words might have failed, but they'd given me an idea. I checked to make sure Orlen and Peck were safely in the rucksack strapped to my chest, and then I grabbed Beaman's hand and started crawling up the side of the nest.

"Come on!" I yelled, ignoring the pain in my foot and yanking him behind me.

Mother Batteral was not happy. She kicked with her talons and beat her wings until all of us—nestlings, travelers, and all—were flung against the other side of the nest. Should I throw the wizard knife? If I did and missed, I'd have nothing left to defend us.

With my free hand I frantically searched through the rocks in my rucksack, searching for the triangle-shaped, icy one. Instead I felt the searing pain of a spiky thorn.

It would have to do. Feeling warm blood already dripping down the pricks in my hand, I took aim at the crouching batteral and, with all my might, hurled the horn nut toward the center of its four eyes. I only needed to hit one.

The batteral straightened as the nut sailed through the air. Too low. The spikes clung to its body fur like a harmless bramble.

"You missed!" yelled Orlen.

I crawled to the top of the nest, pulling Beaman after me. "You think I don't know that?"

"So do something else!" he shouted, swaying from my earlobe. "And you, Beaman! Throw your cleaver!"

"I can't!" His voice was high-pitched and hysterical. "It's my only knife left! And it's my favorite! Mother gave it to me! I use the flat side to crush garlic and—"

"Throw it!" Orlen screamed. "Why do you think your mother learned to throw knives in the first place? It wasn't for crushing garlic! JUST THROW IT!"

I tore through the bag again, looking for the icy rock. There it was! Nobody, not even a batteral, would like a sharp piece of ice digging into their eye.

I took aim again. The beast lunged forward. I felt a slight wind whistle past my cheek as Beaman's cleaver went spinning through the air.

A thunderous roar tore through the sky as the knife and my rock both hit the target. The batteral shook its head, screaming and turning in a pained circle.

"Let's go!" I yelled, pulling Beaman close. "Get ready!"

He frowned. "Get ready for what?"

"Flying lessons." I placed a vine in his hand, wrapped it around three times, and then shoved him over the edge of the nest.

10

How to Meet a Swamp Queen

❧

It's important to stay quiet while desperately holding on to swinging vines beneath a nest full of raging, shrieking creatures that want to eat you. Beaman was likely aware of this, but as he clung to the vine beside me, he whimpered like a pirate about to be thrown overboard.

I caught his watery, traumatized eyes. "Just hold on," I whispered, the way I would to a panicked Peck. "It'll be okay. Try to be quiet. When you're ready, start going down."

"I'm not ready." He slowed his breathing. "But I'll go anyway."

"Good."

Hand over hand we descended. At first I kept my eyes firmly up, past Beaman, toward the nest. What would we do if the batteral saw us? I was out of plans. I hesitated. When I glanced below, I saw nothing but a landscape too dark and murky to make out. Was I leading us from one danger into another?

"It's all right," Orlen said, crawling from his perch enough to touch my own shaking hands. "Peck and I will keep watch."

Above me, on his own vine, Beaman babbled softly in between exhausted, choked sobs. "You should be a Roamer, not me," he said. "You're good at sleeping outside and not eating much, you didn't bring a blanket, and you don't even mind not wearing shoes. And you haven't complained once about the cold or the wind or the wolves. I care about the queen and the Peace, but I want my knives back. And my pans—all of them, not just the ones I brought. And I miss my pillow from home. I miss Pap's songs. I want my mother!"

"Your mother will be proud of you," I said, trying to bolster him. "I'm sure she misses you."

"Your family must miss you, too."

I felt my grip loosen. Quickly, I took my right hand off the vine and wiped the sweat away. I did the same with the left. Better. The trees in the forest were taller and wider than any I'd seen. My arms ached from switching from vine to vine as they ran out of length. Whenever possible, I tried to find footholds in the massive trunks we traveled alongside, to give my arms a rest. When we ran out of vines, ten feet remained to the ground. I pulled Peck from the pack with one hand.

Orlen slid from my shoulder and onto the chicken's back,

where he gripped her feathers. "I'll go with her. It'll be less bumpy that way."

I stifled an exhausted laugh at the strange scene and tossed Peck gently to the ground. Her flapping wings let her settle with a little cushion onto a patch of moss covering the nearby roots of a giant tree.

I had no such wings. I threw my pack to the ground, then let go.

The ground squished beneath my bottom like one colossal pile of sheep manure. It didn't smell much better. I felt a light stinging on my arm, then my cheek. Then more. I flinched, and swiped the air, but it did little to dissuade the tiny, flying insects.

"Ow!" Beaman landed with a squelchy thump beside me. He looked down. "Am I sinking?"

"You both are," said Orlen, crawling off Peck and into my apron. "And so are your packs. Come over here."

Peck clucked behind me. She was still perched on an island of roots sprawling from the nearest tree. "Get over by Peck," I told Beaman. With effort, I stood up in the heavy muck and fetched our supplies.

When I reached the safety of the tree roots, Beaman was crouched with both arms around his knees. He shivered, though the air felt much warmer than the nest had. I handed him his blanket and dug for cheese in my pack. I wiped feathers from a piece of brick bread and broke it in two. I handed him a piece. He looked down at it mournfully. "I don't suppose any of my bread is left? Or sausage?"

"You didn't want to ration," I reminded him.

He nodded sadly. "Right. I forgot about that." He slapped at his neck, then at his own cheek. "Stupid bugs." He uncorked a bottle from his pack and held it over his mouth. Nothing came out. "I don't suppose I can have some water?"

I handed him my flask. I was parched, but we had to be smart. "Just a couple of sips."

I broke the sawdusty excuse for bread into crumbs for Orlen and Peck, and we chewed and slapped the bugs away. I studied our surroundings.

The lower parts of the trees were all pocked on the same side with strange-looking growths, like the barnacles that gathered on the dock pilings in Trapper's Cove. Beyond the root islands and muck was an endless blackwater pool. Sluggish bubbles journeyed up from someplace far below. The bubbles formed thick domes that burst with steam and stench.

There was no birdsong. No scurrying ground animals. No wind. Only a swamp that seemed to go on forever.

"I can't take it!" Beaman shouted, waving his arms. "They're all over!" He looked at me miserably.

I leaned forward over the roots, scooped a handful of

muck, and rubbed it all over my face and neck. Then I scooped another handful and held it out to Beaman. "Coat yourself in this—they won't bother you. Pigs do it, to keep flies away."

He wrinkled his nose. "The stench is unbearable."

"You already stink. Both of us do."

Beaman looked offended, then lifted his arm and took a deep sniff of his armpit. He gagged a little, then gave me a sheepish grin. "Okay. But this stuff smells worse than me." Reluctantly, he took the muck and smoothed it on his skin.

I picked Peck up for a soothing cuddle. She nestled against my dirty neck, and our hearts pressed against each other until both beats slowed. I breathed through my mouth, though it did little to halt the smell of the caustic, acrid air. "Are we still in Maradon?" I asked.

Orlen rose from the root he'd settled upon. He twisted his bracelet in thought. "Oh, you can be certain we are," he said, gesturing around them. "May I present . . . the Bangolin Swamplands."

"They were on Mother's map," said Beaman.

Orlen nodded, peering around with apprehension. "There are books about them in the castle library. During times of war, the swamplands were used as both a safe haven and a dangerous weapon."

Beaman looked around warily. "How can a place be safe and dangerous at the same time?"

The wizard arched an eyebrow while grooming his mud-flecked sideburns with his fingers. "It's more common than you might think. A select few Maradonians—who knew the swamp's secrets—were recruited to lead rival war bands in."

With a sigh and a groan, Beaman sat up. He rubbed his exhausted arms. "Then what?"

Orlen shrugged. "Then they didn't come out again."

Beaman looked around and gulped. "Why didn't they come out?"

"Let's hope we don't find out," Orlen said darkly.

Beaman sighed and took out his mother's journal. I joined him and we both studied the map. Orlen jumped down and landed on the book. He studied the landscape below his feet and squinted at the words.

"Here are the swamplands," he said, stomping his feet on a large shaded area.

I could hardly believe it. We'd traveled over more than nearly half the queendom. The border of the swamp looked to be only a day's walk or so from our final destination.

"This is great!" Beaman said excitedly. "The batteral saved us time."

Orlen shook his head. "Not necessarily." He stood at one end of the swamp drawing and took four short steps to the other end. "It can be a four-day walk across this mess. There's no telling where we are within it. And we have no way of knowing direction. We could end up traveling the wrong way. Or walking in circles."

He looked longingly at the castle on the map, and the words *Maradon Cross*. His face was worn as he stepped off the pages and onto my bent knee. "And Peace Day grows nearer with each sunset. I have five days to make it to the wizard district, discover the details of the plot against the queendom, and find a way to stop it."

As though sensing his mood, the swamp began to darken, early afternoon turning toward evening.

"If you can't stop Lacera, what will happen to Maradon?" Beaman asked.

Orlen grimaced at the question. "I don't know. First I need to find out how Renart is involved and what the two of them have planned." He walked along the thick root, stopping on a patch of moss. "As for Lacera, there's no map to navigate the dark forests of her intentions."

Navigating dark forests. I had flipped past a page in the journal with a drawing of a large tree with expansive roots. It matched the trees in the swamp, I was certain. I released Peck and held my hand out to Beaman.

"Beaman, can I see the journal?" He handed it over. I lit the claw rock and paged through until I found the drawing. I thrust the page back to him. "Read this."

Puzzled, he took the journal and read aloud.

*Forests in Maradon are often thick and dense. Do
not enter any unexplored wood without substantial
supplies. Moss and edible growths will grow all over
trunks, but those in places with little access to light
will always be thickest on the east side of the trunks.*

Well. We didn't have substantial supplies, but we certainly had tree growths. I scanned the trees around us, then
pointed. "There you go. Let's head east."

I put Peck back into my satchel, and Orlen slipped into
my pocket.

We advanced slowly, avoiding the sinking muck and
using the far-reaching roots and mossy islands as pathways.
At times the black pools rippled with the movement of things
unknown. Hours passed before I felt my nose twitch with a
prickling sensation.

I pulled on Beaman's tunic. "Stop."

"Why?" He looked around nervously.

"I don't know."

An eerie, lilting moan came from somewhere in front
of us.

"What was that?" Beaman jerked away from the noise.

The chilling sound came again, louder. And to the left.

Beaman gulped. "A swamp bird, maybe?"

I searched the moss island we stood upon, seeing nothing

of note. Then, in the outer reaches of the glow rock's beacon, I saw the outline of a moving shape. It crouched and shifted. Barely visible were limbs—arms and legs and a head.

Beaman saw me freeze and clutched my arm. "What is it? Do you see something?"

I shook free of Beaman's hold. "Something's out there," I whispered, feeling Orlen shift as he peered over the lip of my apron pocket. "Look to the right of that far tree, straight ahead."

But when we both looked back, it was gone.

Seconds later, a splash sounded behind us.

"Oh, *do* be careful!" called a scratchy voice. "Watch out for bumpy, stumpy roots, the ones that grab you by the boots!"

"I think it's a *who*, not a what," Beaman whispered nervously. "Not a bad rhymer, either."

"Who are you?" I shouted, holding the glow rock high and searching the shoreline of the mossy island. "Show yourself."

Orlen set his jaw. "I very much doubt it's anyone we'd like to acquaint ourselves with." He slipped back into the apron pocket.

"Now, don't step there!" the voice croaked. "You'll be sucked down. Please don't! I don't want to be alone again."

I pulled Beaman back, just as the branch he'd tested the ground with became stuck. He yanked, but it wouldn't budge.

"Please," I called. "Show yourself."

There was another splash in the water, a moving shadow, and then an ancient woman stepped from behind a tall tree on our small trunk-and-root island.

Her face was like cracked earth, with wrinkles so deep that I could barely locate her mouth. Long gray hair, matted with muck, hung from her head. Her ears were small and shaped like withered mushrooms, as was her nose. Her eyes, when they widened enough to be seen, were wild and watery.

The expression on her face was a strange combination of pleased and worried and fierce. In one hand, the old woman held a thin, sharp bone. She nibbled its edges.

"I heard you coming," she said, "so I put on all my pretties. You only get one chance to make a first impression. Or a last one, if things end badly." She coughed, then cackled and grinned. "As they sometimes do."

She wore mud-caked trousers under a sullied gown with only one sleeve. A long, embroidered vest covered the top of the gown. Many beaded bracelets adorned her bare arm, and similar necklaces were draped across the top half of her chest like armor. A diamond-shaped jewel pierced the skin below her bottom lip. "I don't get many occasions to dress up."

The black pools bubbled just beyond her as she approached. The same prickling sensation as before crawled up my neck, tickling my ears. Peck poked me in the back, her beak tapping insistently.

"Th-thank you for helping us," I said. "With where to step, I mean."

"Ah, but maybe I haven't helped you," said the woman, licking her lips. "Maybe you'll end up like some of the others. Maybe you'll stay here forever."

"Tread carefully with this one," Orlen said, still out of sight. "She's clearly lost her mind."

The old woman frowned and hobbled forward. "Who said that? *You* should tread carefully."

Beaman tapped my elbow and tilted his head toward a nearby root island.

I placed one hand over Orlen. My other hand curled awkwardly around my pack, feeling for Peck. "Where shall we step, then?" I asked.

The woman zigzagged toward me. "Follow the swampland's poetry." She saw me studying where she stepped and smiled a gap-toothed smile. "You can't be in a hurry."

"Unfortunately, we are." I stepped back. "We are on a mission, my lady. May I ask your name?"

"My lady!" The elderly voice crackled in delight. "Oh, I like that. It sounds royal! But I fear the only title I own is Swamp Queen. My Duran used to call me that and bow."

"Duran?" Orlen whispered, shifting in my pocket.

The old woman squinted at me. "What's that?"

"Nothing," I said, nervously tapping my pocket to get Orlen

to stop talking. I reached into my rucksack as she rose. "Would you like some bread before we continue our travels . . . Your Highness?" I held out our last piece of brick bread.

The Swamp Queen nodded. "I will accept your offering. You may bow, too," she said grandly. When we did nothing, she frowned. "I said to bow!"

I shoved Beaman over so that we were both bent at the waist as she snatched the bread from my hand. "Pardon our manners, Your Highness."

"You may rise." Her eyes rolled up in bliss as she ate. Her chewing slowed, then stopped. She sighed. "The game's not as fun without my husband. Thank you for the bread. I haven't had any since a kind lady passed through last year. She shared her food. I tried to help her out of the swamp, but a gator came and . . . I was too late." She blinked. "I do hate it when I'm too late."

The woman stepped carefully across a bridge of roots to the island opposite the one that we stood on. "Your well-meaning friend is leading you the wrong way. He may know his way around a kitchen, but he's clearly lost here."

Beaman's jaw dropped. "How did you know that I can cook?"

She pointed. "The burns on your arms from the stove and oven. I once knew someone who had burns like that. He smelled like butter." A sad look swept over her face. "I miss him terribly. I saw the tragedy before it happened. But I thought I could change it. You can sometimes, you know."

"Can what?" I asked, stepping toward Beaman.

"Change things." She sighed, then shrugged. "But some things are written so stubbornly that they can't be erased."

This woman had clearly been alone too long. But she'd somehow survived—that might be a help to us. "How long have you been here?" I asked. I glanced into my rucksack at our meager food supply. "And what do you eat?"

"Oh, I've been here for years," she said rather secretively. "I eat swamp mussels and greens and—BAH!" With astonishing speed, the old woman spun, snatched up a dried vine, and used it to beat a bumpy, reptilian snout that had burst from the water in a nearby pool.

"BACK!" the old lady shouted. "BACK, BACK, BACK!"

The gator's mouth clamped onto the Swamp Queen's dress. It dragged her toward the pool, even as the *thwaps* of vine, rained down. I rushed forward to help, but tripped over a root. The flap on my rucksack opened and Peck flew out.

The gator's snout twitched upward, snatching for the hen. The Swamp Queen lunged forward and batted Peck back toward the island. I reached from the ground and pulled hard on the hem of the old woman's dress. Both Peck and the woman landed on top of me in a heaving pile.

"Thank you, dear." She pushed herself up and looked at my face. She frowned, then suddenly clutched my cheeks in her wrinkled hands, as though seeing me for the first time. "My goodness, you're a child! I couldn't quite tell under all that muck on your face." Her head jerked toward Beaman. "And him, too?" She let out a joyful laugh. "Finally! I've been—ahh!"

A second snout burst from the pool and chomped again on the dress, dragging her back to the water. The first gator joined it.

"Both of you? Oh, bother!" The old woman thrust a hand into the pockets of her dress. It emerged from the cloth folds with two long sticks that looked like candles. She pointed her free fingers at the candlewicks and muttered low words. The wicks lit, then fizzed with a brilliant burst of light. She cackled even as the swamp gators pulled her into the sludge. "I've been saving these for you, Lumpy and Bumpy!"

"Firebursts!" yelled Beaman. He threw himself over me as two thunderous *BOOM*s rang out over the swamp.

Thick, silvery-blue smoke lingered where the Swamp Queen and the gators had been.

The smoke cleared. The gators were gone. Only the old woman remained. I stared at her fingers—the ones that had lit the fireburst wicks.

"You're a wizard," I managed to sputter.

She was certainly old enough to have experience that could help Orlen. I tapped him, but he poked my hand away and remained still.

The Swamp Queen wizard hefted herself up. "I believe 'thank you' is a more traditional response to being rescued, but yes, I am a wizard. Though if you're in need of magic, my skills are very limited. My talent lies in visions. That's how I saw you children coming. I've been waiting decades for you. Now, let's have a small fire to warm these old fingers. Would you two like to discuss your future or not?"

Beaman met my eyes, looking sick to his stomach. He shook his head slightly.

I opened my mouth, but no words came out. I pulled Peck closer. "Yes," I said finally. "Yes, we would."

11

How to Prepare for Impending Doom

〜

I used the wizard blade to slice wood shavings for a small blaze, wondering what I was about to learn of my fate.

We gathered around the neat pile and the Swamp Queen muttered the same sounds we'd heard before, but wiggled her fingers in a different delicate dance. It took a few tries, but soon the smoldering embers caught and turned into a crackling blaze. The swamp was dark enough for phosphorescent plants and insects to begin glowing with dim yellows, greens, and blues.

"My name is Minera. Yours are . . . ?"

I glanced at the lump that was Orlen. "I'm Stub," I said. I tilted my head to the side. "That's Beaman. And my chicken is called Peck."

She nodded, as though it were perfectly normal for a traveler to have a chicken as a companion. That made me slightly less wary. But only slightly.

"The biting bugs are gone at this hour. Clean your faces

so that I can see you properly." The swamp queen produced a water flask from the depths of her layered clothing, along with a cloth.

"So," she said as we wiped ourselves clean, "let's speak of my vision. Two children. That's right enough. But I could have sworn I saw three children in another vision. Perhaps that comes later." She squinted at Peck, looking frustrated. "And a chicken seems off. I saw dragons. And a bird—a small one."

"A swallow?" I asked, remembering the message bird that Orlen had told us about.

She brightened. "Yes! That's it, exactly. The bird is important—you must use it." Her head cocked to one side as she stared at me. "Do you have vision talent as well, dear?"

"No," I said, feeling a blush creep up my cheeks. "I don't have any talents. I just—"

"That's not true," Beaman said sharply. "She has plenty of—"

"Oh, blast and bother!" the old woman said, tapping at her head. "There was supposed to have been a wizard with you as well. Not me, mind you. Oh, I'm all mixed up!" She tapped her head again with insistence. "Perhaps my talents are finally starting to dwindle." She let out a craggy laugh. "Being one hundred and forty tends to do that to a person."

"You were right about the wizard." Orlen pulled himself

out of the apron and raised an arm. "Hello, Minera. It's been a long time."

The woman squinted and gasped. "Orlen? Is that you?" She bent over me, peering onto my apron pocket. "Why, you're tiny! We can talk about that in a bit, but I must say, I never would have expected it to be you." She winked at us. "He was always a bit of a loner." She clapped again. "But now you've adopted yourself children? I thought you didn't particularly like children."

"Don't be ridiculous. We're traveling companions, nothing more."

Beaman and I exchanged glances. He spoke first. "You know each other?"

"We *knew* each other," Orlen corrected. "A lifetime ago. Before we came to Maradon. Minera and I lived in the same village in Wintrel. She used to come into my parents' shop for late-night snacks with her best friend, Duran." He cleared his throat. "That was before you two got married."

A cloud passed over Minera's face. "He died soon after we arrived. The swamp got him. I didn't have enough magic to save him."

Orlen lowered his head. "I'm so sorry."

"So am I. I think I may have gone a bit mad in the years since." Minera shook a finger at him. "But you heard me say his name—you were just going to stay hidden in that pocket until I led you out of the swamp, weren't you? You always avoided me in Wintrel after I foretold of you botching a huge spell one day." A flicker of a grin lifted the edges of her lips. "I didn't know it would involve shrinking yourself." Her face softened. "You were afraid I would tell you something else about the future that you didn't want to hear. You were always such a planner. As a boy, then as a young man."

A shadow passed over Orlen's expression. "Well. I didn't plan well enough for us when it counted, did I?"

Minera fingered a large jewel around her neck and cleared her throat. "There are some things that can't be planned for." Her eyes flickered over to Beaman and me. "I assume you've told them."

Orlen bristled. "I've told them everything I can. I've told them all about the danger their queendom is facing. That's the truth."

Minera studied Orlen. "Part of it, anyway." Then she looked between me and Beaman. Her watery eyes settled on me. "It's *her*," she said firmly.

"Me?" I asked, turning my satchel around and hugging Peck. "What about me?" And what were the two of them hiding? What had Orlen not planned well enough?

Minera walked forward, holding one hip. She placed a hand on my shoulder, scrutinizing me before giving a satisfied nod. "I'm very glad you didn't die. You could have. I saw that possibility several times."

My stomach clenched. Did she mean in the batteral's nest? Or in the mountains? Or . . . as a baby, even? I glanced at my rucksack, suddenly wanting to make sure the roll of paper was still there.

"You still might die, of course. Lots of chances for that left." Minera removed her hand from me and looked down at my apron. "So, Orlen. What do you have to say for yourself? I predicted that you and the children would come here. I know where you're going, so I must assume that the darkest part of my vision is true. Lacera is coming here?"

Orlen nodded. "I need to get to the castle for more details, but I believe so. A letter I saw said that she will arrive on Peace Day." He grimaced. "I can't predict what plans she has with the queen's regent, but nobody will be prepared. Especially not Queen Sonora." He looked up at Minera. "What else have you seen? What will happen with us wizards?"

"I can't say yet." The wizard woman ran her fingers over the bracelets on her arms and the necklaces at her throat. "But let's rest for the night and you'll tell me your journey story so far." She smiled at Beaman's nervous expression. "It's safe here. Trust me. There aren't any other gators for miles, and if I can survive this swamp for decades, you can manage a meal and a journey story." She nodded at Beaman. "You'll cook."

"I'd like to." He blinked hard. "But all my pots are gone. And my knives . . . they're gone too."

"You'll use mine."

"Yes, ma'am." He straightened his spice belt. "I'll do my best."

While we waited for Minera to return, Orlen went to attend to personal business. I leaned over to Beaman. "Do you think they're hiding something?"

His eyebrows rose in alarm. "Like what?"

"I don't know. Orlen was acting strange. I think he and Minera are keeping something from us."

Beaman laughed. "Now you're the one thinking the wizards are planning something." He reached out an arm to pat my shoulder, then pulled it back. "Wizards don't like to talk about themselves—my mother has said that." He raised an eyebrow. "I can think of someone else who's like that. Don't worry so much. They're nice, Stub."

"You think everyone's nice," I muttered, twisting the short strands on my head. "You'd probably think a person who chopped your hair off while you slept was nice."

"You're always looking for the worst thing possible," he scoffed. "Pap says that some people walk through the fields looking for flowers, while others just look for rocks that

might trip them up. You miss the flowers when you're looking for rocks."

Hmph. "Well, you miss the rocks when you're looking
for flowers."

He smiled and shrugged. "Still, it makes for a nicer
walk."

Hours later, I felt the safest I'd felt in maybe forever. Despite
its dangers, Minera was at home in the swamp. And with his
spice belt and talent, Beaman had created a wonder from edible plants. To each of our bowls he added a few of the delicate
shellfish that grew in clusters on submerged vines.

"Not too many," Minera had warned. "Swamp mussels
are delicious, but they have relaxant and sleep-aid proper-
ties. If you eat more than five or six, you'll sleep until noon
tomorrow. And you don't have time for that."

Beaman hummed beside me, sneaking looks at his miniature painting of Queen Sonora while resting on a thick
tangle of tree roots covered in soft moss. Peck had settled
on his belly, and Orlen had settled on top of Peck.

I'd let Beaman do all the storytelling. His version was
long and full of details that I would have dismissed. Details
like his description of enduring leg cramps and hunger
cramps. Details like how I'd saved him, or at least tried to,
before we both went tumbling down over the cliff in the

avalanche. Details like burning the onions and overcooking the grits and Orlen being accidentally yanked around by me when I'd forgotten that we were bound. Details like wanting to prove his worth, so he would earn his mother's respect. I was both embarrassed by and glad for his wordiness. It gave me a chance to breathe and to watch Orlen, who seemed wary of Minera. As though he was afraid of what she might say. Or reveal.

"Will you come with us?" Beaman asked Minera. "To the castle?" He wiped a sleeve across his mouth and set his bowl aside, his stomach full and his eyes bright and hopeful.

Minera shook her head. "Duran's here. I'm a bit lonely, yes, but I'm not ready to leave him yet."

I dipped a hand into my rucksack and pulled out the muttering rock. I handed her the stone. "I know it's not much, but maybe you would like this as payment for helping us? It has a voice. Maybe it could be . . . company?"

Minera took the rock and turned it over in her hand. She smiled with delight. "I haven't seen one of these in years. It's a message rock. My mother made me one to keep in bed. We used to make them as youngsters, to send each other nonsense. You have to press it in the right place to make it louder." She studied it. "It's old, like me. The magic's worn down." She cradled it, then placed it to her ear. Her mouth opened in wonder. "It's a lullaby." She smiled at Orlen. "'All the Nights.' Do you remember? You must. Your mother used to sing it to you and Gwenda at the shop. You two slept in a corner when they worked late."

Orlen gave a curt shake of the head. "I'm not a child anymore."

"Well, you were, once." Minera cupped the rock to her ear and sang softly.

> *First sunrise, my love was with you.*
> *First sunset, my heart was near.*
> *Every day, I will protect you.*
> *All the nights, I will be here.*

As she sang a second verse, the blue, glowing light of an enormous swampfly flitted past. Three small lights followed. I watched them disappear into the darkness together, feeling as though a swamp mussel were stuck in my throat.

The rock kept singing softly as Minera's voice faded away.

Orlen coughed twice and cleared his throat. "A mediocre rhyme," he grumbled. "It would never work in a spell."

Minera blew her nose loudly on a length of her hair. "Well, I think it's sweet. I remember some of the botched spells you invented as a boy. Tried to turn your younger sister into an oven once, didn't you?"

Orlen scowled. "Gwenda used to say she felt ill when it was her turn to bake the shop pies; then she'd run off. I just wanted her to do her share of work."

Beaman brightened. "You bake?"

"No, I *baked*. Past tense. And not by choice." He raised two fingers and swirled them at the nearest tree. "'Lazy sister, full of lies, make her cook all of the pies.' Nope. Still doesn't do a thing. Enough nonsense, Minera. We're running out of time."

All mischief in Minera's expression disappeared.

"That you are," she said. "An end is coming, that is certain. Whether it's someone else's or your own, I cannot say."

In the middle of the night, a stirring sounded beside me as I watched the fire and looked through the Roamer's journal.

Beaman rubbed his eyes, then shot up suddenly, drool dripping down one cheek. "What is it? Are the wolves back?"

"Shh." I poked the coals. "No. Go back to sleep. I'm just looking at the map." I rubbed at the batteral wound on my foot. It was swelling.

Beaman grimaced. "That looks bad. Why didn't you say anything?"

The fire's heat was suddenly too hot. I turned away. "It doesn't matter. Complaining about a thing doesn't make it go away."

"Maybe." Beaman reached for his jar belt. He handed me the tinadub oil that we hadn't used back in the mountains. "But nobody can help you if they don't know that you're hurting."

I stared at my foot. There had been countless times when Matron Tratte knew I was hurting and did nothing to help. But Beaman wouldn't want to hear that any more than I wanted to share it. I tossed the oil back to him. "We might need it later for an emergency."

"That cut looks like one."

"I can take care of myself," I said shortly. "Go back to sleep."

Beaman looked at me for a long, searching moment, then nodded. He lay down, turned his back, and was soon breathing evenly.

I felt a tickle on my foot. Orlen crawled up my trouser leg and settled on my knee. "You can't sleep," he said.

"No."

"Neither can I." He stifled a yawn as he looked at between me and the journal. "You also can't read," he said softly.

I stiffened and pulled my knees up. I wrapped my arms around them.

Orlen clung to my trousers and resettled himself. "That's why you had Beaman read the map in the mountains. And about the trees here."

I looked at the low flames, feeling a blush rush to my cheeks. "I know the letters and the sounds. Most of them, anyway. It's just . . . when they group together, I can't keep them straight."

He patted my leg, then rolled up his sleeves. "Let's fix that. Put me on the journal and hand me a matchstick."

I moved him to the crack between the pages. "I thought you didn't have any magic left."

He sighed. "I'm not going to use magic. I'm going to teach you. We'll start with—"

I held a hand up. "I thought you didn't particularly like children. So don't do me any favors. Because I don't particularly like those."

He crossed his arms. "Maybe I *don't* particularly like children. But I do like books, and I'm not averse to sharing them with others. Books don't interrupt you. They don't argue with you. And they ask very little of you." He scanned the page, then settled the pebble on a word. "In short, books make excellent friends."

"I wouldn't really know about friends."

Orlen stumbled. He straightened himself and his tunic. "Well, that makes two of us, doesn't it. Now pay attention."

I looked at the journal first. Then at Orlen.

And then, in a sinking swamp, by the light of a dying fire and a magical glowing pebble, I had my very first reading lesson.

. . .

"Off to the castle you go, then, to save a queendom!" Minera said.

We'd broken out of the swamp's darkness as the sun rose the next morning. I hadn't seen the sky for two entire days. Like Beaman with his pillow, I hadn't known how much I could miss it until it was taken away. Ahead was a steep embankment, blocking the view of what lay beyond.

Minera looked up. "The hill is steeper and the slope more slippery than it looks. I'll wait here, to see that you don't tumble down again. At the top, you'll be able to see the castle walls in the distance, next to the coastline. You'll pass a stream or two along the way." She looked our motley crew up and down, and grinned. "Maybe wash up a bit. A day's walk and you'll be there."

"It's that close?" I asked, placing Peck into my front-facing sack.

"Yes. When you're in this sunken place, it can feel like there's nothing beyond. But that doesn't mean there isn't."

"You really should come, Minera." Orlen climbed up to my shoulder. "We may need all the wizard help we can get. Everyone in the wizard district would love to see you."

Minera laughed. "I believe that's the nicest thing you've ever said to me. Adversity suits you, Orlen." She shook her head again. "But no. My magic is in seeing possibilities and hoping for the best one. I can do that from here. I'm no good with spells or fighting. Hoping—that I can do."

She pressed the lullaby stone to her heart, gave one long, appraising look at me and Peck, and pulled something from the depths of her skirts. "A present for you, Stub."

I looked down at the blue stick, decorated with the emblem of Maradon: the guardian gates, the book, and the jewel. It was more elaborate than the ones I'd seen in the market in Trapper's Cove. The wizard's mark glinted as I turned it in my hand. "A Peace Night fireburst? But why?"

She smiled. "I'm hoping that you'll have reason to use it. It's a small one, but powerful. It can light up the night." She reached again into the folds of her clothing layers and produced a bulbous coin purse. "I've earned plenty of your Maradonian coin over the years. Take this." She passed the purse to Beaman, then looked Orlen in the eyes. "We all handle it differently," she said, her voice careful. "Don't we?"

I looked between them. "Handle what differently?"

Minera stepped closer to my shoulder. She held her hand out, and Orlen stepped on it. She brought him close. "I'm glad that you shared our struggles concerning Lacera with the children, Orlen. It's really quite extraordinary, isn't it?"

Beaman frowned. "What's so extraordinary about it?"

"Oh, it's just that I know what a solitary boy Orlen was. He should think about sharing more often, you know." She winked at her fellow wizard. "After all, you're magically bound to Stub. Think about that."

Orlen stared at Minera, his gaze hesitant, then searching. He inhaled sharply.

"Good." Minera smiled. She placed him back on my shoulder, stroked Peck, then patted my arm. "Perhaps I was wrong, Stub," she said, looking at me meaningfully. "Maybe it was a chicken I saw, and not a dragon. It's hard to say. Go now, and good luck."

As we crested the hill, I felt a rush of uncertainty. Orlen hadn't given me any real reason to mistrust him. Neither had Minera. The prickle I'd felt when meeting her had likely been due to the gator danger, not her.

So why had my instincts sent such a strong feeling to my chest when Minera had looked at me and Orlen and Peck for the last time?

12

How to Roam a Royal City

❧

G iant pigs and giant flavors!" Beaman grinned at me as we neared the city gates, people jostling us on all sides. "Did you see the pepper pie the size of my head? Spiced peppers and cheese! In a pie! Why didn't I think of it?"

I winced as a passing girl jabbed me with an armful of blue-flowered, thorny Peace Day wreaths.

Beaman nudged me with his elbow while happily munching on a skewer of crispy whole fish and holding a triangle of golden-brown pastry. At his suggestion, I'd bought inexpensive sandals for both of us while Orlen huffed about wasting time.

The shoes felt both right and wrong beneath my feet. It was all a bit too much—like when Orlen was teaching me to read last night and the words swam in my head, each begging for attention. And the salty sea air and the harbor dredged up memories. Part of me felt as though, despite the distance, I might spot Matron Tratte at any moment. Was she terribly angry that I'd left? Was she scouring the village for me? Or had she simply passed my duties to Hut and moved on?

"I still can't believe I'm in Maradon Cross!" Beaman finished his fish and shoved the stick in his pocket. "Did you see the ships in the harbor? Everything's bigger here."

Orlen chuffed. "Maradonians always want things bigger. Bigger is not always better." He crouched within a new handkerchief tied around my neck. With the noise of the crowd, nobody noticed his voice. "There are so many wizards here that enhancement spells are cheaper than horses. I once saw someone try to enhance a cat to pull loads. Imagine a cat the size of a small horse." He snorted. "It didn't work out well. Took a dozen men to hold it down so the wizard could change it back."

The crowd of people entering the city narrowed to pass under the gates of the twenty-foot-high walls. We were horribly squeezed together for ten long feet, then painfully released like newborn babies. And then there I was. Inside the gates of the royal city of Maradon Cross. Carrying a ragged rucksack, a chicken, and a shrunken wizard.

With a queendom to save.

Peck stuck her head out, her beak shifting quickly side to side.

I reached in my apron for a handful of wheat kernels and

sprinkled them into the sack. "Don't worry, Peck," I whispered. "You'll be fine." I lowered my chin to the kerchief. "Which way, Orlen?"

"Stay straight and head toward the castle—past the market square."

Smaller streets and alleys branched off the main thoroughfare. Two- and three-story homes and shops made of timber and stone were packed tightly together, battling for space like nursing kittens. I watched as three girls in navy trousers and tunics scaled the thatched roofs and secured Peace Day decorations, laughing and weaving blue ribbons in elaborate patterns. I blinked, and for a second I saw a ragged-haired girl and her chicken alongside them. I shook myself free of that nonsense as Orlen yanked my handkerchief.

"Stub!" Orlen said. "Head toward that countdown clock. Then cut through the market—it's faster."

A larger version of the sand clock in Trapper's Cove rose high above the marketplace. A board beneath it enthusiastically proclaimed a number and two words. I slowly sounded them out, using the tricks Orlen had taught me the night before.

4 DAYS LEFT!

The number sank in. Only four days until a powerful, evil wizard queen arrived in Maradon. And nobody knew, except us—and the queen's traitorous regent. Below the clock was another large wooden sign, painted with Maradon's emblem in each corner.

Beaman licked the last trace of fish from his skewer and read it intently. I watched him, hoping maybe he would give some indication of what it said. I couldn't make out all the words. I heard a tiny throat clearing beneath my chin, then a low voice:

"Do you want me to read it?" Orlen asked.

My face reddened. Part of me wished that I had my own scarf to hide in. "Yes, please."

I felt the wizard lift slightly to get a better view. He spoke the words softly.

> *One Hundred Years Means One Hundred*
> *Times the Celebration!*
> *Temporary castle Workers Wanted:*
> *Laundry, kitchen, household, errand/*
> *deliveries.*
> *Fair wages offered. Report to the castle gates*
> *for inquiries.*

"That's all," he finished.

"Thank you," I murmured, tucking the information away as we navigated the marketplace.

Instead of tents, it boasted permanent wooden stalls

arranged on three of the square's four sides. Wandering vendors also sold goods from baskets. A middle-aged woman with a beautiful, star-shaped emerald jewel around her wrist sat beside a clay bowl with a few coin inside.

"Look at that!" said Beaman, watching intently as she juggled six apples in intricate patterns, keeping them afloat longer than usual in the air. "She's got to be a wizard."

Orlen snorted. "One would think you'd be used to wizards by now."

Beaman leaned his head close to the handkerchief. "Yes, but this one can actually still do magic. In fact . . . *oh*." His cheeks grew pink, and his eyes locked firmly onto a line of tables selling Peace Day decorations near the edge of the market. Behind them a makeshift wooden wall was full of Peace Queen portraits.

"One hundred years!" shouted a vendor. "Own all the queens of Peace before the holiday! Just three weeks to buy brand-new paintings of Queen Sonora!"

Beaman stared wistfully at a large Sonora painting. The young queen wore a calm, serene smile, and her hands were raised in a magnanimous greeting.

"Rubbish," whispered Orlen. "That child's never held that pose in her life. She's too full of mischief to sit still for portraits."

Beaman blushed even more. "I wasn't looking at her. I

was looking at, um . . ." He searched beyond the table and pointed. "That."

An enormous, official-looking paper was nailed to the center of a large noticeboard at the corner of the market. The words were written in sparkling, wizard-enhanced black ink that grew bolder whenever someone drew near. There were so many passersby that the words seemed to vibrate. This time Beaman read it aloud:

In Honor of Maradon's 100 Years of Peace
Queen Sonora has ordered a Public Feast on
Peace Day
The Queen Herself will mingle among us all!
Market Square ~ Midday to Midnight
All are welcome!

Orlen chuckled at the sign. "Now, that was most definitely *not* Renart's doing. He hates mingling with commoners." He tugged at the handkerchief. "Keep going and turn onto the street on the left. Then turn right on Rampart Lane—that's the wizard district. Gwenda's shop is the last one on the left."

The wizard district was a long, curving street that dead-ended at the city wall. An ancient watchtower loomed over the neighborhood. Beaman and I walked by taverns with colorful names but simple exteriors. The Hungry Goat, the Heartsick Dove, the Mutinous Pig, and the Dragon's Claw were all painted white with doors in various shades of blue. A sign was propped outside a three-story building. Orlen didn't wait for me to ask.

"Boardinghouse, Newcomers Welcome," he murmured.

The shops all had large windows. An elegant shingle with a number and the type of service provided hung above every door. I slowed my walking. Beaman did as well. To my relief, he pointed and read each store's name and service aloud with delight.

The Light Knight—Long-Lasting and Color-
Changing Candles (Peace Day Deals!)

Tarrow's Teas & Tonics: Specializing in Growing
Hair, Plants & Confidence

As You Wish—Temporary Enhancements: Decorative
moles, tattoos, hair, etc. Freckles by the dozen.
Pricing by the hour.

Home & Hearth: Unbreakable Dishware, Self-
Cleaning Chamber Pots, Burn-Again Firewood

*Magical Animal Enhancements: Speed, size,
temperament. Weekly/monthly/yearly spells
available. Inquire within for pricing.*

The Giddy Room—Magical Toys and Games

With each sign, the reason behind our journey faded and
my sense of wonder grew brighter and brighter. Of course I'd
seen wizard goods before, but to be surrounded by them was
a different matter. To think, all that magic had been in my
queendom, and I'd never known. I looked in the toy shop's
window and spotted an enormous dragonfly made of glitter-
ing jewels fluttering around in circles.

"There's my old shop up ahead," said Orlen. "The
Scholar's Closet."

I stopped at the shingle and looked at a display pillow in
the middle of the window. "What's a forever-ink pen?"

A hint of a smile came over Orlen's face. "It's a pen that
lasts a thousand years. It pulls traces of the environment
around it and converts the elements into ink, so it never runs
out. They're extremely expensive and rare. The spell that
produces them is incredibly difficult." He straightened his
shoulders. "Only one wizard in Maradon can do it. You're
lucky enough to be traveling with him."

"A thousand years isn't forever," said Beaman.

Orlen pursed his lips. "It's close enough."

We came to a stone plaque mounted in the center of the lane midway down the street. Rows and rows of tiny slash marks were carved into the stone at the base of the plaque. There must have been thousands of them. A middle-aged man with a jeweled eye patch dipped a cloth inside a bucket, then polished the slashes. As we passed, he pointed his fingers at the rock and waggled them. A thin slash joined the others.

He held his hand to his heart for a moment, then walked back toward the boardinghouse.

"What is that?" I asked.

I felt Orlen shift at my throat. "It's . . . it's a calendar," said Orlen. His voice dropped off when he said "calendar," as though the word weighed a great deal. "Please keep going."

He looked toward the end of the street. "There—the last shop. Jammed right against the wall. That's Gwenda's place."

Three more doors and we were there.

The window was curtained.

Beaman glanced at the shingle above the door. "The Marooned Goose ~ Magical Fixes & Repairs." His eyes drifted to a smaller sign propped in the window.

Studying the letters in the first word, I concentrated and formed the word in my mind, trying it out several times before speaking. "Closed. What do we do now?" I asked. "Wait here?"

Orlen sighed. "No. I was hoping I could take care of this curse problem with minimal mocking, but Gwenda always did like to scuttle out of work early. She can spend hours at meals with her friends. She's probably still having a late lunch. Head to the Hungry Goat. She always eats there." I felt him squirm in the scarf. "And before we go . . . there's something I need to tell you both. I haven't been completely honest with you."

My stomach clenched. I knew he'd been hiding something. "What is it?"

"Well," Orlen said, his voice gathering strength. "You see, back in Trapper's Cove, Beaman was right."

I clutched Peck. "Right about what?"

"Well . . ." Orlen crawled out of the handkerchief and onto my shoulder. "The wizards of Maradon *are* planning a rebellion. I was afraid that if you knew the whole truth, you wouldn't carry me here."

"What?" asked Beaman.

My heart and stomach twisted in knots. I'd been raised among liars and cheats. I'd taught myself not to trust people, because it never came to any good. But I'd been so intent on earning freedom for me and Peck that I'd let my guard down. I'd been stupid enough to believe someone.

I'd been used.

I snatched Orlen from my shoulder and held him firmly in my fist. "Why do you think we're going to take you anywhere but straight to the castle for questioning?" I said evenly.

He looked at me, and I could have sworn there was a hint of regret in his eyes. "Because you and I are magically bound together—only a wizard can fix that. And really, I wasn't lying when I said that your queendom is in danger." He glanced up the street, where two women in fine trousers and tunics marked with the royal emblem were heading our way. "Stop making a scene and find my sister. Then I'll explain the rest. Trust me, you don't have a choice."

The words felt like a slap. My entire life had been spent having no choices. "We're going straight to the queen." I stuffed him into my apron pocket. "And you're right. We're bound together and you're two inches tall. You're the one who doesn't have a choice. Maybe the queen will give me a place just for turning you in."

Orlen squirmed furiously. "But you don't understand—"

"Say one more word and I'll call for a guard right now," I told him.

"Stub." Beaman's hand grazed my shoulder as I turned and marched away. He ran after me, breathing hard. "Stub, maybe we should wait for him to explain."

I ignored him. As we were about to pass the Hungry Goat, I felt a sharp twitch behind my ears. I ignored it, knowing very well that a tavern full of rebel wizards was the reason. But the twitch became a prickle dancing up my spine. Then a buzzing in my left ear. I turned that way and saw something that I couldn't ignore.

My feet became anchors, holding me captive. It couldn't be. But it was.

The tall, broad woman was dressed in a familiar red tunic. She came out of a shop beside the tavern, her face full of anger and frustration. A young boy on the street bumped into her, his arms full of Peace Day items. Matron Tratte turned to snap at him, then smoothed her hair and turned my way.

"Change of plans," I said hastily, grabbing Beaman's hand and yanking him through the door of the Hungry Goat.

13

How to Light a Spark

I slammed the door behind me, breathing hard.

What was Matron Tratte doing in the royal city? I'd been seconds from her seeing me! I could have been caught and sent home to Trapper's Cove! I leaned against the door and pressed a panicked hand to my chest, feeling as though I'd already been shoved back into the broom closet.

"Who was that?" Beaman asked again.

"My owner." I whirled on him. "You told the traders in the mountains where we were going. You said to go to the Fork & Cork. No doubt your mentor made a stink about you being gone and Matron Tratte caught wind of it."

His face flooded with guilt. "I—I'm sorry. I wasn't thinking."

"That's because you don't have worry about things like that," I snapped.

Peck anxiously poked my back and I stood up straight. I reached a reassuring hand behind me. "We're okay," I told her. Though, looking around the dim lighting of the tavern, I wasn't sure our current situation was any better.

The familiar tavern sounds of loud conversation had quieted with our entrance. Three dozen curious faces looked our way.

Make that three dozen *rebellious-wizard* faces.

Outside, there was a woman who owned me—a runaway apprentice was no small thing. If she caught me, I'd only avoid formal punishment by entering into her service for the rest of my life. And I knew very well what sort of informal punishments she was capable of.

Inside was a group of vicious, magical traitors who planned to take over our queendom.

The options were not pleasant. What was worse, the chance of being wizard-cursed, or a reunion with Matron Tratte? I put my hand on the doorknob and scanned the indoor enemy, considering my choices. But actually . . . the wizards didn't look overly threatening.

Candles, cased in glass, stood guard at the center of each table, the lights flickering all manner of colors, bathing the room in a mixture of twilight and sunrise. Wild herbs grew live from the sides of rafters and the eaves above. The leaves and tendrils of the plants swayed gently, as though the room was producing its own kind of magical music. Their savory and sweet scents tangled together, leaving me feeling both calm and hungry.

My fingers relaxed. I let go of the doorknob. I took a single step forward onto a straw-colored mat in the entryway, pulling Beaman beside me, still feeling my heart pounding. A bell above the door rang three times. The mat turned a pale purple.

"INCOMING!" a server bellowed from a nearby table without looking up. His apron turned from white to the same purple color as the mat. "One adult, two children!"

A very tall man behind the bar glanced briefly at me and Beaman and waved. Then he frowned—at us, at the bell, and at the mat. "Just the two of you?" he said "Hmm. Must be in need of an update. Come in, I'll be with you in two minutes!"

Orlen tugged at my apron. "That's Jan, the owner. Ask him where Gwenda is. I don't want anyone else to see me like this."

The owner of the Hungry Goat was a middle-aged man with enormous ears and no hair to speak of. He wiped his hands on the towel tucked in his belt, then wiggled his fingers at a tray full of soup bowls until steam began to rise. His fingers danced again and he picked up the tray as though it weighed no more than a feather. As he wove between tables, the quiet gradually gave way to chatter and the room grew loud with talk once again.

I sat on a bench in a corner nook by the door, fingers clenched, feeling confused. The wizards eating lunch looked far less dangerous than the normal crowd at the Tinderbox. I looked over the room of rebels, waiting for another prickle of any kind, but the only pokes came from Orlen jabbing me in the neck with his tiny finger.

"Ask him!"

I turned my head, as though I was talking to Beaman. I pressed my hand firmly against Orlen, grateful that he was out of magic. "We're not taking orders from wizards who want to take over our queendom," I muttered back. I parted the window curtains. I could see Matron Tratte outside the shop across the way.

Beaman's eyes widened as a woman walked past us with a tray of tea, milk, pastries, and a sweet-smelling golden goo that was letting off low, lilting notes. He let out a chirp of excitement. "Is—is that humming honey?"

Orlen huffed. "Yes, and for queendom's sake, we wizards are not taking over Maradon! You misunderstood me. What I meant to say is that we were sent here for rebelling against Lacera—we're all prisoners here."

"Prisoners!" Beaman clapped a hand over his mouth as a nearby couple looked our way.

I pulled Beaman onto the bench beside me. I took Orlen from my apron and placed him on the windowsill. *"Explain."*

"Lacera banished us years ago with a powerful spell. She's still banishing wizards who try to defy her. None of us can leave Maradon. We're trapped."

I peeked outside again. The matron was still there. "I don't believe you," I whispered. "If that were true, you would have told the Peace Queens years ago."

Orlen took a forceful step toward me, then stumbled over his robe and nearly tumbled off the windowsill. He clung to the curtain for support. "We couldn't! That was part of the spell. Anytime we try to mention the banishment to anyone who's not a wizard, our voice is lost. Any attempt to write down our history results in a blank page. If Lacera is coming here, it's finally our chance to confront her. We can overpower her and force her to break the curse. Our freedom is at stake!"

Freedom. That I understood. My own prison warden was right across the street. "If that's true, then how are you telling us about it right now?" I pressed, keeping my eye on the matron.

"Because of you, Stub. I'm bound to you by magic. I didn't realize it until we were in the swamp and Minera pointed it out. I'm telling you the truth. Look around you— every wizard in this place has some sort of jewelry, even if it isn't in plain sight. Earrings, a bracelet, an anklet, a ring or necklace or nose ring."

Beaman blinked. "So what? We wear jewelry, too." He pulled on his earlobes. "See?"

Orlen let out a bitter laugh. "Yes, but our shiny decorations are *shackles*—beautiful things, so that none of you Maradonians would give them a second thought. They're part of the spell." He thrust out his arm and pulled at the bracelet. "She marked us with jewels from our own queendom. First, because they were formed in a place full of magic. And second," he said, glaring at the jewel on his wrist, "to remind us that we'll never go back."

I looked at the tavern customers. I saw jewel after jewel, just as he said. My mind raced along with my heart. In the swamp, the secretive exchange between Minera and Orlen had made me suspicious. Part of me had been looking for a reason not to trust Orlen, and now that I'd found out what he'd been hiding, I didn't know what to think.

"Tell me more," I said.

"There was a large group of us who'd banded together to overthrow her—she brought us to her castle, claiming she wanted to talk reasonably. I had a plan for us to force her to give up her status as queen. But then we were ambushed. Since then, she's banished anyone who dares to defy her."

Matron Tratte turned, and I let the curtains shut again, my fingers feeling wooden and clumsy.

"Table for you?" Jan smiled, bustling over. "I believe this is your first time here—I'd be happy to recommend something."

I opened my mouth, but nothing came out. I was too

busy processing the large orange jewel hanging around his neck. That and the fact that my instincts hadn't sent a single prickle of warning since we'd stepped into the Hungry Goat. Which meant that I wasn't surrounded by danger. Which meant Orlen wasn't lying.

Beaman leaned in front of me as I snatched Orlen and placed him in my apron pocket. "We're looking for Gwenda. We have something that's, um . . ." He glanced at me. "That's in need of repair. It's an emergency."

To his credit, Jan simply nodded. "She's down in the dungeon room." He pointed to an open doorway and descending staircase beside the bar. He grinned. "That's just what we call it—a little wizard joke. You won't be locked in, I swear."

Beaman managed to grin back, but he looked a little green as he motioned me forward.

I descended first, a single word echoing in my mind: *prisoners*. With a mighty heft, I opened the thick slab of wood at the bottom of the staircase. As we stepped inside, uproarious laughter rang out from the far end of the room.

A high voice called out over the mirth. ". . . and that's when I said, 'Giant duck egg? I'll show *you* a giant duck egg!'"

The room exploded with fresh roars of glee.

Two figures sat on a sofa that faced away from us. Beyond them, a tall, silver-haired, straight-backed woman with an emerald tunic had her back turned. A green-jeweled ring

on her right hand flashed in the flickering light as she drew
something on a large sheet of paper attached to the wall.

Not jewelry, I thought. *Shackles.*

"Who are they?" I whispered.

Orlen shifted. "Part of the first group banished by Lacera. There were nearly one hundred of us then. Few are still
alive."

Nobody seemed to hear us enter. As the woman continued drawing, the others watched her intently, and I looked
around. The first thing I noticed was a large map covering
the right wall, painted with colored details of towns and
geographic features. I silently sounded out the word written
above it. *Win . . . tr . . . el. Wintrel.*

A nearby table held half-full plates, teapots, mugs, and
bottles. Lazy curls of blue and green and purple smoke
rose from dozens of candles with colored flames. The room
smelled faintly of salty sea spray.

The left wall was covered with paintings of people and
village scenes. It also boasted a large fireplace crackling with
multicolored flames.

"Guess who?" the drawing woman called out. An image
of a tall man with a sour expression slowly appeared. The pen
switched between colors as she added a royal emblem to his
flowing robe and a large stack of books at his side. "And one
more thing," she said, drawing quickly. With a twitter of her

fingertips, the image of a pastry appeared. One flick of her finger sent the pastry picture straight into the man's face, where it exploded in a swirl of purple.

"Flying berry pie to the face!" cackled a muscled old man in a sleeveless tunic the color of charcoal. His wrinkled arms were covered in colorful designs—a dragon, a tree, flowers, and more. "Oh, stop," he cried, taking off his glasses and wiping his eyes. "It's too funny! I'll wet my pants, and I haven't managed a proper drying spell for ages!"

I knew who the drawing was of too. The pompous look and wine-colored birthmark gave it away. I bit my lip to keep from laughing.

Orlen cleared his throat, crawling to my shoulder. "Would that be a drawing of me, dear sister?" he called out in a loud voice. "Not terribly original. You made the very same one repeatedly when we were children, and you still draw about as well as you bake."

Silence filled the room, fast as a crack of lightning.

"Now, if I may interrupt your lovely game, I'm in need of a repair—as you all can see."

Gwenda turned slowly. Her gray hair was scattered with thin metallic clips, each one attaching something different to her head—a leaf, a flower, a small curled scroll. She shared a long nose and dimpled chin with her brother. She frowned at me, then gasped and dropped her pen. "Orlen?"

A tall old man with a long mustache and a knitted hat hefted himself up from the sofa first. The muscled wizard joined him. The three elderly wizards stared at my shoulder.

"What on earth have you done to yourself, brother?" Gwenda glanced at Beaman and me. "And who are these two?"

"This is Stub and the boy is Beaman," Orlen said. "We've been traveling together. Introductions first, explanation next." He nodded at his sister. "This is Gwenda. The *artist*, apparently."

She stepped around the sofa, still gaping. She stood inches from me. She had skin like a crinkled paper bag and bright gray eyes. Her eyebrows were marvelous, wild sprays of white and gray. She looked down at my rucksack, where Peck was curiously poking her head out. "What's the chicken for?"

I pulled Peck closer.

"The chicken is with me, Gwenda," Orlen said crisply. "Now, the rest of you, say hello."

Gwenda raised an eyebrow. "Is that an order from the royal wizard who chose to run away and hide in the castle?" She leaned down to look him in the eye. "You haven't spoken to us in fifty years, Orlen. And now you want a *little* favor? I find that interesting. Your spells were always disastrous experiments. Do you remember when you tried to fasten my lips shut and ended up gluing your own?"

She smirked and tapped him on the head. "You know that old saying—magic is often wiser than the wielder. It was the best five hours of my childhood, until Mother fixed you."

Orlen sniffed and recoiled. "Pity I never invented a spell that would cure that terrible breath of yours."

"Well, I see you haven't changed a bit." She whistled a tune. "My brother, the size of a mouse, coming to beg me to fix him because he wrote another mediocre rhyme and tried to do a spell when he was angry." She winked at me.

"*Please*, Gwenda. I have important news to share. It's about the castle regent and—well, first things first. I'm bound to the girl. That will need fixing as well."

Gwenda's eyebrows rose in glee. "Bound to a child!" She rubbed her palms together. "This just gets better and better." She clucked her tongue and patted my empty shoulder. "Not for you, dear. My sincerest apologies for your hardship." She cleared her throat, backed away, and gave a sarcastic bow. "I'm Gwenda, I specialize in fixing broken things." She scrutinized her brother. "Though I've never tried repairing a person. I'm afraid you can't fix arrogance."

As the siblings glowered at each other, the mustached man cleared his throat loudly and lifted his hat. "I'm Bastian. I own the Giddy Room—the toy shop." He dug in his pocket. "Here," he said. He wiggled his fingers and blew on the objects in his hand. Two tiny, colorful dragonflies flew across the room and hovered in front of us expectantly. "Take them. They're just paper. I put a bit of wind inside them, so they'll fly a bit longer."

I held out a hand. The paper landed on it, then wiggled away and flew at Orlen, poking him repeatedly in the bottom until I caught it again.

Beaman's dragonfly flapped around his head while he stared nervously at the cutlery on the tables, as though it, too, might fly up in his face.

"And I'm Verett," said the muscled man, reaching a hand forward. His voice sounded as ancient as he looked—like the creaky opening of a trunk that had been closed for centuries. "Bastian's older, wiser, better-looking brother."

"You're older by three minutes, and that's only because you're pushy. And the only part of you that's good-looking is the tattoo of me that you have on your back."

"Why do you think it's on my back?" Verett snapped. "I don't need to be looking at two of you all day!" He rolled his eyes. "Anyway, I own As You Wish—the tattoo and barber shop down the road. Would you like anything, dearies?" he asked. "Maybe a Peace Day flag right on your forehead? Those are popular right now—and the pain goes away fairly quickly."

I shook my head. "No, thank you."

Beaman looked a little ill. "Poached pickles," he whispered. "What have I gotten myself into?"

"Well! Now that we're introduced," Gwenda said, briskly marching back to the sofa and chairs, "I'll do the repair and then you can share whatever important news you have from the castle." She coughed loudly in the direction of the others and pointed indiscreetly to the drawing she'd done. "About the regent having a softer pillow than you or larger sleeping quarters or whatever it is. Stub, place him on the floor."

I did as asked and backed away.

Gwenda stepped forward and wiggled, waggled, and dangled her fingers over the shrunken wizard. One by one, they tried to break the spell.

Then they tried in pairs.

Then as a trio.

An hour passed, then two. Orlen stood ten feet from me and repeatedly tried to break our bond. His face grew redder and redder with each failed attempt.

"Oh, it's no use!" Verett cried. Sweating with effort, he collapsed into the nearest armchair. "You'd have to be a kincain to break this. What in the world were you trying to do? Tell us more about the spell."

Orlen crumpled into a pile next to a table leg. "I was trying to shrink Renart and send him into my pocket, so I could ask him questions."

Gwenda knelt beside him. "But what was your intent—

your emotion behind it?" Her lips pursed. "You know that controlling that's always been a weakness of yours in spells. And otherwise."

Orlen scowled for a moment. Then he sighed. "You're right. I wanted him to feel threatened—hopeless and alone, with no one to turn to and no way out—so that he'd confess whatever it is he was plotting. I was too upset. It backfired."

Bastian stretched his fingers with a soft moan and sat on the sofa. "But why would the spell send you to Trapper's Cove?"

Orlen grimaced. "I wanted him as far from Queen Sonora as possible. Within Maradon's Borders, that would be Trapper's Cove. As for being bound to Stub's pocket . . ." He looked at me curiously. "I'm not sure why the spell chose her."

My ears burned and my cheeks grew warm. *Hopeless. Alone. No way out.* Those words had sent Orlen to me. I shrugged, then put a hand in my rucksack to pet Peck and felt the roll of paper—the letter from my mother, who'd abandoned me.

"As for needing a kincain to break this, I doubt that Lacera will do the honors when she comes to visit," Orlen said shortly.

Gwenda reached forward and snatched her brother from the floor. "What are you talking about?"

204 · JESSICA LAWSON

The wizard brothers froze, their eyes wide and uncertain.

Orlen squirmed. "Not so tight! She's coming here on Peace Day. I would have told you first, but you're so stubborn, I thought you'd never try to fix me. And yes, the children *know* about us. That we're prisoners here. That we were banished. That we've been here for years with no way to go back to our home."

Gwenda's mouth fell open. Her fingers did as well, and Orlen dropped down to the table.

Bastian gaped at me and Beaman. "But how?"

Glaring at his sister, Orlen rose. "The spell that cursed me to Stub's apron pocket allowed me to tell her our history. She's bound magically to a wizard. And I'm bound to a non-wizard. The combination . . . well, it seems to have poked a hole in Lacera's spell. Beaman can listen as well. Go ahead."

Bastian took a step toward me. "We're . . . trapped here," he said, then winced as though the words might backfire. When they didn't, he slowly smiled. "That's amazing!" he laughed. Then his smile faded. "But what could she possibly want, coming here? She's taken everything from us."

"Not yet," Verett said. All color had left his face. Even his tattoos seemed to pale. "She's coming to finish us off."

His brother nodded. "Maybe she's coming to ruin Maradon's Peace. Because we've managed to make a life here."

"This is not truly a life," said Gwenda curtly. "You know

that. We're good at pretending, but we're imprisoned here."

"But we don't have to be!" Orlen said quickly. "That's my point. I'm telling you, Renart is conspiring with her. Lacera has promised him something in exchange for handing over the queen. Like, like . . ." He floundered for a thought. "I don't know what, but whatever she's offered the traitor is a false promise. She'll be the one to take over, and then Maradonians can say good-bye to their beloved Peace. But we can stop her! We can save both our queendoms! I *have* to get back into the castle. We can find out more and make a plan to ambush her and Renart—"

"You make it sound easy," Gwenda interrupted. "Simply make a plan. Like last time, in Wintrel?"

Orlen's face fell. "No. Not like that."

His sister nodded. "Then we agree. We must do nothing until we're certain. Orlen, you need more details about this letter."

His voice was heavy. "I'm the only one of us who knows the rooms of the castle. What are we going to do? I'm too small to do anything." With extreme effort, he picked up an olive from a plate and threw it an inch. "You see?"

The colored candle flames flickered and dimmed, changing with the mood of the room. *Magic is often wiser than the wielder.* Gwenda had said that. Orlen thought he was too small to be of use.

"Maybe not," I said. "Maybe you're just the right size. Like you said at the city gates, bigger is not always better."

I flushed as the wizards looked at me expectantly. "There was a sign in the street. The castle needs more workers to help with Peace Day preparations. If we go to the castle gates, maybe we can be hired. And Orlen, it's better if you're small—no one will see you. You can tell me where to go." And, I thought, the castle is the last place Matron Tratte would look for me.

"Yes!" An enormous grin practically leaped off Beaman's face. "We can work in the castle kitchens!" he shouted.

I couldn't help but smile along with him. He'd looked fit to vomit earlier, but now he seemed about to explode with excitement.

Orlen frowned. "How can we be certain you'll be chosen? They'll be plenty of peasants willing to do dishes and cut carrots."

Beaman raised an eyebrow. "Yes, but can any other peasants bake like a Cork? Gwenda," he said breathlessly, "do you think the tavern will let me borrow some ingredients and the oven? What should I make? My seed rolls? Or maybe a tart? Or perhaps a butter cake or my sweetrolls, or my special spice pudding, or . . ." Beaman's eyes glazed over as he mulled the possibilities. "Can you imagine, getting to work in royal kitchens, with royal ingredients and royal pots and pans! Maybe we'll get to serve as well—this is my chance! I can make my pudding for Queen Sonora and—"

"This is your chance to save your queen from danger," Orlen scolded. "Not court her with overspiced pudding."

Beaman reddened. "Everyone likes my pudding."

Bastian clapped his hands. "It's perfect!" he cried. "Not your pudding—though I'm sure it's tasty—I mean all of this." He waved aside Gwenda's solemn expression and slapped his brother's back. "Hope, my friends! We've been on short supply for years, and now a spark has been lit."

"I say this very rarely, but my brother is right." Verett clapped a hand on his brother's shoulder. "I'll make a list—there must be at least two hundred capable wizards willing to face Lacera."

Gwenda's lips twitched; then she smiled slowly at me and Beaman. "You'll be a pair. You'll pose as brother and sister. Tell them you're orphans. Everyone knows the queen has a soft spot for orphans, right?"

I stared at her blankly. "Orphans? But why?" I was an orphan, and certainly no one had ever had a soft spot for me.

Verett flexed his muscles, making the dragon tattoo breathe fire. "Because she *is* one, of course. She's a very *lucky* orphan."

I stared at the faces around me. Everyone seemed to be in on the joke. It was a joke, wasn't it? Orphans didn't become queens. Orphans lived on the street or were forced into the service of awful tavern owners. I'd never met a single lucky orphan in my entire life, and there were more than a few of us in Trapper's Cove.

Beaman caught my eye. "You didn't know? Sonora was found in the middle of the market square when she was a newborn. It was Peace Day, and the queen was delivering a speech to the people."

Orlen nodded. "I was there, standing right beside her. We heard a baby crying. Someone must have laid it near the speaking platform and disappeared. Renart bellowed for someone to quiet it."

"I was there too," said Gwenda. "She asked whose child it was, but no one answered."

"That's right," said Orlen. "She never wanted to have children, but she took one look at that baby and changed her mind."

"Didn't you ever notice in the portraits that Sonora's got two sets of earrings?" Beaman asked. "Queen Nadina left the first ones in, out of respect for the birth parents."

Of course Beaman had noticed. He practically slept with one of the portraits. And, come to think of it, I'd noticed as well—when I'd dusted the paintings back in Trapper's Cove. It just hadn't struck me as something worth dwelling on. A vision of Sonora's portrait flashed in my mind. It was strange to think that the queen and I had something in common. Only she'd been abandoned next to a queen and I'd been abandoned on a tavern porch.

Gwenda pointed to Beaman. "Dear, I'll take you up to the oven shortly to bake something. We'll let Jan know what's going on, but no one else—we don't want to get anyone's hopes up until we're certain. That said, I'll make sure we're organized enough to gather everyone at a moment's notice." She considered our clothes, which were dirty and dusty, as well as worn and torn in places. "Easy enough repairs," she murmured. "We'll do something about the... traveling odor as well. Do we have your permission to clean you both up a bit to improve your chances of being hired? Peace colors, I think."

"I'll do it." Bastian cracked his knuckles and shook his fingers. "What shade of blue are we thinking? Sunny-day blue? Sea blue? Stormy-sky blue? And do you want the hair blue, and the eyes blue, or just the clothes?"

"Let me do it," said Verett, clucking his tongue. "I love you, brother, but your style is . . . well, it's a bit like you—antiquated."

Bastian bristled. "We're the same age, you ninny." He smiled at me. "I'm thinking something festive, with patterns. How do you feel about tiny dragons, roaring with flames made of Peace flags?" he asked Beaman, who was looking increasingly ill.

"I'm thinking a simple, matching tattoo for both of them," Verett said, flexing his fingers. "Nothing too large," he said, eyeing Beaman's nervous expression. "Perhaps a spray of freckles here and there? Freckles are *very* in right now."

The two of them crowded closer and closer. Orlen scrambled over to me and crawled up to my apron pocket. When I looked down, he was shaking his fist.

"Stop all this!"

The wizards ignored him.

"STOP!" ordered Gwenda. "Fingers down."

The brothers halted immediately and put their hands behind their backs.

"Let's make a bit more room, shall we? And we haven't even gotten permission," she scolded. "May we, children?"

Beaman kneaded his hands together. "Umm . . ."

Verett looked over at Beaman and winked. "Blue hair for you, I think. Very festive. And a large mole. Or three."

Beaman blinked, then gulped. "Large moles?"

"There may be a *slight* burning sensation," Verett said, raising his hands.

"Oh, you're full of rubbish!" Bastian said. "We'll be gentle. It'll be fun. It'll be great!"

Beaman looked at me. I looked at Orlen.

"Change is always uncomfortable," he said. "Look at

me. This hasn't been pleasant." His expression softened. "It depends on what they do." He turned to his fellow wizards. "Nobody knows these two—there's no need to get silly. Just clean them up and keep it simple."

"Ha!" Bastian laughed. "That's rich advice from you— you've lost your magic. You're as simple as it gets now, aren't you, old friend?"

Orlen blinked. He swallowed hard and didn't respond.

Peck let out a cackle and poked at my chest. I didn't realize I'd been holding her too tightly. I placed her on the floor by the hearth and turned to Gwenda. "You may clean us up."

"Excellent." Gwenda clapped her hands at her fellow wizards. "As Orlen said, there's no need for disguises, so don't get too excited. Small repairs only. Bastian, please, a bit of music to help them relax."

"Stub . . . ," Beaman said, his eyes growing even wider as Bastian twirled his fingers and soft, soothing notes rang out from a music box near the map of Wintrel. "I don't think my mother would like this."

His hand clutched at my tunic, and then at my hand. His fingers curled tightly around mine.

My muscles spasmed at the memory of Matron Tratte grabbing me by the wrist. Her hand clasped tightly around mine. Dragging me to the broom closet. I tried to scrape the image from my mind. Could the wizards do that sort of thing? Erase memories? "No," I whispered. "She wouldn't like it."

"Are you nervous?"

I looked at the boy beside me. He was not Matron Tratte. Taking a deep breath, I let my arm relax. "Shut your eyes. Think of the castle kitchen." I let my own fingers fold around his palm. "Think of Queen Sonora."

Beaman scrunched up his face and closed his eyes. He sighed. "It's not working. I'm just not as brave as you."

"Then stop thinking. It's easier to be brave when you don't think so much. Close your eyes. Just trust them."

He let out a bark of laughter, then looked at me as though I'd grown a second head. "You? Telling me to trust some-one?" He took a deep breath. "Okay." He started to hum the tune he and Pap had hummed in the kitchen in Trapper's Cove.

I focused on his humming and waited for the magic to change me. And, as I felt a tugging at the roots of my hair and a swishing wind whirl around my tunic and trousers, I glanced at Orlen now standing on the far end of the table. He watched his fellow wizards with an expression I couldn't quite read. Then his gaze flickered over to me.

Perhaps it was the bond between us or maybe the magic coursing around me. Or the fact that I was in the midst of undergoing small repairs. Whatever the reason, as Orlen looked at me and I looked at him, I suddenly had an over-whelming urge to mend something that had been long broken—in me or in him, I couldn't say. It was something unnameable, which made it impossible to fix.

I dropped Beaman's hand, closed my eyes, and waited for the feeling to pass.

14

How to Be a Rogue Servant

With three days left until Peace Day, Beaman and I went looking for a job.

Bells rang from the market square, chiming a simple song followed by five solemn notes. The air was thick with the telling moisture of coming rain, and cloud cover dampened the approaching sunrise. The sky began to lighten in the east, but it would be a gray day.

I tugged at the ends of my enhanced hair. At first, the wizards had made it long, with braids. Since my braiding skills were about as good as my reading, I requested something short, just enough to cover my earring-less ears. Enhancements needed something to start with, so while they could change the size of my ears, they couldn't make something out of nothing. Verett had offered an earring tattoo. I declined.

We wore simple matching tunics and trousers. The grayish-blue fabric was the nicest thing I'd ever worn. My neck scarf had been altered to the same color. The sandals I'd bought at market were enhanced to look like Beaman's old pair, with a leather covering over the top half.

I leaned against the castle gate, yawning and trying my best to look like Stub-the-Castle-Worker and not Stub-the-Nuisance.

The guard at the castle gates smirked at me. "You said you were reporting for work," he said. "There aren't any napping jobs." He looked pointedly at Beaman, who'd been babbling questions at the guard for the last hour. "And no flapping-your-tongue jobs either." He looked toward the wide stone path leading to the outer castle walls. "Finally. Here comes Mistress Frana, the stodgy old goat."

Two silhouettes appeared underneath the raised portcullis. One was the guard who'd gone to send word to the kitchen mistress that potential workers had arrived. The other was a middle-aged woman with a stern gait and face. Her black hair was streaked with gray and white, pulled back into two tight buns. Her dark brown eyes were small and close together and sharp. They were the kind of eyes that didn't miss much. She looked over us suspiciously, clutching half of one of Beaman's seed rolls in her hand.

"How old are you, and who told you to report?" she asked crisply.

Beaman's arms snapped to his side. "We're twelve. We heard you were in need of kitchen workers, Mistress. We thought we'd be helpful and show up early. We both have kitchen experience, working in the finest taverns in Trapper's Cove. But . . ." He gulped. "Now we're orphans. We have nowhere else to go."

"You're not apprenticed?" she asked shortly. "I don't have time to deal with runaways."

"Of course not." Beaman elbowed me.

I cleared my throat nervously and kept my gaze to the ground, for fear Mistress Frana would see the lie in my eyes as I recited my line. "It was always our parents' dream to cook for a Peace Queen." I dipped my hands into my rucksack, sweeping over the paper that detailed very clearly in my abandoning mother's words that I was a runaway apprentice. I lifted Peck, grateful that the wizards had lengthened and fluffed her feathers. "And we'll give our best laying hen to the castle. She's the only family we have." At least that was true enough for me. I summoned my courage and looked the mistress in the eye.

She lifted the chicken's wings one by one. "I see. And which of you made this?" She held up the roll.

Beaman raised a hand.

"It's good. What's the spice?"

"Tarrow root." Beaman fumbled with his jar belt and found the source. His eyes shone with admiration as he looked at it. "It's from Lucia—the queendom across the sea.

My mother—*ow*—our mother bought it from—*ow!*" He grunted. "From the market near our tavern. It adds a wonderful savory taste to fish stews as well." He uncorked the jar and thrust it forward. "I've got to tell you, it's not great with pork, but I was experimenting one day and I found that if you mix it with—"

"That's quite enough, boy. As you likely know, the queen is sympathetic to those without guardians." Mistress Frana sniffed the jar, then handed it back. Her eyebrows rose as she studied us. "You're awfully clean for orphans."

Beaman smiled. "Pap says that cooking demands cleanliness." He grunted at my persistent elbow and fixed a distraught expression on his face. "That is, he *used* to say that."

"Hmm," said the matron. "I don't need two cooks." She pointed to me. "You'll wash dishes and serve. This way, you two. Morning duties have already started. Follow me," she said in a clipped voice.

We followed her quick march back toward the castle, passing through the portcullis. The grand entrance of Maradon Castle stood before us, two hundred feet wide and twice as tall, with four round towers rising even higher. A stone plaque over the ten-foot-tall double doors was carved with Maradon's emblem—the guardian gates, the book, and the Peace jewel.

I'd seen that emblem my entire life. If the wizards were right about Lacera, and if we failed to stop her, she might take over the queendom. There would be no more emblem. No more Peace.

The inner grounds were like a small village. Mistress Frana stepped briskly along the courtyard encircling the castle, pointing out the butchery, the blacksmith, the stables, and more. A rumble of thunder sounded overhead. There was so much to take in that I struggled to keep up.

"The lower level of the castle holds the kitchen and laundry," Matron Frana was saying. "You'll use those doors over there. The main level is where the Grand Hall and dining areas are located. Your work will be restricted to those places, unless you're sent on an errand. The upper floors are only for attendants. No workers under thirteen can labor past ten o'clock in the evening, but they always start the early shift. Now, about uniforms—they're all in the laundry chamber. Trousers, tunic, aprons, caps . . ."

Orlen shifted in my apron as we walked along.

The matron arrived at a low, thatched building. "Here are your quarters," she said. "The queendom provides a night guard to ensure your safety. Leave your things on any empty pallet. The weeks leading up to Peace Day are always a challenge, and because of the anniversary, it'll be more like a battle. Delegations coming from every region of Maradon," she grumbled. "Ladies, lords, captains—all of them expecting excellence."

I exchanged nervous glances with Beaman. How would we sneak into the castle at night to search through the regent's things if there was a guard watching over us? And with lords and ladies all over the place?

"Put your chicken in with the laying hens when you're done settling your things. Gather the eggs while you're there, and then report to the kitchen."

"This is unacceptable!" Hours later, Orlen crouched in the handkerchief around my neck, using a smidge of it to wipe sweat from his brow. "What is Beaman doing?"

I glanced around.

The kitchen was one long stone cavern with a ceiling that curved fifteen feet overhead. There were ovens and butchery tables and large stone basins for soaking and scrubbing dishes. Overhead hung lines of onions and garlic and turnips. Barrels of ground wheat and corn stood open, with giant metal scoops thrust in to the hilt. It was hard to concentrate among such abundance.

"He's at a workstation," I whispered. "Chopping things."

"Chopping things? One of you *must* find a way to Renart's quarters! Do you think I made that castle map for him to wipe his nose with? No! Do you know how difficult it is to hold a pen when you're two inches tall? I've still got ink all over my hands!"

"What can I do? The cooks want him there and the scullion wants me here."

"Then stop washing dishes so well—she'll switch you to another job!"

"Or she'll fire me."

"Hmph." Orlen ducked back down. "Unacceptable," he mumbled.

I turned from the conversation to see a child sprinting through the kitchen, ducking around tables and people.

"Watch it!" a voice shouted.

"Ow! No running, you whelp!"

"You nearly cost me a finger!"

The girl had short blond hair that hung over her forehead and ears. A white scarf was tied over the top of her head, in the manner of some of the laundry servants I'd seen carrying linens through the kitchen on the way to the dining rooms.

Her heavily freckled face looked familiar for some reason. She kept looking behind her, which was exactly what she was doing when she slipped on some dishwater and slid right into me. She clutched my tunic for support and we both went tumbling to the floor.

"Oof!" the girl said, scrambling up. "Sorry!"

"Move it!" a man grunted, lifting a kettle of hot water. He poured it into the farthest washing basins, creating a thick roll of steam. The girl dashed off, disappearing in the mist.

"Probably a new one," the kindly scullion muttered, lending a hand to help me up. "New servants always think they have to fetch everything in the biggest of hurries." She studied me and frowned. "You need to watch your grooming." She licked her fingers and smoothed my hair. "The regent is coming today to check in with Mistress Frana. He likes a tidy staff." She jumped as the attention bell near the kitchen entrance rang out.

The kitchen din softened enough that everyone could hear the steady sound of businesslike footsteps approaching.

A broad-chested man strode into the room, his black leather boots clicking on the stone floor. He was dressed in a richly embroidered royal-blue jacket and held an iron box with papers strapped to the top. A thin chain plunged into his shirt, and a large badge over his heart bore Maradon's emblem. A white handkerchief covered his neck, extending up oddly around his right ear. Something yellowish oozed from the fabric.

The man's eyes flitted sharply over the kitchen, as though searching for something.

My heart jumped into my throat. I bent to the floor and pretended to tighten my bootlaces. *"Orlen,"* I whispered. "Is that him?"

Orlen peeked. "Yes," he said grimly. "That's what treachery looks like."

Treachery looked like a tall man with a slightly annoyed expression plastered to his face and a dagger the length of my forearm strapped to his belt. He had a serious face, with thin lips, an ample chin, and high cheekbones. In his lobes, small silver versions of Maradon's flag caught the light. His closely clipped hair was the gray-white of an organized stormy sky, ending neatly below his ears.

I dropped a dish into the water with a loud splash. Renart shot an irritated glance my way. My hands sprang to my apron pocket to cover up the movement within as Orlen ducked back down.

"Mistress Frana," Renart's voice boomed in a sharp, low-pitched tone. "I need another word with you about the Peace Day guests. Follow me."

The mistress dropped a spoon she'd been tasting. "Of course, Your Regency. I'm happy to have another word." She raised her voice. "The rest of you, keep working. The midday meal for guests will be served in an hour." The mistress spoke briefly to the woman stirring the sauce, then followed Renart down a narrow hallway at the back of the kitchen.

"Now's your chance!" Orlen hissed. "Follow him!"

"I can't leave now," I muttered back.

"You must!"

My mind raced as a fresh load of dishes and forks and knives was dumped on my station. Bloodred berry sauce

sprayed off the plates, staining my apron. *Knives and berries*—
that was it! I smeared a line of sauce over my palm. With my
clean hand, I grabbed the handle of a sharp knife in the sink and
coated it in redness as well.

"My hand!" I yelled, letting out a startled cry, holding
the knife near the stain.

"Oh!" The lead scullion sprang forward and swiftly
wrapped my hand in a dish towel. She shoved me toward
the staircase leading down to the laundry. "Go," she hissed.
"And be quiet about it. Take care of that and get a fresh apron
before Mistress Frana sees you! She hates worker's blood in
the kitchen."

I rushed through the kitchen, pausing at a chopping
block to tighten the bandage around my fake wound. Under
the guise of fastening my bandage, I elbowed Beaman's side.

"Ow! Oh, Stub. Hello!" Beaman was sweaty-faced and
pink-cheeked. A dusting of flour powdered his face and hair.
He gestured excitedly to a stain on his apron. "They let me
work the bread and sauces this morning! One of the workers started vomiting, so they sent her off—how wonderful is
that? Then the red sauce for the giant clams was oversalted,
and I suggested adding cream to correct it, which is unusual
for a red sauce, but I'd done it before, and the saucier loved
it! The quality of the butter and cream is—"

"Just stop talking for once!" I urged. A worker beside

him rolled her eyes in agreement, as she hauled a load of potatoes to another station.

He blushed. "Sorry." His lips twitched, like he couldn't keep them closed. "It's just that when I sautéed the onion, it really—"

"*Beaman*. That was Renart who came in."

His knife clattered to the chopping board. "*Toasted turnips*."

"Yes." I put the knife back in his hand. "Orlen and I are following him. Meet me in the bread pantry when you can. And stop looking at my apron."

"Sorry. Again." He gave a nervous chuckle. "I, um, have orders, though . . . how shall I slip away from, um, her?" He nodded to his fellow worker, returning with an empty pot.

"Don't you ever have to go to the bathroom? Find an excuse."

I hurried down the hallway, twisting the towel. Kitchen voices faded, and I saw a doorway on the left. Renart's voice sounded faintly within.

The door was cracked open enough that I could see the regent pacing. Trying to slow my heart, I approached the crack and leaned in to look. Renart was placing sheets of paper on a small table. I couldn't see much. There was a thick woven rug, a desk scattered with goblets, a tall blue

candle marked with hardened drips of wax, and portraits of
the Peace Queen hanging on the wall.

"... only three days until Peace Day... need at least eight
hundred cartloads of wood for the fires and plenty of coal.
Just like last year, but ten times the amounts."

Matron Frana's voice rang out with worry. "But we don't
have that amount of seafood or meat."

"I don't care what you don't have! Just find a way to get
enough food for the feasts. The guests have already arrived
and will need attending to." Renart tapped a sheet of paper.
"I have here the rooming plans for more than seventy visitors
of high status ...."

"Get closer!" Orlen hissed. "Look at the list."

"Yes, I'll just barge in, shall I?" I whispered back. "Stop
talking!"

"... and some will prefer meals in their room. Captain
Yardley has asked that her wife's wine be watered by half after
the dinner hour, and Lady Anders will throw an absolute fit
if you put cheese on her plate." He jabbed at the papers. "Are
you listening?"

"Of course, sir." Mistress Frana sighed. "You've told me
all this before."

"Oh? Have I?" Renart's voice grew icy. "Perhaps you
don't realize that this is an important year for the queendom. I'll be here all evening tomorrow for Sonora's birthday

meal." His lips curled in distaste. "Of course, Nadina had to go and give that little orphan a birthday the day before Peace Day. She could have picked any day, but *no*, she had to complicate things." He paused, then sighed. "She always did try to complicate things. She was always trying to . . ." Renart trailed off for a moment, gazing at Queen Nadina's portrait on the well.

"Sir?"

The regent's head snapped back in Matron Frana's direction. His glare returned. "I will not be around to monitor all aspects of the anniversary feast—there are, after all, so many things to do. *Everything* must go well." Renart gathered up the paper. "And there will be no magic to help. The castle wizard has disappeared, and there aren't any plans to hire another one. And that's another thing. No wizards are to be in the castle on Peace Day—is that understood?"

"What do you mean?" Mistress Frana's voice rose an octave. "No magic? But we depend on it this time of year. How will we keep the dishes warm and such? What if something burns?"

Renart waved away the woman's concern. "Get me a list. I'll send errand runners to the wizard district for any warming salts or pans or flavor enhancements you need and such. Gather everyone in the Grand Hall in ten minutes, and I'll make a quick announcement about the queen's birthday feast." Renart lowered his voice. "Now, one more thing, about the anniversary. Queen Sonora and I will need to step out around sunset, so if . . ."

Around sunset? What else! I couldn't hear! I pressed a light hand against the crack to push it open slightly, then heard a rustling of footsteps down the hall.

I turned to see a laundry worker—a different one than before. This one hurried down the hall toward me, his arms filled with stacks of sheets. As he swept by me, he knocked me from my crouch. I stumbled into the meeting room and fell at Renart's feet.

"What's the meaning of this interruption?" Renart bellowed.

Under the guise of standing up, I yanked hard on the regent's trousers until his knee bent. The iron box fell from his hands to the floor with a crack. It opened, releasing a torrent of papers and an ancient-looking envelope.

"Oh! Sir, I'm so sorry!" I cried, scanning the papers as I gathered them. Where were the rooming plans? There! While Renart and Matron Frana fussed over me loudly, I heard Orlen's voice whispering names.

Captain Ramire. . . Madam Koss. . . Lady Hoyle. Then he let out a small shout. I coughed loudly to cover the sound.

"Explain yourself!" Renart snatched the papers from my hand. His narrowed eyes swept suspiciously over me.

"I . . .um . . ." I rose and thrust my toweled hand in Mistress Frana's face. "I've got a cut. It won't stop bleeding. The dishmaster sent me to you."

Mistress Frana waved a hand in my face. "Go to the seamstress. She'll stitch it up."

"Yes, ma'am." Relief coursed through me as the door was closed firmly behind me. I walked back toward the kitchen.

"I knew it!" Orlen whispered excitedly. "Lacera's name was listed on the west tower with the words 'Meeting Room.' Now's the time to go to his quarters! You won't be missed. Just wait somewhere until everyone leaves."

I spotted Beaman and nudged his side as I walked through the busy room. There were three girls and boys of apprentice age at his station.

"Come with me to the bread pantry," I said loudly. I took his arm and lowered my voice as we moved through the room. "Renart's coming to make an announcement soon."

"What are we doing?" he muttered, looking around nervously.

"We're hiding until everyone's gone; then we're going to search the regent's office."

"But we'll miss what he's going to say," Beaman said anxiously. "It might be important."

I pressed him into a room packed with shelf upon shelf of bread and closed the door behind us. I stuck a hand in my apron and found my claw rock. I shook it, and the room glowed. I'd slept with both glow rocks the night before, the way I'd sometimes done in Trapper's Cove. I slept better, knowing that I carried some way to stave off the darkness. Luckily, I'd forgotten to return them to my pack.

"Fine," said Beaman. "We can skip the meeting. We'll hide behind the flour in case someone comes in." He turned around a row of large barrels, then let out a startled yelp. His arms rose, flailing, then he fell with a loud thump.

"Um, Stub?" Beaman's voice went up a pitch. "Someone's here."

"*Shh!*" said another voice.

I turned the corner to see the laundry girl who had knocked me over in the kitchen. "What are *you* doing here?" I asked, thankful that Orlen hadn't spoken.

"What are *you* doing here?" she countered. "Is Vile Renart gone yet?" She peeked over the barrel toward the light slipping beneath the closed door. "I was about to go back through the kitchen when you came in."

We didn't answer. We were too busy gawking at the girl's face.

"Well?" she asked impatiently.

"Your freckles," Beaman said in a choked voice.

"What about them?" the girl snapped.

"They're disappearing," I supplied.

One by one, the brown spots fluttering all over the child's face faded away. At the same time, something curious was happening to her hair. It darkened more and more, until it matched the black of the barrel behind her. And it was getting longer.

The girl looked down and inhaled sharply, then cursed in a way that rivaled any of the crews I had served back at the Tinderbox.

Beaman's cheeks flamed scarlet. "*Pickled peppers.* It's *you.*"

I'd never tasted a pickled pepper, but I completely agreed. The girl's face was one I'd known for years. I'd cleaned stew and spit and blood and goodness-knows-what-else off it. It was the face of Queen Sonora of Maradon.

Beaman turned to me and shook his head in wonder. "It's the queen. In the pantry."

Flustered, Sonora flung off her head wrapping. "You can't tell on me," she begged. "Please. This castle's already like a prison! It was just a little temporary enhancement. I didn't even go all the way to the wizard district—there was a nice wizard right down the street on her way to the market, and she did it for me. I'll give you anything if you don't tell. Do you need coin? I'll give you a bulging purseful."

Beaman's mouth still hung agape. The redness hadn't faded from his cheeks. "Money?" he asked me, bewildered. "From the queen? In the pantry?"

Sonora groaned. "Yes, I'm the queen. But I turn thirteen tomorrow, and by the looks of things, you're not much older." She eagerly took both my hands in her own. "I'll do anything if you won't mention this to Renart. We all need our little freedoms, don't we? In a way, you and I are exactly alike."

It was difficult to hold back my laughter. The queen and I were nothing alike. I felt a sharp poke in my belly and grimaced. Orlen and I really needed to have a talk about his methods of communication.

"Your Queenship," I said, "I think we all—"

"Sonora—please just call me Sonora. Nobody calls me that anymore." The queen dropped my hands and sighed. "I could order you to be silent, you know."

"You could," I said carefully. "But perhaps, instead of money or orders, maybe you can tell us a little about the castle. We're new and we've only seen the kitchen and our quarters. You could show us places we'll never see—your quarters, or, say, your regent's? Steward Renart?"

Her nose wrinkled. "Why would you want to go there?" Her eyes sparkled. "I know. I'll show you a secret."

I swallowed. Who knew when we'd get another opportunity to search Renart's quarters? "That'll be a good start. But we really—"

"Oh, this is better than good. Do you faint easily?"

I looked at Beaman, who looked as though he might hyperventilate at any moment. "Um . . . not easily."

"Good." Sonora stood and searched the corner of the bread pantry's stone wall. After sticking her fingers into a crack, she moved her hand up and down until a metallic click sounded. She pulled hard and the hidden door opened. She smiled. "Because there's a dragon in the dungeon."

15

How to Face a Dragon

The queen of Maradon stared at us expectantly. Beaman looked half moony-eyed, half terrified. As for me, I wasn't sure I was hearing correctly.

"Ridiculous!" Orlen scoffed, breaking the silence. "Nonsense."

The queen peered at my waist. "What was that you said?"

"Oh my!" I cleared my throat loudly and whapped an open sack of flour, sending a small fog into the air. I gave a rough squeeze to the tiny speaker in my apron. "Did you see that spider?"

Queen Sonora coughed, waving a hand in the air. "Missed it. It's quite dusty in here."

"Floury," Beaman corrected, still staring at Sonora as he picked up a full sack. "Not dusty. Your Dragonship." His cheeks were approaching a shade of red that matched the fake wine he'd made me in Trapper's Cove. "I mean, Sonoraship." He blinked and hugged the flour sack hard, sending a fresh blanket of white powder snowing upon us. "I mean, Your Lady Dragon-Queenship."

Sonora leaned toward me. "Is your friend okay?" she whispered.

I eyed my fake brother's powder filled hair. "My brother is fine. We just started working here and, well, we're basically used to sleeping in a chicken coop behind a tavern. So, um, well, meeting our queen face-to-face is kind of . . . startling."

"Chicken coop?" Beaman frowned at me.

Sonora's face filled with sympathy. "You must have been very poor—I'm so sorry."

"And you did just mention a dragon." I laughed uneasily, still cupping Orlen in my apron to keep him quiet. "Do you mean a toy dragon?" I asked, thinking of the Giddy Room's jeweled dragonfly. As fun as it sounded, we didn't have time to waste playing with royal toys.

"I mean a *real* dragon." Sonora leaned forward with a knowing smile. "They actually exist! I didn't think they were real—of course, there are books in the library that talk about them, but they say they live so far away and keep to themselves so much that few people have ever seen one." She pointed to my glowing rock. "Can I borrow your light, um . . . what are your names?"

Another quick check confirmed that Beaman was still a silly mess. I made our introductions.

th

e to meet you, Stub and Beaman. Follow
ared into the doorway.

ur
he
th
at
d

ed just before entering the passage. He
s to his chest and mouthed two words with a
face. *Queen Sonora!*

the passage and mouthed a single word:

d his expression. "Yes, well, there's that.
?" he whispered.

y
y
.
n
s
o
r
s

n hissed. "She's just playing some silly game.
if a dragon were in the bowels of the castle."
night show us Renart's quarters after," I
e's the queen, Orlen—she can go anywhere."
l reluctant approval. "Fine. Put me in your
can't see down here."

door behind us and took the pebble from my
it until it glowed. What in the world was a
n the castle? And how could Orlen not know

ge was tight—the ceiling was only a hand's
my head, and I could easily reach both walls.
cast a dim light over the stone. I saw scratches,
re had been a battle waged inside the cramped
silent, and the air smelled and tasted stale.
re no steps, just a rough, cobbled dirt path

beneath our feet. We walked for a few minutes; then the p
split. We took the right branch until it split again.

"No, um, chance of getting lost in here, right, Y
Highness—um, Sonoraness?" Beaman asked, coughing
tremble out of his voice. "Not that I mind. I'm fine w
being lost! I feel quite breezy. Not a bit queasy. Oh, ha! T
rhymed. . . ." He turned back to me and desperately jab
his finger back the way we came.

I turned him around.

"Don't worry," laughed Sonora. "I know my w
around. My tutor forced me to write a wretched history es
about the Peace a few weeks ago in honor of the annivers
I found a map of the tunnels and passages pressed betw
the pages of a book from my great-great-grandmoth
time, when we were at war. I think the dragon dates bac
then. Careful!" she called, slowing her pace. "Step wide c
this corner—the floor's just thin, painted wood that dr
straight through to a room full of spikes. Wouldn't want
of us getting impaled, ha!"

Beaman let out a high-pitched giggle. "Getting impa
ha!" he echoed. "Um, speaking of what can kill you, don't
think we should tell someone there's a dragon under the cast

"I'm the queen. Who else needs to know?" Sonora pau
midway down a stone staircase that curved in a spiral. "
look a little green. Are you sure you want to see it?"

I ignored Beaman, who was vehemently shaking his head no. "Yes."

We followed the queen's directions, squeezing through a ten-foot section of passage with thick nails aimed inward from both walls. Behind me, Beaman murmured something about iron horn nuts as he slowly made his way through.

"I don't want to be here," he whispered to me.

"Neither do I," snapped Orlen quietly. "This is ridiculous. Watch that nail!"

"Quiet, Orlen," I muttered. "You're doing fine, Beaman. When we're through this part, you go ahead of me and keep up with Sonora."

He nodded, then leaned close when we got past the trap. A good deal of sweat was beading on his brow. He gulped and glanced down the passage. "She's just, um, a bit different than I thought she'd be."

I raised my glow rock. The passage was empty. "Sonora?"

Light footsteps sounded up ahead. "Sorry—I didn't realize you weren't with me. It's this way. Just a few more steps down after these stairs. Here are the dungeons where Tartínians were kept during the Great War." She said it grandly and with a hint of mischief, as though showing us a banquet table full of delectable treats that she'd taken nibbles out of. "I think they're haunted." She seemed to relish the thought.

I didn't share the sentiment. My sense of unease grew as we descended a stone staircase. The path widened to a hallway. Small rooms were on either side, with doorways made only of vertical iron bars. They were ancient-looking, rusty things. I couldn't help but imagine the prisoners who'd been trapped there.

". . . and here's the Prisoner Hall, for holding entire groups of enemies . . ."

The dungeon hallway opened into a large room of stark, stone walls. It was covered in iron collars chained at short intervals. They looked like the shackles I had to clamp around the sheeps' necks and legs in order to shear them. There were manacles for arms and ankles as well, rusted over with age. It suddenly hit me how important the Peace was.

And the queen still didn't know it was in danger. How could we keep it from her? But what if Orlen was right and she turned Lacera away? Defeating her was the wizards' one chance at freedom.

I bumped into Beaman, who was waiting for Sonora at the end of the Prisoner Hall. She was fiddling with a decrepit wooden torch holder. Reaching up, she pressed a circular stone at its base. When she pushed it in, a five-foot-high rectangle of rock moved inward, into in the wall, revealing a tunnel.

"One more pathway until we get to the sea cave."

Sonora grinned. She pointed above us. "We're at the bottom of the cliff that drops off on one side of the castle. It's a war room, for planning, with barracks and supplies that could last for years. If someone took over the castle, the queen's chosen successor would come down here while the queen joined the battle. Then, if the battle went badly, the successor could come out and reclaim the queendom when the time was right. They only had to use it once during the Tartínian War."

The tunnel grew narrow. "How did they know when the time was right?" I asked.

Sonora shrugged. "Don't know. At some point, they just figured that waiting wasn't an option anymore."

The last passage angled downward. It felt damp and smelled salty. We were nearing the sea. "How did you know how to get into this place?" I asked, holding myself steady on the walls as a light signaled the end of the tunnel.

"Last week I was exploring, using the map I found, and almost got caught when Vile Renart came bumbling down a passage carrying some kind of big book and a strange little bottle. I barely squeezed into a recess as he passed."

A book? A bottle?

"Oh, he's awful," Sonora continued. "Meetings, meetings, meetings. 'Must learn to be like your mother.' Ugh, it's *constant*. He's always having me sign boring papers and lecturing me on the merits of sitting up straight because mother had excellent posture and I sit like a wet noodle." She let out an exasperated huff. "He's actually scheduled a time for me to meet a foreign queen on Peace Day. I *hate* meeting people." She smoothed the back of her hair and flashed a grin our way. "Present company excepted."

Beaman made a sound like a mewling kitten.

As for me, I was too busy with the prickle running up my spine to deal with wayward compliments. "What's the meeting for?" I asked. "Where is the queen from?"

She shrugged. "He didn't say. And the meetings are all the same. I say hello to someone in fancy clothes. I drink some tea while Renart babbles on. He fusses about the smallest things, and says I'm not ready to understand the most important parts of running a queendom. Then he claims he's doing all the work of a queen, just without the title. Then he glances at me with his pompous eyes and talks about how my mother made a perfect leader. Do you know that once, I saw him kick a baby owl that somehow got lost in the castle? He claimed he was startled, but I think he's just terrible. I can't quite figure him out."

"Neither can I," Orlen muttered.

So Renart *was* bitter about not having a title. And he'd been mucking around in the dungeon." About Renart," I said carefully. "He knows about the dragon? How do you know that?"

She shrugged. "I'm guessing. Where else would he have gotten the burn on his neck? He obviously knows his way around the passages, and his family has been the queen's stewards for ages."

So *that* was the oozing wound. "But why would he—" I stopped short as we entered the sea cave.

It was enormous—ten times the size of the Prisoner Hall, with rough, craggy stone floors and a high ceiling that dripped moisture. At the end of the room near us were remnants of barrack beds and piles of rotting wood crates that must have been supplies. I heard the sound of waves crashing against stone in a *shhh, chhh, shhh, chhh* pattern.

At the far end of the cave, the ceiling sloped downward. Instead of ending in a wall, it opened to the sea. When I saw what was between the waves and the barracks, I dropped my pebble. My jaw dropped along with it.

Chained to the rock wall one hundred yards across the way was a creature the size of a pirate ship. It loomed in the dim light offered by the cave's end. When it didn't move, I blinked several times—thinking, hoping, wishing for it to be a trick of the eye. A shadow and nothing more.

I closed my mouth and swallowed, tasting salt and something sulfurous in the air. I already knew all too well that it was a terrifying thing to be forced into facing a deadly beast. It was quite another to go searching for one. We'd made a mistake.

The shadow shifted.

A low, menacing growl echoed through the cave.

"There it is," Sonora said. For the first time, her voice sounded reasonably serious as she pointed.

The creature's skull and snout were angular. Both were covered in a forest of sharp, white horns. Smoke curled from flaring nostril slits. Bloodred and golden scales shimmered along its sharp jaw and down the entire length of its muscled body. Four powerful limbs erupted from its massive core, each ending in curving nails as deadly as battle spears. Leathery red wings, tipped in feathers of gold and crimson, stretched and unfolded. The creature's tail was as long as its body, thick and covered in spikes that made the ones in the passage look like toothpicks.

The dragon's neck and each of its limbs were clamped in shackles, with a chain allowing small amounts of movement. I wrapped my arms around my chest, half wishing I had Peck for comfort, and half grateful that the chicken was safe in her royal coop.

"Dragon," I said hoarsely.

I turned my body away from Sonora. Orlen raised his head up, let out a small gasp, and disappeared into my neck scarf again. The creature paced back and forth in front of a high platform jutting out of the rock.

"Dragon," Beaman agreed miserably, clutching my

side. He looked at Sonora and straightened, puffing out his chest a little. "Impressive. Thanks. Glad to have a look." He aimed a thumb toward the hallway we'd entered through. "We should probably get back now. Don't want to be missed."

I looked at the glow rock I'd dropped. It was a dull gray. At least an hour had passed.

"Isn't it beautiful?" Sonora asked. "I hate that it's chained up like that."

"That's my favorite part about it," Beaman whispered in my ear. "Can we go now?"

When the dragon saw us, it growled again and flapped its wings, sending a fierce wind across the cave, blowing back the queen's loose hair. Straining against the chains, it let out a furious, earthshaking scream, revealing teeth that could rip any batteral to pieces with a single tearing motion.

I backed against the wall. "But why is it here?" I asked.

"I told you—it's probably left over from war times. It was guarding the prisoners."

"What's that?" Beaman asked, pointing to a large iron wheel attached to the cave wall. A long chain was wrapped around it. The end links threaded through a metal circle. They were broken off at the end.

I glanced up. There were more circles—a line of them, like the shackles in the prisoner room. I traced them and saw that they ended on the high platform. The dragon paced in front of it.

"I think it was guarding something." I thought fast. "You said Renart was carrying a book. What book could be that important?"

Sonora's eyes widened. "Stub, you're brilliant. I'll bet it's the Book of Peace—with copies of the Peace letters."

"Do you mean there's really a Book of Peace?" Beaman asked. "I thought it was just part of the emblem. Like a symbol. Or a story."

Sonora shook her head, frustrated. "I can't really remember. My mother told me about it once—it did feel like a bedtime story. How the letters were stored in a safe place, and they were to be brought out only when we needed to reference them to avoid war. She never got a chance to tell me more. I'll bet it's been down here for years, being guarded. What do you think, Stub?"

"Me?" I paused, trying to take in the fact that the queen of Maradon was asking what I thought. Unfortunately, I had nothing to offer.

I didn't understand the Peace letters in the first place. It seemed so implausible, that letters could halt a war. I thought of the conflicts I'd seen in Trapper's Cove. Those battles were on a much smaller scale, but they were only ever settled when one side lost something and the other side won. There'd never been a case where the fighters had simply shaken hands and exchanged notes and forgotten the conflict. So what had we given Tartín to make them stop fighting? "I couldn't say," I finished lamely.

Sonora frowned. "But what would Renart want with a bunch of letters? Tartín hasn't been a problem for years. I'm sure it's for some silly hundredth Peace Day display. He's obsessed. Mother always said that his Maradonian loyalty knows no bounds."

Hmm. Orlen had implied the complete opposite. Was the queen just naïve, or was Orlen wrong? Or was he lying about Renart for some reason?

I didn't know who to believe, or who to trust.

No matter how loyal he was, I didn't think Renart would have faced a dragon simply for a book of letters to put on display. If he was being loyal, perhaps he'd fetched the Peace letters in preparation for his meeting with Lacera. After all, she was a powerful and magical queen. If anyone could break Maradon's Peace, it would be her. Was Renart worried about impending war, and reading up on ways to avoid it?

But Orlen had said that Lacera didn't want her people to have contact with non-magical lands. I was missing something. There was only one way to find out what was going on—we had to get into the regent's quarters.

A low noise knocked me away from my thoughts.

Beaman was humming. Not a good sign. It was soft at first, but the tune got increasingly high-pitched as he looked at the dragon. His nerves wouldn't last much longer down here. I slipped him an elbow and he jumped like it was a dragon tooth.

"Your Highness," I said, "why do you think Renart would need the book—I mean, other than for a display? And do you agree that he seems loyal?"

"I have no idea why he would want the book. As for being loyal, Mother always seemed to think he was, but—"

Before she could finish her thought, Beaman raised a hand. "Er, um, speaking of loyalty, Your Highness, might it be good for us to scoot back to the kitchen?" He grinned weakly and tapped his chest. "Just speaking as a loyal worker to the queendom. Who loves Maradon a whole lot. And who also loves food a whole lot." He gulped. "And who'd love to be in the kitchen. Working. Away from here." At another elbow in the side from me, he finally shut up, looking at the queen with hopeful eyes.

"Do you know where I'd like to be tonight?" Sonora asked instead. "I'd give anything just to stay in my quarters. I'm dreading the welcoming feast—all the pompous lords and ladies! And speeches don't start until nine o'clock; it'll last until midnight." She brightened. "Perhaps I'll fake an illness. I *have* been getting headaches

Beaman gripped my arm. "Speaking of why food is important . . ." He looked around the kitchen, then turned to me and snapped his fingers. "Remember the swamp mussels Minera told us about? They've got plenty here, and it'll be a bit chaotic during the feast preparation. I'll borrow a few ingredients and make a special dish for the guard."

16

How to Ransack a Royal Room

⟨∿⟩

I can't believe it," I whispered. "It's working."

The guard slumped in her rocking chair, snoring like a swarm of buzzing swamp insects. A trickling line of saliva slid slowly down her chin. The rest of the young workers were sound asleep, exhausted from the hours-long feast preparation.

Beaman grinned. "After the stew, I gave her a cup of tea steeped with extra doses of calming herbs. You see, Orlen? Food can be magic too. I'll stay here in case she wakes up." He glanced at a sand clock on the wall. "You have an hour and a half until the feast ends."

"Right. We'll be back soon."

I ducked out of the servants' quarters, then made my way around the back of the courtyard to the entrance farthest from the Grand Hall. A slow trickle of rain was falling, making the dirt-packed yard slippery. As we passed the animal enclosures, I paused. Something stirred in my chest.

It wasn't a prickle. It was an ache. It would only take two minutes to say hello to my best friend. Maybe three.

My feet made the decision for me, jogging softly over to the gate.

"What are you doing?" Orlen whispered.

"Just making sure Peck's all right."

After slipping past dozens of slumbering animals, I stepped into the first large, open coop. All the chickens were slumbering up on roosting bars the height of my head. There were hundreds of nesting boxes built against the walls, but when I looked around, there didn't seem to be enough chickens to use them.

An uneasy chill swept up my back. *Just find a way to get enough food for the feasts,* Renart had said.

"There's no time to look for her," Orlen said, though his own voice sounded stilted, as though he, too, was holding his breath. A *whoosh* of air released from his tiny lungs, sounding like a combination of worry and relief. "Yes, all right. Find her."

I rushed along the roosting bars with my heart in my throat.

Orlen clung to my shoulder as we crept up a narrow staircase in the castle. I peeked down the hallway at the top, seeing nothing but wall torches giving off faint, Peace-blue

254 · JESSICA LAWSON

light. Renart's was the last door on the right, at a dead end.

"I cannot *believe* you brought that chicken with you," he muttered, though he had practically jumped onto Peck's back the moment we spotted her. "And why on earth aren't you wearing shoes—I thought you'd finally come around to them? Your stockinged feet look ridiculous."

"I didn't want to leave our trail in mud! And we're lucky Peck's still alive! There's no way I'm leaving her there to possibly get eaten." I used my head to nudge aside the stack of linens I carried and stuck my face into my rucksack. Peck rested gently on top of a folded sheet. I kissed her feathers. "Please keep quiet, friend."

A light shone beneath Renart's locked quarters at the end of the hall. We crouched just outside it. The smell of lavender wafted under a crack in the door.

I dropped the linens, arranged the uniform I'd stolen from the laundry quarters, and knocked three times. There was no answer.

"He's gone." As quietly as possible, I twisted the doorknob. "It's locked."

"Of course it's locked! He's hiding traitorous letters and who knows what else in there!"

There were two keyholes. I took the wizard match out of my apron pocket and twisted it into both spaces, feeling for something to give. A minute passed, then two.

lately, and I did have a fainting spell last week. The doctor thinks it's because I'm growing, but I think it's from enduring Renart's lectures on being responsible." She let out a scornful laugh. "Honestly, I think he would be better at leading the queendom than me."

I had a feeling that Renart would probably agree. Orlen poked me hard in the belly.

"Oh! Look out!" Sonora shoved me toward the passage entrance.

The dragon reared back against the chains and roared again, shooting a series of fiery flames from its throat. One nearly reached the place where the three of us stood. The restraints that held it in place were attached to the stone. As we watched, the dragon wrenched and writhed. There were already cracks in the cave wall. With each tug, the cracks widened.

"Can we *please* go now!" Beaman shouted, pulling me back as the dragon lunged forward.

"Oops, should have warned you about that," Sonora said. Her nose wrinkled. "Do I smell burned bread?"

"It fell out of my sleeve." Beaman sheepishly pointed to the burned bun on the floor. "I like to keep a nibble handy. Speaking of nibbles, is anyone hungry? Maybe we should go. I could make you a snack—that's my job, and I wouldn't want to lose my job, Your Queenship."

"I said to call me Sonora. That's a royal order. And don't worry, I won't let anyone take your job," she said, patting his shoulder. She lifted a small sand-clock necklace out of her shirt and looked at it. "Bother, I need to get back to my room and change clothes. Let's go."

Beaman clapped his hands. "Sure," he said. "I mean, if you're ready."

We followed her out of the chamber.

Some time later, Sonora pointed to a staircase leading up. "That goes to my room." She pointed to a passage to the right. "And that one leads to the cheese pantry. No traps between here and there, I promise. So, are we even? You won't tell on me?"

"Um, the thing is," I began, "we really need to—"

"I'll show you something else next time. This time you can choose. The library, my rooms, or another place. Even Vile Renart's office. I might have fun sneaking in there. He's such a secretive snapper turtle. I think that's why he's so happy that Orlen left. Now there's no one but him to consult about things."

I cleared her throat. "Orlen?"

"The castle wizard. Twitchy, grumpy old man. He's supposed to look after me at the Peace Day festivities outside of the castle this year." She grinned. "But he's gone now, so maybe I'll get to go by myself! He's a fussy old fuddy-duddy."

I felt Orlen bristling in my apron.

Beaman laughed, then clapped a hand over his mouth. "Sorry."

Sonora laughed back. "What for? It's not like he's here. In any case, I'm off to get ready for dinner. Perhaps I'll see you around." Her fingers curled around her laundry clothes. "I hope I do. I enjoyed our time together. I don't really have any friends." She blushed, then with nimble steps, she walked away.

Beaman smacked me excitedly on the shoulder. He took an awkward leap after her.

"Wait, Your Queenship! I mean, Your Sonoraship! I mean, plain Sonora—not plain," Beaman sputtered. "I just . . ." He took a deep breath. "I'd love to know something. What's your favorite food?"

She turned, looking puzzled for a moment. "I don't know. I don't really think about food."

Beaman recoiled. "But your kitchen is full of anything you could ever want."

She shrugged. "Food's food. It's all the same, isn't it? See you. And please, call me Sonora." With that, she turned again.

Beaman stared after Sonora. "Who doesn't care about food?" He looked at me, slightly horrified. "Especially when you've got all of it?" He leaned against the passage, looking lost.

"Are you okay?" I asked.

"What?" He shook his head and sighed. "I'm fine. I just—I don't understand." He blinked at me. "She—she doesn't care about food."

I nodded. "But she's still very nice, isn't she?"

He looked down the passage that Sonora had taken and let out a long sigh. "I suppose."

"Thank heavens," Orlen said loudly. "The cook has come to his senses. Perhaps we can all now concentrate on finding out when Lacera is arriving, and oh, here's another thought—why the queen's regent has been trying to fetch a book guarded by a *dragon*. You heard Sonora—there's going to be a banquet until midnight. You're both under thirteen and won't have to work after ten—you can sneak into his room then. Try to find the letters from Lacera."

Beaman squeezed past me, glancing once more at the tunnel that Sonora had hurried down. The moony light in his eyes had been firmly snuffed out.

"Cheese," he mumbled, sniffing the air as we pushed hard against a load of cheese wheels to get through the hidden door. "Now, *cheese* is very nice."

Orlen slunk deep into the folds of my scarf as we slid into the busy kitchen. "Yes, well, cheese won't make your wretched night guard go away. And you've got to get past her."

and scanned the rest of the room, looking under the bed and rifling through clothes. There was no book.

I took several sheets of paper from the stack near the windowsill and crumpled them a little, to better match the ones in my shirt, then placed them in the trunk and closed the lid. Renart had already read them—hopefully he wouldn't look too closely at the papers. "Should we take the bird?"

"No, he'll be suspicious. Just get out of here."

I closed the door behind me and waited for Orlen to scoot under to relock it. A buzzing feeling swept through my feet.

Footsteps. Coming faintly up the stairwell. "Orlen, hurry!" I whispered. The hallway was long, but it turned a corner on one end. We could make it. The footsteps grew louder.

"I can't shift the bolt," Orlen said.

"Shh! He's coming! Just leave it!" I twisted the knob and cracked the door enough to grab Orlen. Then, just as I was shutting it, I felt a prickle in my knees so strong that I stumbled, knocking the door open.

The footsteps stopped, then quickened along with my heartbeat. "What is the meaning of this!" Renart bellowed. "Who are you?"

I rolled to see his angry face inches above mine. "I—oh no, I um—" I forgot my line, but managed to stuff Orlen into my pocket and shove myself up to a standing position.

Renart looked at the rucksack still hanging from my

258 · JESSICA LAWSON

shoulder. "Are you *stealing* from me, you filthy little louse?"
He grabbed my arm and threw me against the wall, then tore
the bag from my shoulder and opened it. He stumbled himself as Peck came floundering out and ran into his room. "A
chicken?" he said, temporarily confused. He dug in the bag
again. "And a bedsheet?"

The paper dragonfly from Bastian flew out of the bag
and jabbed him in the chin. "And trinket magic," he mumbled, swatting it roughly to the floor. His eyes narrowed as he
grabbed something at the bottom of the bag. "Ah," he said, his
eyes gleaming dangerously. "What's this you've taken?"

I knew what it was before he pulled it out. An invisible
blow took my breath away.

The paper from Matron Tratte's was clutched in his hand.
Again I cursed myself for not having burned the stupid thing.

I watched, helpless, as he uncurled the page and read the
letter. At first he only looked relieved. But as his eyes drifted
down the paper, a calculating, knowing look took over. He
cleared his throat loudly.

"'To the owner of the Tinderbox Tavern in Trapper's
Cove,'" he said, lowering the paper with a menacing grin.
"How *interesting*. Do you know, I was just going over the
backgrounds of our guests, to better arrange seating order."
He bent before me and took my chin firmly in his hand. "I
came across a Lady Tratte, newly wed to a Captain Vella. As

I recall, she was, until quite recently, a tavern owner from a seedy trading post." He looked down at my feet. "Exactly the kind of place where young scraps don't wear shoes."

The pinch Orlen gave me was enough to produce a passable concerned grimace. "We were dyeing the tablecloths today. Blue water was all over the floor. I didn't want to chance it getting on my shoes and then staining the guests' quarters. And yours, of course, sir." The words came out with surprising fluidity. Inside, I was blocked with two thoughts

He's got my paper.

Matron Tratte got herself a title.

So, she hadn't been in Maradon Cross searching for me. She probably couldn't give a rat's tail about me. But she most certainly would, if the regent to the queen brought it to her attention. I felt a burning sensation in my throat, as though I was about to vomit.

I somehow managed a nonchalant shrug. "It's not mine. I can't even read. I grew up in a chicken coop. I found that paper in an empty room when I was cleaning guest quarters. I was going to take it to the laundry mistress, in case it was important. You can burn it for all I care."

"Really? What a lovely suggestion." Renart took two steps into his room and removed a long wizard match from an urn beside his personal hearth. He swiped it against the wall, sparking a flame. He held the lit match just under the paper and watched me. "Shall I do it now?"

My heart beat faster. I wanted nothing more than to grab the paper from his traitorous hands. It tore at something inside me that he had read the letter, not me.

He clucked his tongue, then blew out the match. "On second thought, I'll keep it for a while. In the meantime, I think we'll both have a word with your mistress. Right now." He yanked me toward the staircase as a slow clap rang out in the hallway behind us.

"Oh, Renart, *really*. You are *too* dramatic." The young voice dripped with sarcasm.

Renart froze, then turned slowly, my arm still gripped firmly in his hand. "Your Highness," he said, his voice respectful and even.

Sonora walked toward us, her face indifferent. "I was wondering where you went. It's not like you to leave a feast with important people."

"I was just returning to my quarters to, ah, draft an urgent letter that must go out to a coming guest. I came across this girl digging about in my room. I'm now escorting the thieving runaway to a guard room."

Sonora tilted her head. "Thieving runaway?" she asked with a frown.

I used my free arm to point to the linen pile, still stacked by the door. "I was just changing the linens." I pleaded with my eyes. *"As you asked,* Your Highness."

To her credit, the queen paused for only a moment before smiling. "Of course you are." She walked over to Renart and playfully slapped the hand gripping my arm. "And now you've ruined my surprise."

His grip on my arm loosened. "Surprise?"

The queen glanced toward the open door to his quarters. "You've been complaining under your breath for nearly a week about that wretched missing wizard and what he did to your room, but you're too busy thinking of others to do anything about it. I wanted to at least have your bedclothes changed while you were at the feast. I thought it would help you sleep." Her lips pouted in sympathy. "You seem very stressed. I can be kind, you know." She nodded at my arm. "Let her go now."

He raised the roll of paper. "Laundry worker or not, I have good reason to believe that this girl is a runaway apprentice. And the law states that—"

Sonora yawned loudly. "Nonsense. Do you think I don't know my own laws? What about the law states that apprentices may be abused?"

"What are you talking about? She doesn't look abused."

"I take the time to seek out all new orphan employees and get to know them a bit. I have a special spot for orphans, as you know. So, how would you like to live in a chicken coop, Renart, like this young girl was forced to do? Because I assure you, it can be arranged."

Renart glowered. I watched as his long fingers curled into a tight fist. "That won't be necessary."

Sonora took a step toward him. "Good. I'd hate to see you covered in straw and feathers." She tapped a finger against her chin. "Though maybe it would suit you. I wonder what sort of egg you would lay." She held out her hand. "Now, I'll take that paper. We can do a proper investigation *after* Peace Day. I know how busy you are. You need a good sleep before running my birthday banquet tomorrow. Hence the new sheet surprise."

Renart released my arm. "I don't want new sheets. Perhaps Lady Tratte does, though. I'll be sure to arrange with the laundry mistress to have your linen girl take her some. Your name?" he asked me. He bared his teeth at me in what might have been a smile, had it not looked so wolfish.

The expression sparked a memory of a familiar face. "I'm called Hut."

The regent raised an eyebrow. "Very well, Hut." He bowed to the queen. "With your permission, I'll keep the letter, Your Highness. It will serve as a reminder not to have unnecessary conversations. And I am, after all," he said, glancing my way, "in charge of the royal paperwork."

Sonora studied him, matching his calculated expression. "For now."

"One question." The regent looked at me, his eyes narrowing again. "How exactly did she get into my room, Your Highness?" He reached to his belt and unbuckled a large ring of bound keys. "I have the only key."

Reaching a hand into her tunic, Sonora pulled out a necklace chain with a small black key attached. "You have the key to many places in the castle, as you've reminded me over the years. You're not alone in that, Regent." She smiled at his expression. "But you didn't think my mother left me with nothing special, did you? This key has been handed down for generations. It can open any keyhole in this castle, I assure you. She told me so herself."

Renart gaped at the key. "She gave that to you?"

Sonora lifted a delicate hand to her mouth in mock concern. "Oh, dear. Did you think she would leave it to you, since you were to be my regent?" Her gaze became stern. "If you insist on knowing, I slipped away and let the girl into your room. You know how I'm always slipping away. The child has stolen nothing. So," she said, dropping the key, "is everything settled here?"

Peck chose that moment to wander hesitantly out into the hallway. She caught sight of Renart and squawked loudly, flapping toward the stairwell.

Renart looked at me with piercing, triumphant eyes. "Oh, but you're wrong, Your Highness," he said, his voice crackling with anticipation. "At the very least, she's stolen a—"

"Chicken!" The breathless voice echoed up the staircase as Beaman launched himself onto Peck, fully dressed in his cook's gear. "We've been looking all over for this one," he grinned, wrestling the hen. His eyes darted toward me in concern. "She's a squirmy one and just escaped getting her head chopped off." He laughed nervously, his voice cracking. "Can't quite blame her for wanting her freedom."

"I found her in the hallway, on my way here," I said quickly. "I was going to bring her back when I finished dressing the regent's bed."

"You'd better go back to the dinner, Renart," Sonora said, locking his door. "No time for letters right now. I'll meet you down there in a moment." She gestured down the hall. "I need to freshen up before the last toast."

Jaw tight, Renart gave a short bow and disappeared down the steps. Beaman tiptoed to the edge of the stairwell and waited, then gave me a nod.

"Thank you, Sonora," I said, finally letting out a long breath. "And you, Beaman. How did you know just the right time to come?"

He wiped at a curl of long hair that had come loose from his bun. "You said you'd be back. You weren't. I was worried about you. So I ran to the laundry and found fresh cook's clothes, and"—he fumbled in his apron—"I followed my map to Renart's room."

Sonora frowned. "Map?"

Inwardly, I groaned. Darn that Beaman and his big mouth.

Beaman coughed loudly. "Um, I'm going back now." He shot me an apologetic glance and handed me Peck. "It's raining buckets out. Good thing Renart didn't notice my wet hair."

I nodded as he turned back down the stairs. "Good thing." *He was worried about us,* I told Peck with five tender squeezes. Just in case she wanted to know.

Sonora linked her arm in mine, then led me down the hallway, away from Renart's room. "We'll get to this mysterious map of Beaman's later. First, what are you doing here?" she whispered. "Did you really live in a chicken coop? And is it true—are you an apprentice?"

A flush of embarrassed heat ran up my neck. "Yes to both of those, but—"

"Yes to both?" Anger flooded Sonora's face. "Why didn't the proctor report your conditions?"

I stared at her blankly. "What proctor?"

She paused in the hall. "An apprentice contract must be registered with the queendom. Each region has proctors that must ensure the contract is acceptable to both parties and are then mandated to check in on the relationship twice a year." Her forehead wrinkled. "Are you saying nobody came?"

My stomach dropped. I felt the hollow space inside me widen. "No. Nobody came."

"Or maybe they did come, and she appeased them?"

I didn't answer. Either way, Matron Tratte must have lied—she'd never registered me as an apprentice or she'd lied about my circumstances. So I wasn't legally bound to her after all. But what about the letter from my mother? It had to be real, based on Renart's reaction. It was all too much to think about.

We turned the corner. Blinking hard, I cleared my throat and lowered my voice even though the hallway was clear. "Never mind all of that. I was looking for the book you described Renart holding—I was . . . curious. It's not there, but I found some papers. Renart has something planned in the west tower room, at sunset. The day after tomorrow."

"On Peace Day? So what's the silly meeting about?"

"Well, um. . . I wouldn't call the meeting . . . silly."

Sonora rubbed her temples. "I have *such* a headache, and this is not making it better." She sighed. "But it's not your fault. You'll have to tell me more about this later. I'd better get going. I have about ten minutes before Renart gets suspicious about my absence. Meet me in the west tower room in two hours and we'll talk."

"What if it's locked?"

Sonora pulled the necklace out of her tunic again. "Let's hope this does the trick. I can't imagine what's left up there. The west tower was badly damaged by cannon fire during the war with Tartín. When the Peace came, it took several years to address damages and rebuild across the queendom. The rest of the castle was built up in a sturdy manner, but that tower was deemed too dangerous to use." Her fingers tapped on folded arms. "Which makes it all the stranger that Renart's planning on having a meeting there."

Yes. It was strange. It was strange that no one was saying a word about a meeting with a wicked wizard queen—one that Sonora had no clue about. I bit my lip hard, trying not to blurt out the truth. How could we keep this a secret from her?

I made my decision. "There's something you should know first. We'll try to make it quick."

Curiosity bloomed on Sonora's face. "Who's *we*?"

"For starters, it's me," said a small, resigned voice. Orlen waited until I lifted him to my shoulder. "Hello, child. I come bearing news."

Sonora stared, openmouthed. "Oh." Her hands rose to her chest. "Orlen." She shook her head, incredulous. "What in the world . . ." And with that, the queen of Maradon fainted.

17

How to Break a Peace Queen's Heart

ⓈⒶⒹ

Beaman and I climbed the tower steps. For once, he
had nothing to say.

Orlen was silent as well, sitting stiffly on my
shoulder, holding on to my apron strap. I found myself missing their chatter. The distinct odor of wetness on stone was
so sharp that I began breathing through my mouth, just to
avoid it. It smelled too much like the mixture I'd spread onto
the crumbling stone wall at the Tinderbox. Like a possible
exit that I'd sealed myself off from.

Sonora had mentioned repairs to the roof, but the west
tower still had spaces between its stacked stones all the way
up. The rain seeped through, despite the wall designed to
keep it out. There came a faint *drip, drip, drip* of a leak on a
stair somewhere ahead. Harsh, moaning winds whistled outside, stealing into the tower as well.

I held the glow pebble ahead of me, but it did little to
ward off the dark and dank and damp. Peck shifted in the
rucksack on my back.

"Hello?" came a familiar voice from below us.

I was grateful for a reason to pause. After everything we'd told her once she'd revived, I wasn't sure Sonora would come.

A flickering light shone faintly below us on the tower steps. It grew brighter and brighter until we saw the queen's flushed face, looking up. She held a glowing ball of glass in her hand—a more elegant version of my pebble.

"Not much farther," she said. She was dressed in simple blue trousers and a tunic with no adornment. "Where's Orlen? Or did I make up everything that you told me?" she asked, sounding almost hopeful.

"I'm here," he called.

Sonora took in a deep breath. "Right. I'm sorry I fainted before."

"It was rather a lot to take in," Orlen conceded. "Beaman almost fainted too. And Stub nearly squashed me."

Two more circular turns and we were at the top, facing a splintered door scarred with deep sword slashes, faintly grown over with gray mold. It looked as though it hadn't been opened for a long time. Sonora removed her necklace and placed the key in the door lock. She turned the key, then twisted the knob and pushed. She grinned nervously. "Mother was right, it seems."

She opened the door and gasped.

I pulled her back, ready to run.

"No!" she pulled me up. "It's fine. It's just—it's . . . well, look." She stepped aside and rubbed the orb in her hand until the light increased.

I looked. The room was not disheveled or damaged. The circular floor was covered in a plush rug emblazoned with the emblem of Maradon. On the rug was a polished wooden table with three chairs. And on the table was a slim book the size of a large serving platter. Beside it was a feather pen and a corked glass vial. The color of its contents was deep red.

Beside the pen was a weathered, opened envelope. It was the one that fell out of Renart's iron box in the office near the castle's kitchen. I concentrated on the words written on the front and sounded them out.

For the . . . cur . . . current queen or king of Maradon.

The book was simple and brown, but in the middle of the cover was an oval of color. A red-yellow sheen with a keyhole right in the center. It was no thicker than a knuckle. I approached the table and set Orlen onto it.

"Is that . . . *it*?" Beaman asked. "The Book of Peace?"

Sonora nodded slowly. "I think so. It's the same size as the one Renart was carrying in the passage. Did my mother ever tell you about the book, Orlen? You were her closest advisor."

"No," he said stiffly. "She never mentioned the book."

Sonora touched the worn leather. "She once told me

about how you two met." Her fingers gripped the edges of the cover, as though they were trying to still the quaver in her voice. "In a bookshop."

"Yes," said Orlen. "She was very young. Queen Rona sometimes had trouble keeping up with her. Being mischievous is inherited trait, it seems." His eyes caught the light of her orb and gave a twinkle that shifted immediately into something more somber. "She once asked me to turn her into an adventure story, because she never wanted to be a queen."

Sonora swallowed. Her eyes grew shiny. "Tell me something else about her. Please."

He stepped around the book and placed a hand on her finger. "She never wanted to be a mother."

The queen's face fell. I touched Orlen on the shoulder. "Tell her something good," I said.

"I'm telling her the truth. That should be good enough." Orlen looked at the book for a long moment, then raised his eyes to meet Sonora's. "She *didn't* want to be a mother. That's true. But that changed the moment she saw you. I was there. I've never seen anything like it. You were like the sun and your mother was like a green-growing seed, drawn to you for light and warmth. You gave her both."

Beaman placed a hand on Sonora's shoulder. It made sense that he knew exactly what to do in that moment. After all, he also had a mother who loved him. I'd had a mother once too. But she'd left me with a stranger and bound me with a contract.

There was only one window in the tower. A large one, facing westward. It had been repaired and was paned with clear glass. Parted white curtains hung on either side like braided hair, tucked neatly into curved iron hooks. Lifting Peck into my arms, I walked a few feet to the window and held her close. *I'm here,* I squeezed. *You're here. We're here together,* she pecked back.

She rustled and ruffled until I let her down. A long feather dropped from her neck. I watched as it shrank an inch. I put it in my apron and turned back to the others. The wizard spell was wearing off.

Sonora pulled her hand away from the book. "I still don't understand," she said. "Why would Lacera want to see the Peace letters? Even if Renart wants to take over from me, what good would those do her?" She picked up the weathered envelope, then set it down again. "Stub, what do you think?"

"I think," I said, "that we should read these first." I pulled the letters from my shirt and handed them to Sonora. We each took a chair as she read through the first one.

> *To the queen of Maradon,*
> *I'm so sorry to hear of the death of your*
> *mother. Please know that you have inherited*

*a queendom dedicated to the protection of
your citizens. It has come to my attention that
you may need guidance during these difficult
times. I understand the challenges of leading a
nation. I, too, have had troubles to address.*

*Perhaps we could help each other. Like
you, I take my role as a leader and protector
most seriously. Due to your mother's unexpected death, I wonder whether you are aware of
our standing arrangement.*

*If not, take comfort in your lineage, and
the queens that have come before you. . . .*

The rest of the letter described an agreement that had
been in place since Queen Alessa created the Peace between
Maradon and Tartín with her graceful, imploring words.
Except . . . according to the correspondence, she hadn't *created* the Peace. She'd traded for it. Sonora read the next letter.

*Dear Queen Sonora,
Thank you for your response and inquiries.
I understand that you may not have been
informed of certain particulars related to
the arrangement. In terms of procedure,
the following instructions may be of service.
First, you will find the required materials in*

a large cavern below the castle. I will send the
necessary deterrents to make their retrieval
possible.

Second, please arrange for the book to be
in the highest tower in your castle, as viewing
the sunset will be a factor in enhancing the
spell.

I thank you for your queendom's
commitment and look forward to our
continued relationship. I will see you at the
appointed time and place. No need to prepare
sleeping quarters for me. I won't be staying
long.

You'll find full details in the following
pages. I trust you and the generations that
follow you will do the right thing.

I commend you for protecting your people,
as I protect mine.
Yours in Peace,
Queen Lacera of Wintrel

"But how was she writing to me?" Sonora gasped. She threw
the letters on the table and paced back and forth. "I don't understand. I didn't respond or make inquiries. I didn't write letters to
her at all!" She wrung her hands together.

"You didn't have to write her letters." I said it softly. "You just had to sign them."

"But I didn't!" she insisted.

"You did. In the dungeons, you told us about the stacks of boring paperwork Renart would have you sign."

"Those were about castle payments and worker payments and Peace Day costs and . . . oh *no.*" Her voice faltered. "But these letters are still just a bundle of things about keeping our people safe and making sure the Book of Peace and other things are here for a meeting." She picked up the book and looked at Orlen. "Were you here when the Peace letters were written?"

He shook his head. "When the first wizards were banished by Lacera, your queendom was still recovering from the war with Tartín. I didn't begin to learn about your history until I became the castle wizard and scholar."

It was strange to think that I knew so little of my queendom's history. And that Orlen, a prisoner, knew more. But then, he'd been here much longer. I thought of the calendar in the wizard district, and the man who'd added another slash. There must have been thousands of them.

Oh.

Oh *no.*

"Orlen," I said slowly. "Exactly how many years have you been here? You said you were here before the Peace began."

"We were. Things were in chaos still. Many of us thought that was why Lacera banished us here. I was young. In my twenties."

I looked at Sonora. "You said it took time to recover and rebuild things like the castle after the war with Tartín."

She put the book back on the table. "Yes. Even though the Peace had started, it took several years to become stable again."

I laid down my palm. Orlen stepped on, holding my thumb for support. I raised him to my eye level. "You told us in the swamp that you're nearly one-hundred and twenty-seven now. Which makes you one-hundred and twenty-six. Which means . . ."

His face drained. He looked at the Book of Peace. Then at the chain around Sonora's neck. "I remember that key."

I thought of the portraits in the Tinderbox. I'd always noticed the necklace key on Queen Barra and Queen Rona, because they looked so alike. But the same chain had been painted around the neck of every Peace queen. Except the first.

Why wouldn't she have had a key to every room in the castle as well? Unless the key was created after her coronation. As a tool that wouldn't be questioned.

My fingers grazed the wizard blade strapped to my waist. *Did you see the maker's signed paper—the contract that it was valid?* Matron Tratte had snapped at her son. *Magic doesn't last forever.*

Magic couldn't last. Not the good kind and not the bad.

"The book isn't full of Peace letters," I said. "Nothing was sent to Tartín. The book is a trade. A magical contract." I picked up the corked vial. "And the spell has finally worn out. That's why she's here. To renew it, at sunset on Peace Day."

Sonora shook her head. "But a contract requires more than one person—this book has been around for a century. Unless Alessa . . ." Her face fell.

"She made a trade." Orlen held his chest with both hands, as though trying to stop his whole self from tearing in two. "Your queendom's freedom, for our imprisonment."

"No," Sonora whispered.

"Yes." Orlen's voice grew hoarse. "The scale on the book is from a baby dragon. Look at that feather pen. It matches the dragon. The vial must be full of dragon blood—a most powerful magical substance. She must have caught it young, taken its blood, and brought it here. That's why we all show up in Maradon Cross at first. We're pulled to the spell's source. It all makes sense. Terrible, awful sense."

Lightning flashed outside the westward window.

"She was a new queen, at war," Orlen said softly. "She was desperate to save her people. She would have done anything." He walked over to the wrinkled envelope.

I handed it to Sonora. "Renart's people have been stewards for generations. Perhaps his family passed it on to him for safekeeping. Or . . . your mother could have entrusted it to him. It's for you now."

She opened it with shaking hands and read it silently.

"It's about the war," she said quietly. She folded the sheet of paper and placed it back on the table. "It's an explanation of why she did it. She wrote it on her deathbed. Lacera never contacted her again. She left this for the rulers who came after her, so that if the wizard queen reached out, they would know. So they would renew the contract." She touched the Book of Peace and winced.

"Read it," I said. "Please." I scooped Peck into my arms.

"I don't want to," she whispered. "I can't."

"You can," Beaman said, moving to her side.

Sonora took a deep breath. She nodded.

She read the book aloud, as rain pummeled the tower and thunder boomed all around.

"'A negotiated, binding contract between the Queendom of Maradon and the Queendom of Wintrel,'" she began. Her voice shook at times, but the young queen of Maradon was an exceptionally good reader.

Unfortunately, the tale that the Book of Peace laid out was brief and most unpleasant. The first page of the contract sent to Alessa was written in an elegant script that matched the color of the liquid in the vial.

Once the contract is in place, all Maradonian borders will be closed to armed forces. All enemy forces already in Maradon will be expelled. No leader of any queendom, including Wintrel, may enter Maradon's borders, except by direct invitation. Maradonians may come and go as they please. In exchange, Maradon will harbor ongoing influxes of select Wintrellians. No force of magic will ever be used against Maradon by the Queendom of Wintrel. None will know of Maradon's involvement. The wizards harbored by Maradon will be stripped of their ability to explain their origins.

The queen of Maradon will be master of the contract key, and the queen of Wintrel will be master of communication.

This book shall be kept safe by the gifted guardian until such time when it becomes necessary to reevaluate needs.

This is a contract made in good faith. Renewal shall take place every hundred years. At the time of each renewal, Maradon will retain the option to cancel the arrangement. If the sitting queen or king of Maradon makes that choice, Tartin will be free to invade the queendom at will. Wintrel will be free to address any grievances as well. This is a warning and a promise.

The room grew silent as Sonora closed the book.

"So," she said quietly. "This is what's keeping Tartín from invading our queendom. My great-grandmother signed it. No one else has had to yet. But now I'm supposed to." She looked at Orlen. "I'm so sorry we did this to you."

"It's not your fault."

"Do you think the others knew? Do you think my mother knew?"

Orlen lowered his eyes. "I . . . I can't say."

"She did. She had to have known." Sonora traced a line on the page and bit her lip. "I'm supposed to sign it. To keep my people safe."

She looked up at me, her face riddled with fear and doubt and helplessness—all the feelings I'd been intimate with for twelve years.

She looked trapped. I'd been wrong back in the bread pantry. The queen and I were more alike than I'd thought. I put my hand on hers.

"Can't we just throw it out the window?" she asked.

Orlen shook his head. "Renart may come to check for it before the meeting. Nothing can be amiss. We must use the time when Lacera is in here to catch her off guard. Draw out the meeting as long as you can."

Her lips trembled. "I don't know how."

"We'll come up with a plan. Sonora," Orlen said softly.

"I knew your mother when she was your age. You remind me of her. She was bright and brave. She did not yet know that she carried the weight of a queendom on her shoulders. That weight can crush so many things. If it is too much for you, it would be understandable."

"It's not too much for me," Sonora said quickly, her voice tinged in anger. "Even if it were, it wouldn't matter, would it? It's despicable, what Alessa did. And now I'm responsible. Me, alone."

Beaman took her hand. "You're not alone."

She pulled it back. "I am." She stepped toward the door and paused. She shook her head. "I'm sorry." She took a deep breath. "I don't care if the Peace is broken. It's wrong." She placed her hand on the knob. "This way, I'll finally get my title. I'll be Sonora the Peace Breaker."

She looked out the western window of the tower. "You have my word that I won't sign the contract. Whatever you wizards need to do to defeat Lacera, I'll support it. Send me a note if you need anything. Otherwise, I'll do my part. Perhaps it's best if we aren't seen together again. I wish you luck." She straightened the envelope and book and vial so that they were in the same position as when we entered. Then she picked up her light orb and opened the door.

"Is she mad at us?" he asked.

"She's scared," said Orlen. "She's making a difficult

choice. Time for bed. You two will need to find a way to slip off to the wizard district tomorrow, and you'll need your wits about you to do it."

Beaman and Orlen and I crept back into the workers' quarters. I cradled Peck close to me, whispering the need to remain quiet. She knew that speech well from our time in Trapper's Cove, and nestled against me easily. Orlen's snoring was muffled by his head-down position on her back feathers. Sleep wouldn't come to me, no matter how exhausted my body was. Sonora's birthday was tomorrow. And the next day was Peace Day. What was in store for Maradon? For me and Peck?

Sonora sounded so sure. So ready to help the wizards. But the fact remained that Maradon would be her queendom. Hers alone, without any regent to guide her decisions. And she would be responsible for her people's safety.

What would I do, if I were in her situation? It was hard to say. I wasn't responsible for anyone except myself. I didn't have any people. Not really, other than Peck. Peck was my people. I'd do anything to prevent someone from hurting her. If I had been given an ultimatum like Alessa, would I have chosen to take away the freedom of others to protect my best friend?

Orlen was right. The weight of the queendom's fate was not on me or Beaman or Orlen. It was on Sonora. She would be the one dealing with the loss of the Peace when she didn't sign the contract. *If* she didn't sign it.

It made sense, then, that when I had left the tower room that night, I'd seen a flicker of uncertainty in her eyes, as though even she wasn't sure what the right thing to do was. The flicker was small.

But it was there.

18

How to Be Surprised

ake up, both of you!"

For a second I thought that the low voice and rough arm jostling me belonged to Hut Tratte. But no, I opened my eyes to the bleary gaze of the guardian we'd overstuffed with mussels the night before. She shined a lamp in my face. Others in the room groaned at the barked order.

"Turn the light off!" one groaned.

"Wake up, who? What? What time is it?" another grumbled.

"I only need Stub and Beaman," said the guard. "The rest of you still have an hour until you report at six." She nudged me again.

"I'm awake," I said, rolling out of bed. I felt like I'd never gone to sleep. I pulled my apron from its hook and fastened it.

Beaman was not so responsive. He remained curled up

on the thin mattress placed beside mine, muttering something about pancake toppings.

"*Up!*" yelled the guard.

He startled awake and nearly bonked heads with the guard. He rubbed his neck and looked around. "The others aren't up yet."

"No, and I shouldn't be up either," she said. "But word came from the castle. There's an attendant waiting outside for you two." She raised a thick eyebrow. "What sort of trouble are you in?"

As though I was going to answer that. In any case, I wasn't sure what the trouble was. It was far too early for Renart to hand me over to the matron. Wasn't it?

"We're coming." I pulled Beaman out of bed and grabbed the bulbous rucksack from under my bed. "In case I'm sent to market," I explained, coughing hard to cover up Orlen's weak protests.

He'd fallen asleep on Peck the moment we'd returned from the tower. I plucked him from her back and placed him in my apron as we hurried down the hall. Hoping Peck would stay quiet, I threaded one arm into the sack's straps and swung it onto my shoulder.

"What's going on? Who's summoning us?" Beaman asked as we walked down the short corridor.

His apron still hung from his hand as we met the

attendant, a worried-faced girl with thick plaits of hair. Her deep blue uniform was rumpled, as though she, too, had been sleeping.

"Stub and Beaman Cork?" she asked.

"Yes," I said.

"Queen Sonora requests your presence. I'm one of her attendants."

"The queen?" I asked, both shocked and relieved.

Beaman rubbed his eyes. "At five o'clock in the morning?" He tied his apron strings. "She can't want breakfast this early. She doesn't even care about food."

"The queen is feeling quite ill. She's refused the castle healer. She's locked her doors and refused all help. She insists on seeing you. Follow me."

For the third time, I knocked on the door and got no answer. "Sonora," I called. "It's us. Stub and Beaman. Are you okay?"

Footsteps thudded across the room. A bolt slid open with a clang. Sonora opened the door an inch. She peeked out with wide, feverish, frightened eyes. "Are you alone?" She caught sight of the attendant behind us. "You! Go away!"

The attendant bobbed a bow and scurried down the hall.

"Come in." Sonora breathed in and out, then fanned herself.

She wore loose trousers the color of summer grass, and a

flowing tunic that matched. Her hair hung long and free, absent of its usual adornments. On her feet were soft leather sandals. She opened the door just enough for us to squeeze through, then slammed it shut and turned the bolt to lock it once more.

The large, open room smelled of sweetbriar soap and something slightly savory and spicy, like the royal city's market square. Peck flew from my arms and settled onto a thick green rug.

Beaman sniffed the air. "Why do I smell corn fritters?"

"I don't know!" Sonora spun around. "I don't know what's happening. I've felt nauseous and dizzy all night long. I don't think I even fell asleep—I think I fainted again. When I came to, I looked like this." She pointed to herself. "And come see this!"

She pulled us through a small doorway to an alcove filled with piles and piles of trousers and tunics in different colors. Several dresses hung as well, made of fine silk but without any embroidery. "This was full of horrid, fancy dresses. And awful shoes!" Her face was covered in a thin sheen of sweat. "They've all changed." She stabbed a finger at rows upon rows of expensive dress shoes and boots. "They're all comfortable now!" She let out a strange, garbled laugh. "I tried them! Every pair!"

"Sonora," Orlen said evenly. "Perhaps you need to lie down."

"Ha! Yes! The bed!" Sonora laughed wildly. "Look at the bed."

She yanked us into her quarters and pointed to the bed, large and lush, hung with the thinnest of gray silk curtains. Each curtain was pulled to a post. Enchanted fans hung, softly circulating the air.

If she had a problem with that bed, I was half tempted to ask her to trade for the one I'd gotten. "It's . . . very nice," I said.

Sonora stared at us "It *is* very nice. That's the problem! It's nice now. Nice and squishy, with pillows that aren't just for decoration. And it's *bouncy*. Go on—jump on it."

Beaman shrugged and leaped onto the bed. He bounced twice, then fell. "It *is* squishy."

"But it wasn't like that before." Sonora marched over to the unlit hearth, touching items and muttering about how they'd changed. She slumped into a brown sofa and pumped a fist against it, half laughing, half crying. "Even these cushions have changed! They used to be terribly stiff. I don't understand! What's going on?"

Orlen crawled from my scarf, his eyes wide. "Sonora, pull back your hair, dear, and turn around. Please," he said gently. "Mm-hmm," he murmured, his gaze lingering on her ears. "Have you ever taken those bottom earrings out—the jewels?"

She shook her head. "Mother left them in, according to custom—to honor my birth parents."

Orlen touched the jewel on his bracelet, then raised a hand to his chin. "I see. And how long have you been fainting, dear?"

Sonora let out a breath and wiped her eyes. "Just the last month or so."

Orlen stroked his chin, his expression blank, then bewildered. "But no," he said softly. "That's preposterous."

"What is?" asked Beaman.

"Quiet, Beaman. Sonora, you're thirteen today?" Orlen asked.

"Yes. Why?"

He mumbled to himself for a moment. Then, slowly, his face changed from baffled to hopeful. "Yes," he whispered. His breath came faster as he looked around the room. "Oh, my word. *That's it.*"

"What?" all of us demanded.

He clasped his hands. "I can't believe I didn't see it before. I've known you your entire life." He laughed. "Or nearly."

"What are you talking about?" Sonora asked.

"I never would have guessed," Orlen said, his breaths coming hard and fast. "You've been fainting, light-headed, feeling like you're going to jump out of your skin, yes?"

Sonora nodded.

"It normally happens much earlier. There's only one reason why your magic would come in so late."

"My magic? You think I did this?" Sonora took a step
away from me. She looked at Orlen warily. Then she turned
to me. "What's happening?"

I stared back at the queen of my queendom. She was asking me, Stub-the-Nuisance, for my thoughts. I knew a tiny
bit about hope and I knew a lot about liars. I knew very little
else about the world, and even less about magic.

"What's going on?" Sonora shook her fingers and her
clothing changed from green to blue to red, and then back to
green. She jumped, as though trying to run away from herself.

"I'm not sure . . . clearly, you're a wizard, but you've
been here since you were a baby." Orlen agreed. "It's possible that one of your birth parents passed along the power
here in Maradon, but in that case, your magic should have
come in years ago." He frowned. "And though you're clearly
out of control, I couldn't do this level of magic until I was a
grown man. Unless . . ."

Something Orlen had mentioned in the mountains
stirred in my brain. What was it that he'd said about wizards
coming into magic?

Orlen let out a sudden gasp. His chin quivered with

some sort of withheld knowledge. "Sonora . . . do you happen to have any marks on your arms? Stub, walk closer to her." He fumbled against the scarf's cloth. "Take me out of this thing!"

I did as he asked as, puzzled, Sonora lifted her loose tunic sleeve and pushed it all the way up. "I have a small birthmark on my shoulder," she said.

He nodded, holding his breath. He studied her arm for a long moment, then let loose with a strange burst of laughter at the sight of the reddish triangle. A huge smile stretched over Orlen's face. He rubbed his hands together. "It's true," he whispered excitedly. He danced an odd sort of jig. "Ha!" he cried. "Ha-*ha!*"

Beaman frowned and glanced my way. "Should we be worried about him?"

"Quiet, Cork!" Orlen barked. "Sonora, my dear, don't you see? You're a *kincain*! That's why Lacera banished you. She wouldn't have wanted any competition when you grew up."

"A kincain? Oh!" Beaman enthusiastically waved his hand in the air. "I know that one! The nasty, evil wizard— she's a kincain." He patted himself on the shoulder, then picked up Peck, who was bobbling around his feet. Then his face fell. "Oh . . . so, um, well . . ." He took three large steps away from Sonora.

Sonora looked horrified. "I'm a nasty, evil wizard?"

"Don't be ridiculous, dear! You're neither nasty nor evil." Orlen said. "You're just a very *talented* wizard!" His voice bubbled over with excitement.

Beaman relaxed and sniffed the air. "It definitely smells like corn fritters in here. Did you make that happen?" He sniffed again, then followed the scent to the top of a wardrobe. "You did! There's a whole pile up here! I knew you had to have a favorite food!" he cried triumphantly, stuffing a few in his mouth.

"Those were plain biscuits before," Sonora said miserably. "Oh, I don't feel well."

"But why would Lacera banish a powerful wizard here?" I asked, placing Orlen on my shoulder. "Wouldn't she think it would help you break the spell that keeps all the wizards in Maradon?

He waved a dismissive hand. "She needed Sonora out of the way. Also, wizards, even kincains, require proper training to hone their skills. She likely thought that Sonora would get none of that here. And there's no possible way that Lacera would know that the baby she banished would turn out to be the queen!"

He clapped his hands. "Sonora, with your talent, we might just restrain her! We'll have a chance! We've got, what . . ." He started to count on his fingers, but quickly stopped. "A day to train. Not much, but it'll have to do." He leaped from my shoulder to Sonora's. "Please try something for me. Do you see this space in front of the hearth?"

Sonora nodded.

"Now, don't think," said Orlen. "*Feel*. Harness your energy. See what's there—what's all around you. Shift things to what you need. Whatever *you* need."

Sonora's frantic breaths became more even. She raised her hands. They remained there, suspended for a moment. Then her fingers began to move. Her arms swayed.

I felt myself dragged forward as the brown sofa became a soft, moss-covered log. Beaman was also pulled to the rug, which was now growing with real grass. The hearth sprang forward and reformed in a circle. The room darkened, and the ceiling filled with stars.

Sonora opened her eyes. She stepped forward into the cozy circle in wonder and sat beside me. The grass continued to grow past our ankles, then past our waists, then our shoulders.

"STOP!" yelled Orlen.

Sonora shook her hands and everything vanished. We all lay sprawled on a circular blue rug in front of an unlit hearth. Peck poked at a piece of the rug's yarn, then looked up at me, disappointed.

Beaman stared at Sonora with renewed awe. "Orlen, maybe she could return you to your size."

"Absolutely not! Not yet, anyway. I don't want to take any chances. Sonora, please hold your hands together. Stand up, dear. Press your fingers against your heart. The magic will filter back into you."

Sonora pressed her hands to her heart and stood. Her dress grew bright; then its colors swirled and shifted, turning into the one she'd worn at the banquet. She pulled at the neck and stepped in circles. "How did I do that?" she said.

"By magic." Orlen slid down to my apron pocket. "Do keep those hands up like I told you. You're going to need some lessons," he said. "I know just the place. The wizard district."

"But her birthday feast is tonight," Beaman protested. "How can she go anywhere?"

Orlen frowned. "She'll have to be sick."

"I definitely feel sick," said Sonora.

"There you go," Orlen said quickly. "She's sick today. The birthday feast will have to happen without her. Renart can preside. He'll enjoy it. Meanwhile, Stub and I will slip her out of the castle, using those marvelous passages, and Beaman, you'll stay here and make excuses. Don't let anyone in."

That plan was fine with me. I hadn't been looking forward to the possibility of serving Matron—no *Lady*—Tratte at the queen's birthday banquet.

Beaman looked disappointed. "What am I supposed to do if people ask for her?"

Orlen waved a hand in the air. "Moan and groan in a voice that sounds less like yours and more like hers. Then just say that she won't let you open the door. She's the queen. She gives the orders, right? Right."

Beaman let out a long sigh. "Fine. Can I at least have more fritters?"

"You've eaten them all," Orlen pointed out. "She can't conjure them from nothing—enhancements always require a base matter. And how can you think of food at an exhilarating time like this? Yes, I feel decidedly exhilarated!"

Beaman frowned. "Food is exhilarating too," he muttered.

Orlen climbed from my pocket and slid down to Peck, who was gobbling corn-fritter crumbs. He gave her a hearty pat on the feathers. "I suddenly feel like I'm eighty years old! You're one of us, Sonora! You're going to have the chance to help save your own true people. Isn't it wonderful?"

Sonora looked at a painting on the wall—one of her and her mother. She was three or four, and Queen Nadina was holding her. They were on a picnic blanket spread beneath a leafy tree. They were both laughing. "Wonderful," she murmured, her voice tinged with doubt as she looked at me. "Isn't it?"

I nodded. It *was* wonderful. Now the wizards stood a much better chance against their captor. Sonora was a queen. And a powerful wizard. Just like Lacera.

She belonged to two queendoms now. I hardly belonged to one. Sonora was bold and brave and, now, magical. Beaman was so sure of the place he belonged. And I . . . well, Peck and I were a team. Nothing else mattered. Well, except saving the queendoms. That was what mattered most.

"Are you okay?" Beaman tapped my shoulder. "Why are you rubbing your ear like that?"

"What? Oh. No reason." I pulled my hand down, picked up Peck, and placed her in my rucksack. "We better go."

"All right." Beaman looked wistfully at the empty plate on the wardrobe. He fumbled inside his trouser pocket. "Sonora?"

Sonora pulled down on a wall torch and pressed against the stone. A passage opened. "Yes?" she said, turning.

He held out a stale lump of bread. "Any chance you can make this into a snack?"

19

How to Be a Wizard

$\backsim$

Your tunic's changing color again," I whispered to
Sonora as we swerved through the market square.
"Try to keep it gray and pull up your hood. The
wizard district isn't far."

"I can't help it!" she said, rubbing her hands against her
shirt. It shifted from pale green to pale yellow. "Everything's
changing. I can't stop it."

"It's because you're anxious," Orlen said, his voice
impatient. He sat atop Peck in my rucksack.

"And you're bossy and stodgy."

"Yes," Orlen grumbled. "Well, let's try shrinking you
and taking away your powers and see how you feel." He
blinked. "Keep your changes to shades of blue and nobody
will notice."

He was right. Maradon Cross was a sea of Peace-blue
tones. Every home and shop sported flags and flowers. A
royal wagon drawn by a single enormous hog was filled to

the brim with ribbons. It stopped every fifty feet to let attendants jump off and drape them across windows and over
doors. Three young girls splashed each other with blue flecks
as they repainted the outside of a shop. One waved a happy
brush and smiled at us as we turned down the alley to the
wizard district.

Large banners were strung across the entire street. I
squinted at the words and was grateful when Orlen crawled
up my shoulder and read them aloud:

> *Happy Peace Day, Maradon!*
> *In honor of the momentous anniversary,*
> *the wizard district will be closed for the entirety*
> *of the holiday. Peace be with you!*

"Excellent," Orlen declared. "That means Gwenda has
alerted everyone." He pointed toward the Hungry Goat.
"What are you waiting for? Go in!"

As we stepped inside, Sonora looked warily at the crowd
of wizards in the tavern. Every table was occupied, and other
wizards were milling around.

"It's all right," I said. "This way." I waved to Jan at the
bar. "Is Gwenda down there?"

"Yes—with Bastian and Verett." He looked puzzled at
the sight of Sonora, but tipped his hat and tilted his head

toward the staircase in the back. "Any news?" he asked anxiously.

"Lots."

He swung the towel he'd been wiping the counter with onto his shoulder. "Any of it good?"

I glanced at Sonora. "Very good. Give us some time; then I'm sure they'll share everything."

"I'll be waiting." He nodded to the tavern tables. "We all will."

A single-stringed instrument sent delicate music down from the candle orbs, striking notes that waxed and waned. The three old wizards swarmed around the drawing board, each with a glass in hand as they argued over a large map of the castle.

"No, no," Gwenda insisted. "We must have more than one entry. Look again. Think." She took a sip of water, wiped her brow with a free hand, then smiled at us. "There you are." She looked at the person next to me and choked on her water.

All arguments halted.

"Queen Sonora," said Verett. He raised his glass. The others followed suit.

"Hello," she said quietly. Her tunic blushed along with her.

"*Kincain* Sonora," Orlen said. He scrambled from my

scarf to my shoulder. "The tides are turning in our favor. It seems Lacera banished her here as a baby. Her powers came in just this morning. I've brought her for a day of training." His smile melted away. "Because a day is all we have."

Gwenda, Bastian, and Verett all stared in astonishment.

"A kincain!" repeated Bastian, twirling his mustache. His lips curled up with glee. "Are you sure?"

"A kincain?" asked Verett. "Are you serious?"

"Yes and yes," Orlen said abruptly. "I'll explain shortly. First, a demonstration." He clapped his hands. "Watch this. Sonora! Do you see that empty teacup on the table? Make it a wooden bucket."

Sonora raised her hand. She nibbled on her lip and closed her eyes. The teacup swelled to the size of a bucket. A warm, spicy scent filled the air. Steam curled up from the liquid inside. It became a bowl of soup, then a wooden feeding trough. Then the trough caught on fire.

"No worries," cried Bastian, dousing the flames with a pitcher of water. "Still impressive!"

Verett looked skeptical.

"Well," Orlen said sheepishly, "We've got a bit of work to do."

"Yes, we do," said Gwenda. "But it's about time we had some good news. Welcome."

· · ·

Hours later, Peck happily ate table scraps while Sonora practiced magic.

She made plates the size of tables and candles that stretched as high as the room. Once she caused her tunic to grow until the entire Dungeon Room was hidden in a green cloth nest. She hardened things, softened things, brightened shadows, darkened lights. At one point I looked up to see that the sofa had changed into Sonora's bed, and the queen was buried under the covers. "Stub!" she cried. "Help me!"

I crawled into the bed next to her. "You're doing great. This the best bed I've ever been in."

"It's no use!" Sonora yelled. The bed turned back into a sofa. She let out a cry of rage, then turned a bowl of soup into a table full of large vegetables. "I can't control it!"

"Give it time, dear," Bastian said.

"That's one thing we don't have," Verett argued.

"I can't fight a wizard." She sighed and looked over her teachers. "I don't know what to do. And the Peace . . ." She rubbed her temples and looked at me. "I have such a headache."

"Yes," said Gwenda. "That's your magic coming in. Yours is stronger than most, but now that it's come in, the shifting inside you will settle by day's end." She took Sonora by the shoulders. "My dear, you are among your own. You're one of us. And we are so happy to have you on our side."

Sonora didn't meet Gwenda's eyes. Instead she looked down. "Thank you. May I have a break?"

"In a moment, dear. I just want you to try one more thing. Take a quick sip of tea while I tell you what we'll be doing."

Sonora's eyes flickered with the same uncertainty I'd seen that morning. It was slight, but I saw it. Suddenly my jealousy shifted into something softer. She wasn't only *part* of two queendoms. She was *responsible* for them.

"She's doing well," Orlen said.

I flinched. I hadn't even realized that he'd crawled back into my scarf. "She is," I said.

I watched as Sonora took in her orders. Her fingers flexed the whole time, and the mug of tea in her hand grew and shrank with her breaths. I knew what it was like to be told what to do. To have consequences for failing. To feel like you had no choices.

I felt a rustling in my apron. I put my hand in and pulled out a weakly wiggling paper dragonfly—the one that Bastian had made. "The tower's staircase is narrow—will you all go up in a line to confront her?"

Orlen grimaced. "I won't be doing anything at all. I'm useless."

"You're not. You're the reason everyone has a chance at freedom."

"No," he said ruefully. "I'm the reason everyone is here. I shouldn't even be helping to plan."

"What about the plan?" Gwenda asked. She wiped her forehead and lifted a glass of water. The other wizards joined her on a break. "Have you come up with something, brother?"

"No—well, yes, but . . . it's not my place." He stared at his feet.

"It's everyone's place." Gwenda sat at the table beside him.

"She's right," said Verett. "We're in this together."

"Tell us," urged Bastien.

Orlen cleared his throat. "I was thinking," he said slowly, "that you all could enter through the sea cave where the dragon is, and then—"

Crash! A cup exploded on the floor. Verrett stared at the shards of glass sailing across the room, then at Orlen. "Pardon? Dragon?"

"Dragon?" echoed Bastien.

Gwenda looked at him sharply. "A *dragon*? Below the castle? Are you serious?"

"Yes, a dragon. I'll explain more later. The point is, we'll need to get the passage maps Sonora spoke of. There are cracks in the wall the dragon is chained to—that means it will be all the more dangerous.

"There are younger wizards among us, but none are equipped to subdue a dragon. We'll have to hope that together we can subdue it. As for Lacera, our best bet is to take her by surprise, like she did with us. The Peace Day feast is going to be held outside. We'll gather in the Grand Hall and somehow draw her into the room."

"But," Gwenda argued, "what if the dragon tears itself free of its bindings? If it breaks loose, we'll need all the magic we can get to face it. Can't Sonora come with us?"

Sonora shook her head. "I need to be in the market square during the day, as usual, if you don't want anything to seem amiss—and I need to be at the meeting. How can I be in two places at once?" she asked.

"I have an idea for that." Orlen began pacing on the table. "Sonora's a kincain. A very powerful one, particularly in illusions, if today is any indication. So . . ."

The other wizards looked baffled, except Bastian, who grinned hugely.

"Aha! Now *that* would be some clever magic," he said. "Do you think Sonora can do it?" He nodded at me. "And can *you* do it? Can you act like her?"

"Do what?" I asked nervously. "And act like who?" Then I saw the direction this was going. "Oh . . . oh *no*. No, I couldn't."

"You could." Orlen smiled. "Stub, how would you like to be a queen for a day?"

I laughed. "You want me to be the queen of Maradon?

They'll see through me in a second! It's ridiculous! I can't." I met Sonora's eyes, looking for confirmation.

Instead she gave me a grim nod. "I feel the same way every day."

"You'll do fine," Gwenda said gently, putting a hand on Sonora's shoulder. "If we're going to break the contract, we'll need your help." She shook her head. "It still astounds me that I actually thought Maradon's Peace could have been made simply with letters."

The paper dragonfly fluttered over to Orlen and poked his back. I plucked it away and held it in front of me. I couldn't quite believe it was made of paper, just like a letter. As the magical object squirmed between my fingers, wheels turned in my mind. Maybe letters *could* make a difference.

The letter my mother had left for Matron Tratte was evidence of that—it had dictated my very life.

"Orlen," I said, tugging on my scarf. "How fast can Wintrellian swallows fly?"

He gripped the fabric. "Settle down, you'll make me fall and break a hip. So fast it would make your head spin. Why?"

"And how far is it from Tartín's royal city to our own?"

His eyes rolled up in thought. "It would be approximately a three-day march from the mountain border."

"And will the swallow really send messages wherever you tell it to?"

"Yes." Orlen studied me curiously. "Stub . . . why are you asking these very specific questions?"

"You'll see. Sonora?"

She turned to me with an exhausted sigh. "What?"

I held up the dragonfly. "Do you think you can make this look like a Wintrellian swallow?"

"A what?"

"A *this*." Bastian pulled up his sleeve, revealing a swallow tattoo. He blushed. "It's my only one." He tilted his head toward his brother. "You-know-who over there did it."

I grinned. "It's perfect. Sonora, if you can manage it, I have an idea. Orlen and I will have to hurry to the castle and back. I'll need to borrow your necklace. And I'll need your help writing a letter. . . ."

I curled my body toward the fire in Gwenda's quarters over her room. Peck and Orlen and I had completed our daytime mission to steal the swallow. Only time would tell if it had any impact. My evening had been filled with drills on how to act during the public feast and tower meeting. Early the next day, I was to sneak into the castle and emerge as a feeling-much-better Sonora. My mind felt muddled with the knowledge that I, Stub-the-Nuisance—a nobody by trade— would be wearing the mask of a queen.

A flutter of wings interrupted the thought. A comforting

thump landed on my belly. I raised a hand and stroked Peck's new feathers. She looked lovely in her disguise as a miniature owl with a broken wing. After Peck had been transformed, we realized that we weren't sure how long Sonora's illusions would last, so my transformation wouldn't come until the early hours of morning.

I squeezed Peck twice. "I'm here," I told her. "You're here."

Instead of poking back, Peck's beak nuzzled my tunic pocket for treats. Finding none, she fluttered down to the floor and settled next to Orlen.

"Sorry, girl. I don't have anything. Beaman's not here, or he'd give you something," I whispered. I hoped he was well. It couldn't have been easy, covering for the two of us and the queen all day and evening. He was cheered, however, when I told him that Sonora said that he could sleep in her fancy bed.

I startled as Gwenda placed a woven quilt over me and handed me a full mug.

"To help you sleep," she said. "It's warm milk." She winked. "Not magic, but it can work wonders."

"Thank you," I said, sitting up.

"You look like you're up worrying."

I blew steam from the liquid and took a small sip. It tasted like a warm blanket in a cup. I took a longer sip. "I was thinking . . . what if it rains tomorrow and they have to change the feast to being inside? Or what if your magic isn't strong enough, even with Sonora? Or what if Lacera hurts all of you? Or does something even worse than that?"

The old wizard tilted her head thoughtfully. "Those things could all happen. I've spent time being afraid of the worst. I've spent time hoping for the best. I've done both at times." She placed a handkerchief over her tiny, sleeping brother, then sat on the chair beside me. "Tonight I'm just hoping."

I took another sip and looked at her fingers. "Can I ask something else?"

"Certainly, dear."

I wrapped my hands around my knees. "Where does your magic come from?"

Gwenda's gaze shifted to a framed painting on the wall. It matched the map of Wintrel that hung in the lower room of the Hungry Goat.

"As a girl, I often wondered why a certain flock of geese would fly the same path each year over our queendom." She stood and traced her homeland's borders. "One year, I traveled to another northern island with my aunt and saw their nesting grounds. My aunt told me that after creating nests, the parents gave birth, taught their young to forage, and then died.

"The young grew strong and flew back over Wintrel to whatever place they were going back and forth to. I thought I was seeing the same birds, but it was their children." She leaned down and smoothed my hair. "How in the world did they know the way to go, do you think?"

"I don't know."

"Neither do I." She smiled softly. "And that was a long way of saying that I don't know where our magic comes from either, dear. We are given what we are given. Talents and shortcomings. Then we get to choose what we do with both."

Orlen sputtered in his sleep, then rolled over to his other side, nestling against Peck's downy feathers.

"He thinks it's his fault that you're stuck here," I said quietly. "That's why he left you and went to the castle. That's why he stayed away."

Gwenda nodded. "I think I knew that." She looked at Orlen. Then at me. "Get some sleep," she said softly. "You will need your strength tomorrow. You and my brother both. Good night." She leaned close and kissed me gently, just over my nose.

I drifted to sleep, touching the tingling spot on my forehead.

20

How to Be a Peace Queen

〰️

I was wrong to worry about the weather. All day long in market square, the sun had shone brightly. And now, as I sat alone at my own raised table at the head of the Peace Day feast, the sea was calm and the sky was clear. Both were shades of Maradon's chosen Peace color. The day, at least, was cooperating. Unlike my clothing and adornments.

I pulled at the neck of my tight-fitting, bejeweled tunic and fiddled with the bracelets on my arms. The royal dining chair that had been created especially for the anniversary was itchy against my bottom and back. I sat upon the grooves of a carving of the Peace flag, and at my back the chiseled faces of previous Peace Queens bore into me. Like my first glimpse of Maradon City, it was all too much, even without the fate of my queendom to fret over.

I stroked the owl in my lap for comfort and slipped her a piece of bread. Renart had sent the altered version of Peck more than one irritated glance, but as Sonora had suggested,

I simply smiled sweetly with my own altered face and said, "Look what turned up in the back garden! It was left behind and needed a home. Don't you just *love* owls, Renart?"

He'd only scowled in response. Or maybe it was his attempt at a smile. I really couldn't tell.

I'd asked to keep my larger glow rock and Minera's fireburst near me as well, and so Sonora had turned my rucksack into a silky carrying bag embroidered with the Peace flag on both sides. I'd stuffed all the empty space inside it with sweets to hand out in order to justify keeping it with me. It seemed a silly time to be passing out candy, but as one of the children had said, *You probably get so much candy that you can't stand it anymore!*

I'd laughed, but the young boy's words had rung true. I was free . . . but I'd learned so much that made me feel the opposite. I felt like the wall around the tavern in Trapper's Cove had grown higher. And now I had many more people stuck inside with me to save. That kind of freedom came with the responsibility to give it to others.

"I promised you we'd see the lights," I whispered to Peck. "I haven't forgotten. But first, once again, we've got to get through tonight. My eyes steady, your beak ready, friend."

Perhaps by the end of the night, all would be well. I'd place a lit wizard match against the fireburst that remained at the bottom of the bag and I'd celebrate being brave and foolish and free as it sailed into the sky. And the rest of Maradon would join me in sending singing lights all the way to the stars. Perhaps. But my life had taught me enough to give me serious doubts.

I felt a tug in my trouser pocket. I tugged back twice, the signal to say it was safe for Orlen to speak.

"How close are we to sunset?" he whispered.

The sun was less than an hour from kissing the horizon. "Close," I whispered back.

I scanned the crowd. Despite my letter, the queen of Tartín had not yet arrived. My only comfort was the sight of Beaman. As we'd planned, he'd offered to take my place as server when I'd failed to show up for my kitchen duties.

"Do you see that boy over there?" I called to a nearby attendant. "I like the look of the dish he's serving. Please tell him to come here."

The attendant left my side and soon Beaman hurried over, easily outpacing her. He placed a heavy tray on my table.

"More fish, Your Highness?" he asked, scooping a portion neatly onto my plate. He lowered his voice. "It's almost time." He reached into his pocket and handed me a twig with short green needles. "It's rosemary," he said. A forced smile slipped slowly from his face. "For remembrance. That's what Pap says. Rosemary for remembrance. Take it. Just in case."

I took the green frond and sniffed it. It smelled woody and pungent. Like the pine trees that rose above the swamp. "In case of what?"

His voice wavered. "In case, well . . . in case something happens and we don't see each other again. You know what I mean."

I did. I reached out and squeezed the hand that had passed me the token.

He squeezed back. "Are you ready to meet with her?"

"It's like you said when I shoved you out of the batteral's nest . . ." I lifted Peck and placed her into the decorated bag. "I'm not ready. But I'll go anyway." I put the rosemary next to the fireburst. "Thank you. I'll see you soon."

Beaman's eyes grew wide. He picked up the tray quickly and bowed as a stiff finger pressed the edge of my shoulder.

"Pardon, Your Highness. I'm afraid I'll have to steal you away from the feast for a bit. Rest assured, you'll be back in time for the fireburst display."

I turned to see Renart, resplendent in a brilliant blue tunic embroidered with silver thread and tassels. His hair and serious expression both looked freshly oiled as he scrutinized the retreating figure of Beaman.

I placed a fisted hand on my belly and smiled, the way Sonora had told me to do even if I was frustrated with the duties that came with being a queen. But the truth was, my gut had been clenching all day from duties that had little to do with normal royal tasks.

It had clenched in the morning while I was sneaking into Sonora's room and dismissing Beaman to his kitchen service.

It had clenched while I was convincing Beaman that his future career as a chef wouldn't be ruined by him disappearing before the feast was fully over in order to meet the wizards in the tunnels below the castle.

It had clenched while I was being bombarded with clothing choices and attendants and choosing a flowy tunic with deep hand pockets for Orlen's sake, while I was making conversation at the public feast in Market Square, and now at the banquet . . . my stomach had turned inside out and back again more times than I could count.

Still, I did what I'd managed to do all day. I cleared my throat and spoke. "Certainly, Renart." I rose. It was still odd to hear Sonora's voice coming out of my mouth.

"Please, let me escort you." He held out his hand.

As we walked toward the royal entrance from the garden, a voice called out—a horribly familiar voice.

"Your Highness! Oh, Your Highness, a brief word! May I just say, before you go, that—"

I turned and raised my eyebrows. "Lady Tratte. Previously of Trapper's Cove. Owner of the Tinderbox Tavern."

The former matron's cheeks pinked with pleasure as she

bowed to me. "That was last week. My son owns the tavern now, and I have new business ventures to pursue. But you know of me?"

I smiled. "I do indeed. Renart, give me and Lady Tratte a moment alone, won't you?"

Renart looked anxiously at the sky. It wouldn't be more than half an hour before the sun sank into the horizon. He offered me a jerky bow and an annoyed glare. "Of course, Queen Sonora. A *moment*."

As he turned, I linked arms with my former captor and strolled toward a tall hedge. "Yes, Lady Tratte, my regent makes it a point to have me memorize people's names." I rolled my eyes. "A silly practice, I think. Giving people titles is overrated, don't you think?"

Her brow wrinkled in confusion. "Oh, I—well, um . . ."

"In fact, I once knew a woman who thought giving any name at all was overrated. She thought it was quite the *nuisance*."

Lady Tratte stumbled at the word.

"Tell me, do you have any other children that you've left behind in Trapper's Cove? Or perhaps an apprentice?"

Now she stiffened. "No. There's nobody else there."

"Really?" As we rounded a hedge, I clucked my tongue in an excellent imitation of Renart. "That's interesting. Speaking of interesting, I know a story about an apprentice—a child abandoned by her mother." I laughed. "Forgive me, I am drawn to such stories, being an orphan myself. In any case, it's brief. Would you like to hear it?"

Lady Tratte's voice was soft and cautious now. "I—I should like to hear anything the queen has to tell me."

"Oh, good," I said, pulling her arm tighter as we circled back toward the feast. "This child was left on the porch of a tavern, with a letter indicating that the tavern owner was to raise the child and make her a proper apprentice. But the woman simply made the girl a servant. She kept her in a chicken shed and let her believe she had no choices. She told the child that she was an apprentice, but in truth she'd never registered the contract with the queendom. Why do you think a person would be so cruel?"

My former owner paled. She pressed herself against a hedgerow. "Perhaps . . . perhaps the woman herself had been raised with no choices. Perhaps she felt trapped in her own life."

I watched her squirm for half a minute. "Or perhaps the story is a false one, with no merit."

Lady Tratte recovered herself and nodded eagerly. "That's likely the case."

I nodded in agreement. "After all, it's completely unlikely—nobody in my queendom would act that wretchedly. It's as unlikely as that same poor child running away and befriending a cook and a queen and a group of wizards."

I stopped walking and patted Lady Tratte's arm. "Or as unlikely as the barefoot servant in the story wearing these," I said, lifting my dress trousers to show the bejeweled flat moccasins. I leaned close. "An unlikely change, yes. But an impossible change, no."

I looked into the matron's eyes and, for once, did not feel inclined to cower. "You did say that I'd get some shoes if you married the captain. But I'm afraid that I'm no longer available to clean your manor. And as you can see, I have my own shoes."

Lady Tratte stared openly at me now. Her eyes swept from my feet to my face. She stumbled, as though a fireburst had exploded right in front of her. "I-I don't understand," she stammered.

I smiled. "Nobody would believe you if you did."

From the corner of my eye, I saw Renart standing by the nearest banquet table. An irritated twitch about his mouth told me that he was ready for my moment to be over. I cleared my throat and smiled at the shocked face across from my own.

"Lady Tratte, someone once told me that the best way to get where you're going is by walking away from where you've been. I think they were right." I inclined my head. "So goodbye."

Ignoring my former captor's stunned expression, I walked purposely over to Renart. "I'm ready," I lied.

"Excellent. Follow me." He glanced down at Peck poking out of my bag as we left the garden and stalked down the castle halls. "Have you had that filthy animal near you all day?"

I patted his arm. "It's Peace Day, Renart—a time to embrace all people and creatures. So please do try to restrain yourself and refrain from kicking this owl, the way you did the last time one was in the castle," I said. "Now, please remind me, what is this meeting about?" I was trying to suss out exactly what Renart's motives were.

"Yes, about the meeting . . ." He cleared his throat, and looked . . . nervous? Or upset? I couldn't tell which. "I didn't want you getting apprehensive, so I withheld certain details."

I glared at him with my best Sonora glare. "I'm the queen. You're just the regent. I should be given all the details you have."

He paused and started to argue. He wanted to, I could tell. Then something odd happened. His pursed lips collapsed into a frown, and his expression grew weary. "Really, Sonora, you're much too young to have to worry about this. Your mother would have hated it." His voice grew less clipped as we passed through the back hallways of the castle. "That's why she entrusted the knowledge to me. She didn't think you'd have to deal with it at such a young age. It kept her up at night."

"What did?"

"The contract." He nodded grimly and his jaw tightened. "I never thought I'd have to deal with it either, but here we are. She left you in my care. Your duties and burdens are mine, child. The time has come to renew it, and we must do our duty."

"Contract with who?" I asked, playing dumb. I wanted to see exactly how honest he would be.

"Another queen. One who's been helping us. And we've been helping her. Don't be nervous. I'll do the talking."

It was strange. Renart's voice had softened, and there wasn't even a hint of a sneer around his lips. He was the one who looked fearful. And genuinely overwhelmed. He didn't look like he was relishing Peace Day at all. Suddenly I wondered whether we'd misjudged the regent.

"I'll explain when we get there," he said hurriedly, pulling me along with one hand and dabbing at the nervous sweat on his brow with the other. "But it's all in Maradon's best interest. All you need to do is sign your name to a document and you can get back to the festivities."

We met a hallway crossroads and I pulled him to the left— from the map I'd gone over time and time again, I knew there was a shortcut to the west tower through the Grand Hall.

I ducked beneath a tapestry, and opened the door beneath. I pulled him within the hidden staircase that we'd found on Sonora's map.

"What are you doing?" he asked.

"It's a shortcut. I know where I'm going. And I already knew about the contract, Renart."

He stopped in his tracks as the door closed behind us. I sifted beneath Peck to find one of my glow rocks. I shook it gently. "That's right. I know about the wizard queen and the dragon blood and the nature of our Peace. And I know about the letters you exchanged. I thank you for your work. I'm glad that Queen Lacera is coming. But you should have told me yourself."

"What? How . . . how do you know?" he asked, his voice hollow.

Sonora, I called in my head. *What would you say?* I got no answer, other than a reassuring poke on my side from my chicken-owl. "Listen closely," I said. "I am young. But I am the queen of Maradon. This meeting is between two queens. So I'll do the talking."

Instead of a knock on the tower door, there was a single chime.

I rose from my chair as Renart opened the tower room door to reveal a small, unaccompanied woman with long white hair, adorned in jewels. She appeared as elderly as Orlen and Gwenda, but stood straight and firm and bright. She looked kind, but I knew very well that appearances could be deceiving.

She ignored Renart, strode straight toward me, and grasped my hands in a motherly manner. "My dear Queen Sonora," she said, "I am so pleased to be here with you."

I curtsied, then gestured to the other seat at the table. "As you can see, my regent, Renart, is here. Alas, I am too young for certain official duties."

Lacera smiled warmly. "Not for this one, I assure you. But certainly, he can stay."

"Thank you." I waited for her to sit, then did the same. "I do wonder, can you tell me how the spell works and why it's worn out?" I tapped the table. "I've brought the materials, but I would love to know more about the process. I find it utterly fascinating, and my mother passed from the world before she could tell me many things."

I ignored a tickle and a pushing sensation from the pack that leaned against my leg. Orlen was no doubt trying to resist staring down the person who'd made him a prisoner.

Lacera paused. She studied me carefully. "What a charming queen you are, child." She glanced out the window facing the sea, checking the sun's position. Her lips rose in a pleased smile. "Of course I'll tell you. There are several things that can make a spell more binding. Time of day, for instance. Sunrise or sunset suits a spell that changes things. I prefer sunset." She laughed and raised the vial from the table. "As you read in my letter, this is dragon blood. An especially strong binding tool. The scale on the contract book is from the same dragon. It helps to bind my wizards to a source. I captured and gifted the young dragon to your queen Alessa."

I nodded. "To guard the Book of Peace."

Lacera's smile widened. "The Book of Peace. Such a clever name. Yes, the binding spell keeps you free. Our biggest duty as queens is keeping our people safe. It's really quite a simple trade. It only requires commitment." She raised the pen. "We both sign the book, then I perform a spell, and that's that."

She stroked the book along the iron hole in the middle. "Now, where is the key to the contract book?"

I felt the necklace chain around my throat. "Should we reevaluate the spell's borders and terms this year?" I asked. "What if the borders have changed? And what if our relationship with the wizards has changed?"

Lacera laughed gently. She traced a finger along my arm. "You are very young. Queendoms do not change. Not unless you let them." Her eyebrows rose, and she tilted my chin up with a long finger. "Which I'm certain you will not do." She spoke the last sentence with a hint of a challenge.

My heart beat faster. I stood and walked to the west window. I let my fingers graze the rough stone sill. The sun was close to the horizon. My eyes flicked toward the closed door. Beaman should be coming at any minute to interrupt the signing. I turned. "I have a question for my regent. He's my counsel."

Lacera's iron eyes locked onto me, then Renart. "Go on."

"Would my mother have signed her name in this book? Answer me honestly."

Renart did not meet my eyes. Instead, he took stock of his fine boots. Then the room. Then the book. Finally, he stood. His fingers tightened around the top of my empty chair.

"No," he said quietly. "She would not have." He cleared his throat. "But she also wouldn't want you having to lead your queendom in a time of hardship, especially not at your age."

"That's right," Lacera said firmly. "Listen to your regent. Now, unlock the book."

I lifted the chain from my neck and held the small black key in my hand. I stepped to the table. "No age is well-suited for hardship."

Where was Beaman? My mind raced, trying to think of a way to delay the meeting.

"What if," I said carefully, "we did not need the Peace? What if Tartín became an ally?"

Lacera laughed. "Oh, child. This is exactly why you require a regent. As I just said, people don't change. Nor do queendoms."

"But what if they do?" I asked, keeping my voice light and innocent. "What if I sent the queen of Tartín a letter, explaining our queendom's situation and asking for a new start? It has, after all, been a hundred years. Couldn't it make a difference?"

The queen of Wintrel rose slightly, taking one of my hands in both of hers. "My dear girl," she said, "don't bother. Sending that letter would only show weakness." She cupped my cheek. "You must protect your people."

A fireburst exploded outside the western window, where the sun had finally touched the sea. Lacera's lips pursed. "Now let's get this book signed. So that your celebration can continue."

Celebration. A fireburst might travel far enough to buy us time. And, thanks to Minera, I happened to have one handy. My carrying bag lay against my chair.

I lowered my eyes and nodded humbly. "Yes, I'm sure you know best. I must protect all the people in my queendom. That's exactly why I borrowed your Wintrellian swallow and sent the letter I just mentioned."

Lacera frowned. "You did what? Give me that key, child."

"Peck, stick!" I yelled.

While the queen of Wintrel stared at me with a mixture of confusion and annoyance, my small chicken-owl dug with all her might in the purse and flung into the air the only stick she found. With one hand I caught the fireburst she tossed to me. I wrapped the keychain around it and reached into my pocket. Orlen passed me his wizard match.

"What is this nonsense?" Lacera snapped.

Renart looked uncertainly between me and Lacera.

I struck the match.

With growing clarity, Lacera's mouth dropped open. "What are you *doing*?"

I smiled as I lit the fuse. "Happy Peace Day."

I held the spitting, sputtering, sparkling bundle out the window. As Lacera sprang forward, the flame hit powder. I released my hold, and the fireburst sailed over the sea. I tracked the smoke line and watched it burst with brilliant blue light.

I braced myself for some sort of blow. None came. I turned, wondering why Lacera wasn't angrier.

It didn't take long to find out.

"Interesting choice." She lifted a delicate chain off her own neck. "Good thing I made an extra key. You can't trust anyone in this world, you know." She unlocked the book, then grabbed my wrist and yanked me to the table.

Renart rushed forward to pull her back. "Take your hands off her!" he cried.

Lacera flicked her wrist, and he flew against the wall and slumped to the floor, groaning.

"Sign it," she said, forcing my hand to hold the pen. Dipping it into the dragon-blood vial, she spoke in an eerie, soothing voice. "It's for the best. Your first Peace queen knew that. You're doing the right thing."

I fought as hard as I could, but my body had frozen. Only my hand moved.

Queen Sonora of Maradon, it wrote without my permission.

Lacera let out a satisfied sigh and signed her name below.

She frowned. "What's going on?" she asked sharply. "Why isn't it glowing?" She glared at me. Then her glare turned to bewilderment. "Your face," she breathed. "It's changing."

My face wasn't the only thing. I felt a faint melting sensation and lifted a hand to my head. My hair was shrinking as well.

Renart gasped. "It's *you*," he said, trying to rise.

Lacera forced him against the wall once again. As she did, my hand shot out to the table so quickly that it would have been applauded by any thief in the Trapper's Cove night market. I closed the book and snatched the key. By the time the wizard queen turned to me with gritted teeth, the same hand was combing through my motley excuse for hair.

Lacera seized my hand and twisted. "Who are you?"

I grimaced. "The queen was worried," I said quickly. "She sent me in her place. I don't know where she is."

The queen of Wintrel watched me as my clothing became the simple garb of a kitchen worker. My fancy purse was now a rustic rucksack with a chicken poking out.

She narrowed her eyes and raised a hand again.

Before she could blast me against the wall, the tower door flew open.

Beaman stumbled in, breathless. My disguise had faded and Renart was collapsed on the floor. Still, my friend kept his wits about him. He bent over, breathing hard, pretending to bow and see nothing of the spectacle in the tower room. "Your Highnesses! There are twenty wizards in the Grand Hall. They're awfully mad!"

"Who are you? How did you know where we were? Twenty what?" Lacera asked.

"Queen Sonora sent me! There are twenty wizards who've taken over! We've got to help her!" Beaman shot me a meaningful glance, then bolted back down the stairs.

Renart moaned and rubbed his head, then rose.

Lacera crooked her finger and he collapsed once again. "Worthless," she said lightly. She looked at me, frozen at the table. "You're worthless too. I don't know how this has been managed, but I do hope the real Queen Sonora has true courage when I find her." She gathered the book and vial and pen in her arms and marched back down the tower staircase.

I felt my muscles slowly unwind as I watched her disappear down the passage. "I hope she does too," I murmured.

"As do I," said Orlen. "Go after her. Please."

I didn't respond, not even to acknowledge the odd timing of Orlen finally using the word "please."

I was too busy checking to see that Renart was still breathing, and then sweeping aside a tapestry that matched the one far below. I gathered my rucksack and gave Peck a quick squeeze. "It's time to be bold and foolish." With that, I rushed down the secret steps that led to the hidden door in the Grand Hall.

21

How to Face Your Fears

ᔕᔕ

I beat Lacera by a second. The moment I peeked from behind the tapestry, getting a brief, bracing glimpse of what she would meet, the tall doors of the Grand Hall blasted open. She lifted one hand casually as she entered. It took only a flick of the wrist to make every torch on the wall and candle in the room shine brighter. She strode into the Grand Hall, where the wizards stood in a straight line.

I quickly ducked past the tapestry and under a cloth-draped side table right next to the remainder of the wall hanging.

"Well, well, well!" Lacera called, taking in the display. "From one problem to another, I see."

Holding Peck close, I peeked through a gap in the cloth and saw the wizards, their faces filled with fear. Sonora was there in the middle of them, disguised in simple trousers and a tunic.

Orlen crawled to my shoulder. "Where are the other wizards?" he asked anxiously.

"I don't know. Beaman was supposed to hide them close by."

Sunset colors were starting to flood through the tall windows of the Grand Hall. And though I was no wizard, I could see why a spell might be at its most powerful during a day's end or beginning. The raised platform for royals on one side of the room was curtained with thick, crimson velvet. The day's dying light shone upon it, turning one shade of red into five.

A thunderous boom echoed throughout the Grand Hall as the doors slammed shut. Lacera's shoes clicked closer and, for a moment, I was back in my shelter in Trapper's Cove, dreading Hut's arrival. But this version of Hut could wield magic.

She placed the book, vial, and pen on the table where I hid.

"*So,*" Lacera said lightly, turning back to the group. "What's all the ruckus about? Having a secret meeting, are we?" She clucked her tongue. "This is the kind of thing that got you into trouble in the first place. Where's Queen Sonora?"

"Hurry!" Gwenda cried, her voice full of panic. "Do it now!"

The wizards' hands rose as one, and they all began to mutter. All except Sonora.

Lacera stumbled back. Her face fell for a moment; then she grimaced and smiled. With a single finger, she pointed at the empty dining tables. The tables grew and bent, then formed a fence pinning the wizards together. She lowered her head and murmured.

"My fingers!" cried a wizard. "I can't move them! They're stuck together!"

"Yes," Lacera said, raising her hands and shaking them out casually. "You're all stuck together. And stuck, stuck, stuck in Maradon you'll stay."

"We have to do something!" I whispered. Why wasn't Sonora doing anything? She looked frozen in fear.

A frantic banging sounded on the hall's outer doors. Muted screaming and shouting could be heard beyond them. "Let us in!" someone yelled. "There's a dragon outside!"

Lacera sighed. "Pity it got free. I do loathe an escaped prisoner." With an almost-bored expression, Lacera raised her pinky. The doors opened and a flood of Maradonian royals rushed into the room.

"A dragon flew over the banquet!" one of the lords cried, running so hard that he fell to the floor. "Shooting flames like you've never seen!"

"Teeth the size of swords!" shouted another man, who promptly fainted.

"It's still circling!" shouted a woman.

"It's flying away!" yelled a servant who'd just run in. "It's flying north!"

"Calm down!" Lacera shouted. She parted the people with a finger and strode through the room, up to the throne on the far end. "Everyone, stay calm! It was a wizard who brought the dragon. The wizards in this room are staging a rebellion. They want to break your Peace."

Cries of protest erupted.

"Stop!" Lacera cried. "I am here to help. I am a wizard queen from afar. Your queen and I have formed an alliance to see that these *dangerous* wizards don't break your Peace and try to take over."

The crowd quieted under the presence of the wizard queen. Whether it was her magic or her confidence or a combination, it was difficult to say.

"I can save your Peace!" Lacera called. "But I can't do that if you're all in here. I can't risk your lives." She gazed over the crowd and spread her arms in a wide sweeping motion, then drew them in. The Maradonians sprang together in a clump. With the same thrusting motion, Lacera shoved the Maradonians out of the Grand Hall with an invisible wind, ignoring their baffled murmurs and muffled hysteria as she shut the doors behind them. "You're welcome." She waved her hand and the noise outside ceased. The room was quiet once more.

Through the windows, I saw blue firebursts rising.

Around the royal city, Peace Night celebrations had begun.

"So," Lacera said, strolling over to the pinned wizards. She lifted her hands and the tables sprang aside. "Ah, there you are, Gwenda. Yes, I remember you. Are you leading this sad effort?" She clucked her tongue. "It's going about as well as the last one, isn't it?" She crooked her fingers inward and muttered a phrase.

In a frenzy of twists and turns and bumps, every wizard except Sonora was pulled toward Lacera. Sonora looked around her and stumbled forward. Was she doing it for show? Where on earth were the other wizards? I searched for Verett and Bastian among the group, but didn't see them.

Orlen clung to my ear. "Help!"

I cupped a protective hand around him and strained to pull him close. "I've got you."

Lacera pointed two fingers and dampened every wick in the hall. The only light came from the setting sun through the windows. "How shall I punish you?" she said, her voice booming through the hall. "Any ideas?"

"I have an idea." The voice came from the center of the wizards. A young girl emerged.

"You're awfully young to have ideas." Lacera laughed, then stopped abruptly when she saw Sonora's face, the one that matched mine before I'd melted back to my plain self.

She looked puzzled. "What's going on? Are you idiot Wintrellians taking the queen hostage?"

"They're not," Sonora said. "I wanted them for protection. In case . . . you tried to make me do something I didn't want to. I'm sorry," Sonora said, her voice shaking. Her jaw was tight. She made fists of her hands and placed them behind her back. "Where is my servant girl? The one I sent in my place?"

Lacera rolled her eyes. "She's probably running away from the castle. There is no real loyalty, you know. As a queen, you can only depend on yourself." Lacera clasped her hands together. "Now, I suppose this isn't really your fault," she said. Her voice grew smooth and silky. "You're so young. It's hard to know who to trust in this world. But come! Let me dress you properly and we'll renew your Peace." She crooked her finger and Sonora's clothing shimmered, then became a replica of Lacera's. She looked out the west-facing windows. "There's still time, but let's hurry. The sun has nearly set." She turned back to the table and picked up the book.

"I'm sorry," Sonora repeated. "But I can't sign it."

Lacera stepped forward, opening her arms in a motherly gesture. "Oh, my dear girl—did I hurt your hand when I slammed you and these silly servant wizards against the wall? I do apologize. I've been told that I've got an awful temper. Let me see it. I'll heal it for you straightaway."

"I *can* sign it," Sonora clarified. "But I won't."

Lacera cocked her head to one side. "Well. Here's what I think about that." The pen flew into Sonora's hand. "I think that you'll do exactly as I—" Her declaration was cut short when she saw a figure emerge from a small door that blended into the wall. "You again? Where did you come from? What are you doing?"

Beaman gulped. He looked somewhat disheveled but managed to keep his composure. He was pushing a squeaky cart topped with a full silver tea service, complete with teapot, cups, saucers, and several delectable pastries.

While Lacera watched him, I slipped the Book of Peace and other items beneath the table. It was locked again. As for the key, it was in my pocket. Things were looking up.

Then again, I knew better than anyone that good things never lasted. As long as the key was here, she might find a way to get it back. Unless . . .

"Never do what I'm about to do, Peck," I whispered. Hastily, I unstrung the key from the necklace. "Bold and foolish," I murmured, then swallowed it whole. It burned on the way down.

Orlen winced. "Better hope she doesn't slice you open to get it back."

"Shut up," I said, sticking the pen and vial into my pockets. "Save your hopes for Beaman."

I expected my cook friend to look as nervous as he'd been facing the wolves. But he seemed surprisingly in his element.

"I'm bringing the tea, Your Highness," he said. "Your Highness*es*," he corrected, with a high-pitched twitter. He made no indication that he thought anything was amiss, despite the fact that there was no formally dressed table to set the tray upon, nor chairs for them to sit at. "We just wanted to let you know how grateful we are that you are here." He nodded to Lacera. "And for your friendship. Any guest of the queen is a guest of the queendom!" he quipped. "I'll just put this on the throne platform, Queen Mara."

Lacera's anger melted into confusion. "Queen who?"

"Queen Mara of Tartín. Isn't that you?" Beaman took the tray up the short set of platform stairs with slow, deliberate steps. He sighed deeply. "Oh no, that's right! Silly me. Queen Mara is behind the curtain. Listening and waiting to sign a peace treaty."

Lacera frowned. "What are you talking about, you strange little—"

Beaman tossed the tray aside and leaped off the platform. "NOW!" he shouted.

A feral cry of war rang out, echoing over the room. The wizards trapped by the tables roared again, and their wall flew back.

"LIGHTS!" Gwenda screamed.

Every candle Lacera had extinguished flared. The lights spun in the air, then rushed toward Lacera in one great fireball.

Lacera stumbled back for a moment before straightening. She raised one hand and spoke a single word. The fireball halted in midair. She smiled. "Really? That's what you've got?" She leaned forward and blew on the flame. The light disappeared like a candle on a cake. "Listen to me carefully. You are *never* leaving."

"Beaman!" Gwenda yelled in a choked voice. "Now!"

Beaman held the servant entrance door open. A writhing torrent of bodies poured into the room.

Lacera's grin faltered as two hundred more wizards burst into the Grand Hall among a barrage of flying objects: dragonflies, plants, plates, and cups. The wizards all raised their hands once more. Everything not tied down began to fly around the room. Tapestries, tables, chairs. Candles, draperies, centerpieces. Table coverings, including the one blanketing the table I hit beneath. A chandelier's chain lowered and swooped toward Lacera. She shrieked and shattered it, spraying shards of glass everywhere.

"*ENOUGH!*" she screamed. Everything and everyone in the room froze. Lacera caught sight of me, Book of Peace in hand. "BOOK!" she yelled.

The book tore at my hands, then pulled me from under the table. I flew across the floor, still holding it.

"*You,*" Lacera sneered. "I have had enough of you." She flung her hand.

My body slammed against the raised platform. I stood weakly, and checked on Peck. She was breathing, but in bad shape.

"And *you,*" she said to Sonora. She clapped her hands and Sonora sprang to her side. "You need to learn to be a better leader. Your servant got rid of your key." She glanced at the place where the table had been. For the first time she looked flustered. She looked out the window at the setting sun. She closed her eyes and held up both hands.

The pen and vial in my pockets began to burn. So did the key in my belly. Hot, then hotter, until it felt like a dragon was blasting my entire body with flames. It was excruciating.

I fell to my knees and cried out.

"Well," Lacera said silkily. She crooked her finger and my body flew within inches of hers. "This is unexpected." She looked me over. "Empty your pockets."

My legs and insides were scorching. I did as she asked. If I hadn't, she would find Orlen.

"And the *key?*" she asked icily. When I didn't answer, she grabbed me by what little hair I had and yanked my face to hers. "The key?"

Peck's beak gently tapped my back. I forced myself to stare up at Lacera, betting on my ability to lie with a straight face. It was a skill honed over years, thanks to Matron Tratte. It was the only magic I had. "Gone," I croaked, clutching the place where the vial and pen had burned my sides. "Into the sea."

Fury and doubt filled her expression, followed by a glimmer of worry. With one finger, she flung me back into the platform.

"I don't have time for this. I hate wasting dragon blood. I need it for my banishing spell. But desperate times call for desperate measures. This will only take a moment." She fluttered her fingers, and Sonora slid across the floor, slamming into me.

Lacera marched to the table next to the tapestry and poured the entire contents of the dragon-blood vial onto the book's lock. She held out all ten fingers and muttered words. Her face strained with effort.

"Stub," whispered Orlen, who had barely spoken. He was straight as a board, and his voice came out weak and strained. "I have no magic. But I have an idea. It's an illusion spell for Sonora. I just don't know where she'll get a source."

As Orlen spoke, Peck shifted within my rucksack, as though we were back in the thief-ridden market in Trapper's Cove and she was ready to strike at any danger.

My eyes steady, your beak ready, I thought.

"I know a source," I said. I nudged Sonora. "Are you all right?"

"I am," she whispered. "But I don't know what to do. She's too powerful for me."

Still on the floor, I lifted Peck from my rucksack and gave her a kiss. "We'll see about that," I said.

After explaining my plan, while Lacera continued to struggle with the book, I squeezed both of Sonora's hands. "It'll have to be extremely fast. But you can do it. I believe in you, friend."

Sonora blinked hard. She squeezed my hands back. A determined expression filled her face. "Then I suppose I can believe in me, too. Give me five seconds."

I shouted three words as loud as I could.

"EVERYBODY GET DOWN!"

All the wizards turned to me, their eyes full of questions. But they did as I said.

Which was a lucky thing for them.

22

How to Save a Queendom

〰️

The explosion came without warning.

Peck-the-Dragon burst up through the ceiling, then down, in a tempest of red and yellow scales and feathers that glittered like jewels. Fragments of stone rained down on the Grand Hall like a hailstorm as the beast landed with a deafening bang. Smoke poured from her nostrils. Claws the length of swords clicked over the rubble-ridden room.

Each footfall shook the room. A low growling noise grew louder and louder. The dragon reared back and blazing orange flames shot through the air as her front legs met the floor once again. Her wild eyes focused on the wizard queen. She slammed a thundering foot inches from Lacera.

Then she roared.

Lacera threw her arms over her head as the force rippled through her hair, sending her stumbling backward against the table. Sonora raised both her hands. The room grew light once more. Peck-the-Dragon roared again.

The walls trembled. Lacera gasped for breath. "Nobody can summon a dragon. I don't . . . I don't believe it."

"Believe it." Sonora walked steadily toward her.

Peck opened her mouth right over Lacera's head. Her jaws glistened with saliva.

"Oh dear," Sonora said in mock concern. "I think she's hungry."

Lacera ran toward the door. Peck flew, and landed in front of her. She opened her jaws, growling and revealing teeth that put her claws to shame. The trapped wizards began to move their limbs. They all quietly pressed forward. As they did, I crept toward the platform's curtain, hoping that Beaman hadn't been bluffing.

"She wants to know how afraid you are," Sonora said. "Like you, she enjoys the flavor of fear." She took a deep breath and twirled her fingers.

Lacera gasped as her fingers sprang together. She strained to pull them apart. "How? The only way," she grunted, "is if . . ." Realization dawned on her face. "It's *you*. You're that wretched infant." She cleared her throat and attempted a shaky smile. "Talented infant, rather. How fortunate. How clever you must be to have managed to become queen. You and I are so very much alike," she said, her voice frantic. "We're both clever. Both powerful. Sonora, you can join me."

A look of disgust crossed Sonora's gentle features. "Join *you?*"

"Yes," Lacera said, her voice growing stronger and calmer—confident and charming and snakelike all at once. "We can rule both queendoms together. After all, you're not a Maradonian."

"Yes I am," she said firmly. "My mother raised me as one."

A high cackle filled the air. "Ha! Your mother would never have loved you if she knew what you are. She loathed wizards, didn't she?"

Sonora's expression faltered. "She didn't loathe anyone. She was good. She just . . . she just . . ."

Lacera smiled sadly. "She just imprisoned all the wizards I could send her way, then used their magic. Mmm, yes. So, really, if she was alive, you'd be a prisoner right now rather than a queen. Wouldn't you?"

Peck-the-Dragon began to shrink as Sonora lowered her hands, the trembling now shifting to her lips.

"I knew it," Lacera said in a quiet, satisfied voice. "I knew it was only an enhancement. You're young, Sonora. We can build your strength together. And we can build so much more. There are magical riches in Wintrel like you wouldn't believe. And Maradon has its own. We can share them. All you have to do is sign the book. What do you say?"

The queen of Maradon hesitated. Then she looked back at me, as though she hoped I could magically send her courage.

But I wasn't magical, and her eyes remained full of fear and doubt.

Fear and doubt. Well, I had plenty of experience with those two things. And I was tired of them both. With shoulders and legs aching as though I'd been through another avalanche, I stood. "She says no."

Sonora nodded gratefully and turned back. "I say no."

"Foolish child." Lacera thrust out her hand. Sonora collapsed. She picked up the fallen girl's hand. With a snap, the book and pen flew to her. "Sign it."

I glanced behind us, toward the westward windows. The sun had nearly disappeared over the horizon. The other wizards were moving. They only needed an opportunity to overpower Lacera.

Be brave, I told myself.

I lunged.

Lacera cried out as I collided with her. I wrestled her to the floor, then felt an excruciating pain as she caught my throat in both her hands. "You're too late," I said, even as I gagged and felt my vision growing dim. There was something behind Lacera's head—the outline of a girl, slowly rising. It began to fade.

Just when I was about to lose consciousness, something dropped on my forehead with a plink, then fell to the floor.

The hands around my throat weakened. Using what

remained of my strength, I twisted my body. Lacera let out a low moan as I rolled free. The room had grown strangely quiet.

My sight returned enough to see the object that had hit me.

An earring.

"My friend is right," Sonora said. "You're far too late."

In the hush that followed, a metallic clink sounded on the floor. Sonora raised her hand to her left ear. She bent down and picked up a small object that matched the one I'd seen.

Then she raised an open hand at the wizard queen, who was staring at the earring in horror. Still holding the delicate jewel, Sonora closed her fingers in a sudden fist, as though crushing a scorpion.

Lacera froze.

The room flooded with the clink of metal hitting the floor, as the other wizards' shackles fell away. Sonora swept an arm in one heaving motion, sending a flood of binding jewels onto Lacera until the wizard queen was covered in a blinding sea of treasure, wrapping her in a cage.

"There," Sonora said, wiping sweat from her brow. "There are your riches. You can have them all."

She pointed one determined finger at the Book of Peace. It shrank, then changed color. Then it reformed itself into a tube with a string hanging from the bottom.

346 · JESSICA LAWSON

"Orlen?" Sonora said. "Would you do the honors?"

"Gladly." Orlen took the wizard match from my apron and swiped it on the floor. "What was that clever line from back in the tower, Stub? Oh yes. Happy Peace Day." He lit the wick.

The fireburst zoomed through the top of the hall that had been blown open by my chicken. The lights blazed into the twilight sky above the castle, erupting in a glorious pattern of colors that looked like magical shooting stars.

"You see, Peck," I whispered. "I told you we'd see the lights."

As the wizards started to talk among themselves, I walked slowly over to Lacera, who was motionless lying completely still on the floor below the platform, covered in jewels.

I sat on the step beside her and looked over the room. I recognized people from my time spent in the wizard district. There was Jan, from the Hungry Goat. And there was Minera, talking with Gwenda. Somehow she'd made it out of the swamp after all.

A wild-eyed, chicken-sized Peck bobbed over, looking more than a little rattled. She flattened her back and I scooped her up. Beaman limped over and plopped beside me.

"What happened?" I asked, looking at his torn trousers.

He winced, then shrugged. "Oh, it's nothing."

I gave him an admonishing look. "No one can help you if they don't know that you're hurt."

He smiled. "Where did you hear that bit of genius?"

"Oh, just from this brilliant castle cook I know." I laid my head on his shoulder.

"Speaking of which," said Beaman, glancing at the tea tray on the throne table. "Does anyone want a pastry? I hate to see food go to waste. I made them using the most brilliant combination of cinnamon, cardamom, vanilla, a little extra butter—not too much, mind you, and—"

"No!"

Beaman scowled at Orlen. "Okay, I was only—"

"NO!" Orlen jumped down and landed on Lacera's finger, which was poking out of the jewelry casing. He leaned over and bit down hard.

Lacera shrieked and pulled her finger back.

Sonora hurried over and, with a twist of her fingers, secured the cage of jewels. Gwenda, Verret, and Bastian came over and repeated the spell until a thick casing was formed. By the time they were done, Lacera's fists looked like the few remaining Peace baubles hanging in the Grand Hall.

"Thank you, brother," said Gwenda. "That could have ended badly."

Orlen straightened, looking pleased. "Well, it wasn't magic. But it did the trick."

A knock sounded on the Grand Hall doors near the platform.

"Hello," a voice called. "Can someone let me in? My name is Mara. I received a letter. I've traveled from Tartín to talk."

23

How to Find Your Place

ᘓᘔ

One month after Maradon's hundredth and final Peace Day, I realized something: sunrises were growing on me. A new one was on the cusp of blooming when I heard the library door creak open. I smiled, knowing exactly who had entered. Wonderful sweet and savory scents filled the room.

"Is it breakfast time already?" I asked, turning from the east-facing window. I shuffled the papers on a nearby table into a neat stack, then looked up and laughed. "I can't eat all that!"

"You'll have to. I'm trying out new recipes." Beaman peeked his head from behind a high stack of fresh baked goods on the large tray of food he carried. He wore linens marked with the crest of Maradon Cross. His hair was pulled back in a single low braid. "Get hungry," he said. "Pap is bringing the rest in a bit. He's still getting used to his new quarters. Can you believe he agreed to continue my apprenticeship here at the castle?"

I snorted. "The queen herself offered him a high position in her kitchen, so, yes, I can believe it." I lowered my voice. "Did you make *it*?"

Beaman winked. "Under the cloth."

I peeked. It looked perfect. "Orlen, I had Beaman bake you something."

The wizard sat by the fire, holding a pen, cuddling Peck, and making notes in the margins of a small book. Above him, a stuffed dragon toy flew in lazy circles. Orlen set aside his things and stood. "Come along, Peck."

"I still can't get used to how tall you are," Beaman remarked. "And what's that?" He pointed to the hovering toy.

"Bastian brought it yesterday. He thought Peck might like it." Orlen smoothed his maroon tunic and straightened. "I'm still getting used to my height as well. I think Sonora gave me an extra inch or two by mistake. She's still learning. I wonder how she's doing. Any word from your mother, Beaman? She returned, didn't she? It was kind of her to take all those letters to Wintrel."

"Yes, she brought you a note from your sister."

Gwenda had led a contingent of wizards to Wintrel to deliver the news of Lacera's defeat.

Of the wizards who'd helped defeat Lacera, around fifty had decided to stay in Maradon. Other families with Wintrellian heritage planned to visit their homeland soon. Verett and Minera had volunteered to go with a small delegation of Maradonians to Tartín and other queendoms to let them know the truth about the wizards and the Peace, and to try to breed better relationships. Orlen and I would be going with them.

Beaman laughed. "Mother was so excited to go. She wanted me to come, but I told her that one Roamer in the family was enough. She said that Sonora is doing well—she found her birth mother and father. She's staying there for a few months and letting Renart rule in her absence. She wrote me that she's having a hard time figuring out where she belongs." He tossed me a roll.

"I think maybe you can belong in more than one place." I caught it and took a bite. It was soft and filled with spicy melted cheese and peppers.

"When are you going there?"

I swallowed. "In a month or so, after we get back from touring the queendoms. I'll tell her you said hello."

He chomped on a pastry. "I'll make her some treats. I'm declaring it my personal duty to show her that food is just as important as magic. Corn fritters were only the start."

"Speaking of food . . ." I lifted the cloth on the tray again and picked up the tart. I handed it to Orlen. "The crust is *cow* butter, not goat. I had Beaman make it specially for you."

He took the plate and fork, then looked up at me with an unreadable expression. He sniffed the pastry, then took a bite. He smiled instantly. "Buttercrust berry pie! You remembered. Thank you."

While Orlen dug in with gusto, Beaman perched on the table's edge, licking his fingers. He glanced up at a sand clock hovering over Orlen's work space. "I better go check on Pap. He's so nervous to be working at the castle that he's burned three pies already. He thinks Matron Frana's going to kick him out."

"She very well might," Orlen said, through a mouthful of tart. "She's got a nasty temper and no patience whatsoever."

Beaman raised an eyebrow. "Reminds me of someone I know." He put a small plate on the floor for Peck, then reached into his back pocket. "By the way, Renart handed this to me in the kitchen last night. He couldn't find you, so he went to Matron Frana and asked for me, since he knows we're friends." He passed me a wrinkled roll of paper. "I didn't read it. I'll . . . give you some privacy." He walked away, then turned at the door and gave me a lopsided grin. "I'll be back soon. I've got something new I want you both to try. I call it wizard milk. The secret's humming honey." He winked at Orlen, then left the room.

My breath faltered as I unrolled the letter. My reading was much better now, after having had more lessons with

Orlen. Still, I glanced his way. Another bite of tart was frozen halfway to his mouth

I asked a silent question. He put down his fork and came to my side, clearing his throat before reading in a low, soft voice:

> To the Owner of the Tinderbox Tavern in
> Trapper's Cove:
> I am the captain of the Seabird—a trading
> ship about to leave port. We are making an
> attempt to visit queendoms unknown, and our
> course is unpredictable.
>
> One of our crew members gave birth
> two days ago. She was too weak to leave the
> ship with the child, so I left her behind with
> another sailor while we stayed in your tavern.
> When we came back to the crew member, her
> condition had worsened. Tragically, she has
> passed from this world.
>
> Before she left, she insisted that she
> wanted the child to be raised well and then
> given a choice of apprenticeships, on sea or
> shore. I am entrusting you to this task. If you
> feel unable to fulfill it, please pass her along
> to someone who can.
>
> According to the sailor who stayed with

her until the end, the child's mother had these
last words to say:

  "Let her know how much I love her,
always and forever.

  "Let her have adventures.

  "Let her find her place."

  She did not get a chance to give the child
a name. In this troubled time, the entire crew
and I have banded together to choose one for her.

  Please call the child Taran, after her
mother.

Fare well, and fair weather to you both,
Captain Tin A. Mainer

I touched the words until they grew blurry. The letter
wasn't from my mother after all. Still, it held a piece of her.
And a piece of me as well.

I folded the paper carefully. "Well. It seems I have a first
name."

"It seems you do." Orlen patted my hand. "It's very nice
to meet you, Taran."

It was nice to meet me too.

Beside me, Peck gobbled the bread. Her red feathers had
kept some of the brilliance they'd had during her brief time as

another creature—it seemed that Sonora's powers were particularly strong when it came to anything related to dragons. Peck's eyes had become considerably less wild, but she still occasionally let out a small flame while laying golden eggs. She'd given most of them willingly to Beaman, but last week had rolled one into the library fireplace, where it remained intact and glowing. I peered at it.

"How's it doing?"

"Growling and clucking a bit. Unlike chickens, dragons don't need another dragon to produce their young. I suspect that something quite unusual is growing in that egg. We'll find out what it is soon enough." He stroked Peck's feathers fondly. "I've already been thinking of names."

I looked at the piles of books and papers by the fire. "How's your project coming along?"

He cast a weary look at the mess. "It's not easy editing history books to include the truth. But the queen ordered it. I should be done by the time we leave."

I scanned the bookshelves. "It would be nice to have a history of our story. We could call it . . . I don't know. *Chicken-Dragon Saves the Day?*"

Orlen snorted. "You should write it. Your handwriting is getting quite good. Speaking of which, I made you something." He patted my hand and turned away, picking up a small carved box. He held it out to me. "Open it."

The lid opened with a slight creak. Inside, resting on a bed of green velvet, was a feather, ending in a sharp tip. "A forever-ink pen?"

Orlen straightened his collar. "It's a very difficult spell, you know. Only one wizard has ever managed it."

I laughed. "So I've heard. It's beautiful. Thank you." I slowly turned it over in my hands. "I'll miss you when you move to your homeland," I said quietly. "So will Peck." I put the gift back in its case and set it on the table.

"Yes. Well. About that." Orlen cleared his throat. "I was thinking that instead of staying in Wintrel, maybe I would . . . not."

I stared at him. "What?"

"I was wondering, if you might consider . . . finding a family."

"What do you mean?"

"That didn't come out right," Orlen sputtered. He sighed and shook his fingers as though trying to remedy a cramp. "There is a custom here in Maradon that I'm familiar with. A parent gives something to their child, to let them know that they are loved." He met my eyes, then drew another, smaller box from the sofa cushions.

He passed me the box. "I've been wondering if, well, maybe, just by chance, you might . . . you might like to have a last name. And if, perhaps, well . . . if you would like, that is . . . I was thinking, perhaps you might consider . . . *my* last name?"

I cracked the box open.

Inside were two silver earrings.

Orlen cleared his throat again. "Despite what Minera said in the swamp, I happen to think I'd make a decent father figure. Or great-great-grandfather figure, rather. In any case, well . . ." He looked at me with anxious eyes. "What do you think?"

I touched the earrings. They were shaped like feathers. I stared up at him. "I didn't even know wizards had last names."

His lips twitched in amusement. "Yes, well, you never asked, did you. It's Underbell. Nothing fancy, but if you'd like to share it, I wouldn't be opposed. I only mean . . . it would make Maradon more of a home to me if I had family here. So . . . would you like to be my family?" He looked down at Peck, then raised his nervous eyes to me. "Both of you?"

I didn't know what to say. For the last several days, the strangest feeling had been rising inside me. It was like the magic of Peace Nights spent with Peck or like eating Beaman's cooking. But this was different. Like something that could last much longer than an hour or an evening or a week. Like something that just might last forever.

The library grew brighter, bathed in the soft, warm colors of a sunrise.

Of a new day.

"Yes," I said. "I'd like that."

Peck wormed her way between the two of us. And as Beaman bustled back into the library, humming along with three fragrant, steaming mugs, I leaned against my family and squeezed once, twice, three times.

I'm here.

You're here.

We're here together.

THE END

ACKNOWLEDGMENTS

It takes a Queendom's worth of people to bring a story to life, and this book took more than a little publishing magic to make it into the world.

My heartfelt thanks go to:

Tina Dubois, my literary agent. I wouldn't be on this journey without you.

Liz Kossnar, my editor. Thank you for taking the lead on building a bridge between this story and its readers. I'm forever grateful for your input and humor and heart, and so very happy to have had you as my editor for a time.

Amanda Ramirez, my second editor. You're a rock star for taking the reins and expertly guiding this novel to the finish line. You made the final months of working on this book feel fresh again. And you let me send you more than a few puppy pictures.

Dainese Santos, assistant editor and so much more. Your communication skills and humor and positive attitude made me smile more than you know.

Karen Sherman, my copyeditor. Your keen editorial eye saved me from making more typos and errors than I care to admit here ☺.

Chloë Foglia, book designer extraordinaire. I'm so grateful to have had your skills be a part of this story.

Marco Guadalupi, who illustrated a spirited cover that made my heart leap. You are a true artist!

Justin Chanda and all of the folks at Simon & Schuster Books for Young Readers, who do so much for children's literature. I am ever grateful for your talent and hard work.

My critique partners and super support crew: Joy McCullough-Carranza, Tara Dairman, Becky Wallace, Ann Braden, and Linda Williams Jackson. You ladies are my publishing-journey rocks, and the best mental hand-holders ever!

Charlotte Lawson and Maisey Carr, who helped brainstorm creatures. And Tess Lawson, who is an expert cuddlebug—something every author should have access to!

Finally, the character Gwenda is named for Colorado librarian Gwenda Rosebush, who is missed dearly. She was a wonderful, nurturing wizard of a woman in too many ways to count.